VAMPIRES

IN

PARK CIRCUS

Luke Belcourt

To everyone we lost,

and to all of us left behind

A vampire moves to Scotland and makes friends with a local human at a bar.

'It's hard, not being able to go out in direct sunlight,' the vampire says.

'How long has it been since you've seen the sun?' the local asks.

'Since I died, nine years ago.' the vampire says. 'You?'

The local finishes his drink. 'Fifteen long years. I remember it like it was yesterday.'

- *Anonymous*

chapter 1

The sun had not yet risen to cut through the morning fog, as the rain hammered the motorway over their heads.

Two women stood in the silhouette of Anderston train station. They cast very different shadows — Bella, tall and thin and mousy. And Munro, clad in fur, and bigger than any human had right to be. They huddled under the motorway. They would've stood out, if there had been anyone walking past. Bella swept over the concrete with her broom. Munro leaned on the structure, watching her love as though she was tending a garden.

The train station was an enormous structure of concrete nestled in the ventricles of the M8. Even at this time of the morning, a car drove past every minute or so. It was inevitable, the huge motorway dug across the city centre like scar tissue. But the witch and her selkie partner were hidden in the glare of the headlights.

This was part of their commute. Every day, a different section of the road. Because the Bridge to Nowhere had been completed.

Argyle Street, the oldest thoroughfare in Glasgow, had run from the Merchant City along the river through to Finnieston, merging with Dumbarton Road like two raindrops on a car window. But in the 1980's, the government had built a motorway through it, severing it in two. All that foot traffic, all that power, had been unseated.

The original plan had been to connect them via a bridge, but the money ran out, or the will dried up, or the government decided it wasn't worth doing. In the end, the Anderston Footbridge floated over the bypass half-finished for 30 years, reaching out the whole time to close the wound.

Until, in 2013, the bone of the bridge had finally been set. It still had hanging half-bridges, but you could walk from one side to the other. Finnieston's now-gentrified palace of sandstone, reintegrated with the city centre that had changed so much on the other side. The Bridge, in its bizarre twisting shape, held dangerous magical potential.

Bella dropped to the ground and placed her hands upon the concrete, smiling to Munro as they made eye contact. Arabella liked when Munro watched her workings — the quiet, stalwart comfort felt like sharing something vulnerable. And Munro had, after all, spent hundreds of years watching witches in ritual.

Bella could feel the energy in the ground, twisted. And then she spoke her witch's spell.

"Mountain clefts the Clyde in twain, river flows past the Crane, artery running into vein, what power rests in this domain?"

Healing.

There was a flow.

The two energies were still distinct, but they worked.

"I think it's..." Bella almost didn't want to say it out loud in case she jinxed it. "I think it's stable. Weird. But stable."

"Isn't that a good thing?"

"I don't know. I didn't expect it to heal by itself. And it's powerful..."

"Well, I suppose that's what happens when you connect things together. They get stronger."

Arabella felt the skeleton of the city. The capillary of the river, the newly built Hydro on one side and the old Finnieston Crane on the other, obscured by the horizon, dozing over the dock like sleeping lions.

A shadow passed over them. "We're not alone." Munro tensed,

flexing, eyes darting. She could feel it, like a cat in the dark.

"Demon of the Crossroads, make yourself known," Arabella said.

The figure that emerged was lanky and horned. He hunched at seven feet tall and wore a tattered patchwork cloak that looked as though it had once been bright and multi-coloured but had been left by the side of the road until it had been bleached by the years. The demon's fur burst from under its stitches like grass through paving. It was matted and clogged with motorway dust. He walked on hobbling goat legs, examining them with large goat eyes that were too far apart and too big for his skull.

"I have a name you know," he said, a smile creeping across his face.

Bella didn't relax. "Sorry. What's your name?"

"I'm a Demon of the Crossroads. We're all called Preston." He laughed. It sounded like a car backfiring.

So much for getting his true name for an exorcism. At least this one wanted to talk.

"What do you want?" she asked.

"What do *you* want? I'm just hanging out."

"Why here?" Munro stepped forward.

"Well, I can't stand *there,* can I?" He pointed back towards Four Corners. "I'd get swallowed in an instant, I'm just one demon." He dropped to his knees and pressed his bearded face against the ground. "Here I can still feel its warmth, but from a safe distance. And everyone says this place is up-and-coming!"

"Yeah, they've been saying that since before I was born. It up and came."

Munro stepped between Bella and the demon, hunched, her arms clenched. "Tell me why I shouldn't throw you over the river."

"I haven't done anything!" The demon raised his hands, cowering. "You trying to poach my spot? What are a witch and a selkie doing sniffing about?"

"We're just checking the Bridge... for *infection*," Munro said.

"Are you calling me an infection?" the demon guffawed. "I grant wishes, you know."

"I expect they don't end well," Munro said.

"You ever wanted to stretch that borrowed time of yours?" The demon reached forward, stretching to touch Munro's selkie furs, but she pulled back like a boxer.

Bella flinched. Whether it held any temptation for Munro, it definitely tempted her. Bella had watched Munro's life wax and wane with the moon for too long now and wondered when eventually it would be snuffed out. Nicnevin had said they couldn't know how long it would last – but she hadn't implied it would be long. It had been four years since they'd snatched Munro back from the brink, but it felt like yesterday. She tried not to think about it too much.

She did her best to hide her reaction, but Munro definitely saw it.

"I've borrowed enough time as it is," Munro said. "Besides, the help you could give wouldn't be nearly strong enough."

"Oh, you'd be surprised..." the demon purred, in his element now. "I can be quite... persuasive for that old universe. And I have all this power now..." The thread of power lit up, across the roads, into the city and over the bridge, like a glowing x-ray showing Glasgow's bones.

"I've done enough necromancy," Munro said, still stony-faced. "No more."

"Alright," the demon shrugged. "Well, if you change your mind..." He looked to Bella this time, pointedly. "You know where to find me."

And before Bella could snatch him in a ritual circle, he vanished in a puff of sooty carbon monoxide.

"Are you okay?" Munro asked, fussing over Bella like an overprotective parent.

Bella put a boney hand on Munro's big mitt and rubbed the back of her knuckles. "I'm good. Really."

Munro hugged her, and she leaned into the tight embrace, smelling the spiced scent of the furs on her shoulder and her chest.

"I'm good," she repeated. But her ears were ringing, filling with static. "No wait…" And it was good Munro was holding her, because she felt her balance start to go as the world smeared like oil paints—

Iona was in the Archive alone. Bella could see the white paper and the plastic bag strewn across the little table in the back of the room, smell grease, and espresso starting to bubble as Iona cut and riffle-shuffled her cards with hands that had practiced the motion for thousands of hours.

Split, press, shuffle. Split, press, shuffle.

Bella had assumed it was a reading, but it wasn't. She was playing Clock Patience.

"Iona?"

Iona took a deep, ragged breath as her eyelids and the lights in the room flickered. She dropped her cards and started to tip but grabbed the table for balance. And then she saw Bella.

"Bella?"

"What's going on?"

"This is—"

But before she could explain, the room was already fading.

And then, a series of images. Of feelings.

A woman is hurtled bodily by some dark magic from the top of a hill. She streaks across the sky like a comet, striking the ground in the centre of Kelvingrove Park. Lying in the inky night, in a smoking crater. She is wearing a white ritual gown.

The woman staggers to her feet, somehow in one piece. She is starving. She has been starving for a long time.

There is something dead that hangs on her.

But she needs help.

She is rattling through the streets. Rattling across the city. Rattling—

"—towards us!" She realised she was speaking out loud. The world was coming back to her now. Munro was cradling her, face paler than usual. "What happened?"

"You were rambling! It was mostly gibberish, are you okay?"

"We have to go," Bella said, pushing against Munro, but her grip was too strong, even if Bella's limbs didn't feel like noodles. "We have to get home. Iona... she's in the house by herself."

***

The Coven of Merchant City did not have shared premonitions often. The unwritten future is so rarely certain. When you glimpse something yet to come, it is either happening very soon or is very dangerous. Usually both.

Though Munro was born to swim, she could still move fast on a rooftop. Bella's heart rose through her throat every time she watched Munro leap between the buildings. One wrong move and she'd topple into the road below and get eaten by a Hyundai. And yet she never put a foot out of place. She smiled, despite knowing the danger they were about to walk in on. So long as she and Munro were together, they were unstoppable.

She shook herself, refocusing before the wind knocked her off her broomstick. The two of them flew home like cannon fire.

Bella pushed open the door into the archive, brandishing her broomstick like a bayonet as the bell over the door rang to announce their arrival.

It was just like she'd seen in her vision. The incense that burned habitually had been overpowered by the smell of last night's fish supper, the tang of the morning coffee still warm in the pot.

"Bella..." Iona said. She was still lying on the floor but tried again to get up. "Someone is coming. Someone is coming." Like a mantra, to focus herself until she could word her intention: *"Not born in a barn, but the barn's in danger."* She threw her spell, and the door slammed shut behind Bella, creaking as it magically locked.

"Who was that?" Bella shouted. "Who was that woman?" Now that the door was locked, and she could see Iona safe in front of her, she could think. She waved her hand and the rain that had soaked her and Munro evaporated into steam.

"Bad news," Iona said. She peeked around the window blinds, trying to check on the street.

The door to the Archive banged three times, shaking on its hinges with each strike.

Arabella jumped, clutching the pendant around her neck, before taking a deep breath. "Getting jumpy!"

Iona snatched her wrist. "Don't answer it." Her eyes were still glazed over, but she was looking at the door like she could see through it. "Don't go out there." A shock went through Arabella. To hear Iona's voice go tempered, like steel. The High Priestess was issuing a decree. "Whatever's out there... it came from up on the hill. It's a vampire."

***

Cold.

Dark.

Shaking.

Body groaning in protest.

Verity had hit the ground hard.

The orange streetlight bathed the brick road in a glow like amber, and everything was shades of brown and darkness. Verity pulled her soaking, dirty cloak around the shivering lace dress of the ritual, as the world span and she staggered to the only place she knew she could go.

Even in her stupor, a vampire's eyes could see well in the dark. She could move fast, and though her balance was off, she was moving through the night quickly.

Her every muscle, her bones, screamed at her. Gasping for air. Her strength, turning against itself. A venomous snake, chewing on its own tail.

Hell mend her, her only recourse was this den of witches.

The wind was howling, and it looked warm inside. The glow through the windows in the doorway, like a fireplace. Above, a black placard with silver calligraphy: *The Archive of Merchant City*.

There was no answer, but Verity could see movement. She could smell the people inside there, feel her killer instinct tickling in the back of her brain. She heaved, and then the pain overtook her, and she doubled-over. She banged on the door again then fell against it.

Clinging to the door jamb for support, she pressed her back against it and looked up at the sky.

"Please..." she said, though she'd already given up. "Help."

No matter how many times she saw the sky now, she never got tired of it. Vampirism had taken the sun taken from her, but these new eyes had shown her the real night sky. Not black, but purple, and blue — like the world was trapped at dusk. Millions, uncountable stars burned across it like fire catching over an oil spill. Gaseous clouds drifted on cosmic winds. She could feel the earth moving under her feet, feel them all tumbling through space. Feel the moon tug against them.

The sun's harsh light hid all that from humans, she thought. Its oppressive heat shouted over every other star in the sky.

"I suppose... there are worse ways to go," she said out loud to herself. She hoped this death would be less painful than the last. She wondered, watching the sun begin to tickle over the rooftops, whether it would kill her or the hunger would.

And then the door opened behind her, and she looked up.

The woman standing over her was tall, and rake-thin, and her hair was long and bushy and mousy. She said something, but Verity couldn't hear much over her own heart pounding in her ears, and she could feel herself starting to tip.

"I don't... If you could..."

And then she passed out.

***

With her free hand, Iona snapped her fingers and summoned her broomstick.

Arabella cleared her throat. "Iona. You're hurting me," she said gently. "You're also scaring me a bit."

"She's not human," Iona whispered. "You can smell it on her."

The woman in the vision. She had been in such pain.

"She's hurt."

Arabella was frozen between the two impulses. Because she could feel it too. Something dead beyond that door.

Another bang, like something had fallen against the frame. "Help!" The voice was meek, quiet. "Please..."

Arabella's better nature won out. "We're coming!" she shouted.

Iona tightened her grip. "Bella!" she hissed. "You don't know what you're doing."

Arabella straightened herself up to her full height. "We made an oath, Iona. Anyone who knocks that door."

She pried her hand free, and Iona looked genuinely afraid. She had seen this woman exorcise demons, stand up to the Seelie Court. What could make her feel this way?

Arabella opened the door to find a pale woman with a dark cloak, crumpled in the doorstep. "Welcome to the Archive of Merchant City."

The woman was wearing the same white gown from her vision, frilled and puffy. Her raven hair was plastered to her face from the rain.

"It's going to be okay..." Bella said, but before the woman could answer, she passed out in the stoop.

chapter 2

Verity opened her eyes slowly. Her mouth was dry, and her limbs still rang when she moved. She wasn't in the rain anymore. It took her a moment to parse what she was seeing.

A room. Dark wood. A large bed. Two doors. Nothing on her left. On her right, a bedside table with some kind of spinning contraption on it, and an armchair. She gasped as she realised someone was sitting in it. The gangly crow woman from before with the bushy hair, hunched up in a ball with a book.

The woman looked up as she heard the gasp, and smiled softly. "Hello," she said, putting the book down on the bedside table. She leaned forward and Verity backed up instinctively. "How're you feeling?"

Verity wet her mouth before speaking. "I need help."

"I know," the woman said. "You came to the right place. Witch's honour. My name's Arabella."

"Verity, House Oakleaf," Verity said, out of muscle memory. She supposed she didn't get to say House Oakleaf anymore. She sat up, and a magic circle around the bed flared like disturbed coals. She looked around like a squirrel.

"Sorry," Arabella said. "It was just a precaution when we brought you in. Though, upon further inspection... you seem like you're in no shape to be any danger to anyone."

"Am I in danger here?" Verity asked. It sounded so childish a question.

"No," Arabella said. Verity found she believed her, something about her face, her eyes. "You haven't fed in, what seems like weeks?"

"Months now," Verity said. "I've been trying to cut down." She smiled weakly.

"We didn't think that was possible," Arabella said.

Verity grimaced as another wave of pain wracked her. "It's not. I'm dying."

"How can we help?" Arabella said.

"I heard you've done powerful spells with bending death."

"Oh." Arabella paused, processing. "Good to see our reputation precedes us."

"It's true then?"

"Once," Arabella said. "And we had... help."

Verity curled up in a ball, riding out a wave of the pain. "Fuck. I don't want to die. I just don't want to eat people anymore." She found she was crying, but it was just the ache in her muscles.

Arabella grabbed her hand in both of hers. "I'll see what we can do. You've done well."

A wave of lethargy took Verity. "I think I'm gonna pass out again..."

"Sleep. Rest. You're safe here, I promise," Arabella said. "I'll be back."

Verity nodded, as Arabella's hands slipped away, and darkness took her once again.

***

"You can't help her," Iona said, as Arabella closed the door.

She'd been standing outside. And from the sounds of it, she'd heard everything.

"You don't know that," Arabella said. "We helped Munro."

"You plan to pull Nicnevin and the Seelie Court in? For this random stranger she doesn't know?" Iona said. "You'd have better luck lifting the tides."

"There is a vampire that's sworn off drinking blood. That's a miracle!"

Iona guided her away from the door, lowering her voice. "I think she'll be gone within the day. That's why her brood kicked her out," Iona said. "Involving ourselves is only going to breed animosity, and the treaty between vampires and witches is always hanging by a thread."

"What? Listen to yourself," Arabella said. "We're going to let this woman die because of politics?"

"Bella!" Iona hissed, as insistently as she could while not being overheard. "She's *already* dead! That person on the bed has been dead for centuries; if nature had its course she would've been long since gone!"

Arabella tensed. "You thought the same thing about Munro."

Iona covered her eyes, hiding that she was welling up. "Oh, Lord and Lady, I've failed you. Munro, is an *impossibly rare* exception. Vampires are necromancy as ancestry, Bella. Necromancy as culture. Institutional necromancy. It's evil, petal."

"I don't believe anyone is evil by nature," Arabella said, backing away. "And I thought you didn't either."

Iona held her tongue. "I... I'll show you. Later. Let me get my books. In the meantime, please promise you won't do anything rash."

This woman had been like Arabella's mother.

Arabella's stomach turned. She didn't say anything though. A witch's word was her bond. She wouldn't make a promise she couldn't keep. And she knew in her gut, what Iona was saying was wrong.

chapter 3

In swirling smoke and looming church spires, Verity dreamed.

Everywhere she went, a golden thread loomed behind her. Like an umbilical cord.

Her grandfather sat on what could only be described as a throne, right at the top of the hill, looking out over the park and the city alike, its old peaks and its overgrown concrete. He was watching her, no matter where she went. They all were, through the thread. And blood-sated, they were so much stronger than she was.

"Come home, Verity," Breckenridge said coolly, leaning forward in the chair. His voice was soft as walking through a cobweb, with the most received accent you could wring out of a Glaswegian throat. Breckenridge was old money, after all.

"You threw me out," she said, and she wondered if she was saying it out loud, lying in that bed in the Witches' home.

"For your own good, darling." He smiled that viper's smile. "Your mother is worried about you. I'm worried about you. You won't last much longer."

"I'm not doing it anymore," Verity said. It was the only thing she was still certain of. No more. The deaths, accidental or otherwise. The blood, the lineage. It was all rotten. She couldn't have the voices of the people she fed on in her head anymore. It was bad enough having the other vampires rummaging around in her thoughts, her entire family scurrying around in the walls of her mind like mice.

Breckenridge tugged on the golden thread like a leash, and Verity smarted. For a moment the world flashed gold, and she could see them all in a line, spread across the world. The thread which currently ended with her, going through her mother, back through Breckenridge, and off into the centuries past. A flaxen twine passing further back and further back, pinning all their souls to the earth, wrapped around the world thousands of times over. A net, keeping all their spirits on the mortal realm.

The Dark Scaffold revealed.

"It's not your choice to make," Breckenridge said. "Your misguided righteousness is weakening the chain for the rest of us. Even one frayed end can unravel the whole thing."

Verity grabbed the thread herself, and tugged back. But her limbs were weak like a newborn lamb, and she could get no purchase. "Then maybe it doesn't deserve to exist."

Breckenridge sighed, pinched the bridge of his nose. "This is not just a tradition, Verity. This is our lives you are playing with. But you don't have any descendants yourself. So if you want to starve yourself to death..." He took a deep, ragged breath that Verity suspected was just for show. "You're only hurting yourself. We can't stop you." He fixed her with that icy stare. Those bright, piercing grey eyes.

"Then leave me alone," Verity said. "Stay out of my head."

Breckenridge ran his thin fingers along the thread, and suddenly Verity was surrounded by humans. Naked, writhing, they clawed at her, begged her to drink them, squeezing her hands, exposing their necks.

She closed her eyes. "Stop it."

"It is in... our nature..." Breckenridge whispered.

"Stop it!" she shouted, and sat up in the bed.

The room was dark, and she was alone. The spinning contraption on the bedside table ticked and whirred in the silence, slowly measuring the turn of the solar system.

The hunger was always at its worst when she had just woken.

chapter 4

Arabella closed her Book of Shadows as Iona approached – it was bad practice to let anyone else see its pages on the best day, but Bella didn't want Iona knowing what she was working on.

Iona beckoned silently for Arabella to follow her. She had finished getting dressed since Bella had last seen her, a navy dress that she usually reserved for a working, and tied her hair up in a bun.

They padded quietly down the hall so as not to wake Verity, off to a side room where Iona's study was.

Iona pushed a huge book in front of Arabella. "There."

It looked like some kind of family tree. Curlicues of vines, like a monastic mural. And at the end, was Verity Oakleaf.

"What am I looking at?"

"It's her family," Iona said. "I can't believe we haven't taught you this until now."

"How do you have her entire family tree in a book in our house?"

"Because vampires aren't like werewolves, they're not like witches, they're not like ghosts. They're not a group, they're a family. An immortal family."

Iona flipped the page to a diagram of a vampire's mouth, jaw extended like a python, canines sharpened like knives. "Every vampire is a dead person whose soul has been pinned down by the vampire that turned them."

Arabella was getting a sickening feeling in her stomach. "Like what

Nicnevin did to Munro." She clutched her pendant, felt out for Munro's mind. She wasn't in the house – she was at Central Station, picking up Holly and Roman.

"It's worse than that." She flipped back to the family tree. "This vampire pins this one, who pins this one, who pins these two, and each of them turn another and another."

"But Nicnevin made it sound like keeping a soul here was almost impossible to do."

"All of them together work like a dreamcatcher," Iona said. "The line of succession is so convoluted and knotted they all hold each other down. It's why they organise in broods. It's why they're so obsessed with their history. It's why this is so well-documented." She rapped her hand off the book's pages like she was having to pull the words out. "If you were to kill this vampire for example" —she picked one at random— "every vampire under them in the tree would die. And then every other vampire under them. And so on, and so on. They're parasites. Living off each other, by feeding on us. But while they live, they live forever. They don't age, they can heal in minutes, and they do it by siphoning *our blood*."

Arabella sat down in the chair. "But she doesn't want to feed on anyone."

"I suspect that's why she was excommunicated," Iona said. "Her brood father must be waiting for her to crack and feed on someone, change her mind, come back."

"Or... she dies, in that bed," Arabella said.

Iona nodded. "There's nothing we can do for her, petal. She's not supposed to be alive."

Arabella tensed her fists. "But she wants to be different. She's like Munro. She deserves another chance at life."

Iona shifted uncomfortably. "We were lucky with Munro. But no-one deserves a second life. Sometimes you just get lucky. This" —she prodded her finger on the family tree again— "this is an institution deciding that a tiny class of people are allowed to live forever, by drinking the blood of the innocent."

Arabella slumped. She hoped Verity was still asleep, that she couldn't hear this in the other room.

And then, from off down the corridor, the front door jingled.

"Hello!" shouted a sing-song voice from the front room. "Bella, Iona, we're home!"

It was Roman. A little beam of sunshine lit up this grim moral dilemma.

"Is someone helping with these fucking bags or what?" he shouted.

Iona pushed her head out the door. "Wheesht!" she hissed, finger on lips. "We've got a guest sleeping."

"Shit, sorry!" Roman shouted, still no quieter. Bella stepped out and saw him messing about with the door, trying to pull in two suitcases without them getting caught in his skirt.

She crossed the room to her witch-brother and gave him a massive hug.

"Woah!" he said, taken aback before returning the hug. "What happened? Did yous watch Strictly again?"

Arabella laughed, despite herself. "No, we've just... it's complicated."

"Ah right," Roman said, squirming in the hug so he could see behind him. "Munro! Holly! Bella's emotioning!" he shouted, before Iona hissed for quiet again. *'Sorry'*, he mouthed, before going back to lugging his suitcases.

"You alright, babes?" Holly stepped in, a tiny hurricane of a person lugging a case that was taller on its side than she was. It was wrapped tight in chains and padlocks. Her red mohawk had fallen over and she pushed it out of her eyes.

"Dunno," Bella said. "It's been a long night."

"Gies a second," Holly said, reaching up and squeezing her shoulder. "I'm just gonna finish getting this in then I'll be right with you."

Bella nodded, and then Munro filled the doorframe, carrying an enormous telescope over one shoulder padded against her selkie furs, and what looked like a double-bass carry case that Bella suspected they'd borrowed from Julian next door. Munro's face was dour and she was breathing heavily; she must have been carrying the suitcase for miles.

Bella reacted out of instinct, her brain just thinking 'safety', and she wrapped her arms around Munro and squeezed her in a tight hug. "Hi," she whispered into her furs.

"Hi, Bel," Munro said, unable to return the hug with both of her arms full. She nuzzled the top of Arabella's head and left a kiss on her crown.

"Okay, mother needs five minutes before you all start asking things of her," Roman said. He put his suitcases down in front of the kitchen table and stretched out on the couch. He snapped his fingers and the kettle started to boil by itself, before taking a deep breath. "Alright. I'm ready. Hit me."

Holly dumped the chest on him, and he wheezed.

***

The Coven of Merchant City all toddled into Verity's guest room together like estranged relatives coming to the deathbed of a dying family member.

Verity was only half awake, dozing on the bed as the protective circle flared and spat in the dark every time she moved. She was drenched in a cold sweat, and tried to push her hair out of her face but it kept falling back.

What a motley crew these witches were, she thought. All shapes and sizes.

She sat up, head spinning, as the solemn older woman waved her hands and the oil lamps on the surfaces lit by themselves. She stepped in, worrying her hands as she approached. "Are you comfortable?" she asked, trying to broach the gulf between them.

Verity attempted to sit up. "Mm. Well. I'm dying. But, what else is new?" She smiled a thin smile. Her purple vampire eyes passed across them all in turn. This elder witch who didn't seem to like her, and Arabella behind her. In all her years she'd never actually seen a witch. There had been so few chances in House Oakleaf. Their blood, pumping through their bodies, looked just like regular humans, but it smelled... spicy. Distilled.

Beside Arabella were other witches, one a gangly boy-thing with crooked teeth, long blonde tresses of hair and a skirt that clipped his ankles. And the other, was a woman like Verity had never seen before. She was short and stout and square, but her magic seemed the most cured of all; it burned like a fire in her belly. Verity could all but see the flames lick her wide shoulders, her scarlet red hair, her long home-knitted cardigan.

Verity's breath caught. "Who are you?" she asked of the woman on fire.

The boy-thing coughed, inexpertly hiding a cackle. "Sorry," he said, when the older woman scowled at him — "Roman!" — and it seemed to send him into further fits. Roman was his name, she noted.

"I'm Holly," the woman on fire said. She stepped over the protective line, without even a second thought, and stood by the bed. "We're here to help."

"I've... you seem... I've seen you before." She'd never seen this woman before in her life, but something of the fire was familiar.

"I don't think so," Holly said. She smirked. "I think I'd remember meeting *you*."

Roman caught another snort in his hand. "Smooth," he whispered.

"Very smooth."

"Roman, I will escort you from this room," the elder witch hissed.

"Bella says you're a vampire trying to stop feeding?" Holly said. She leaned forward, and Verity put a hand up to push her away.

"It's not working," Verity said. "I can't... you have to stay back."

"Okay," Holly said. There was no urgency though as she stepped out of the circle. "You have your space."

"I thought it would get easier. I thought, maybe, if I could push through the cravings. But my body is starving."

"It will continue to do so, until you die," the elder witch said.

Holly hadn't taken her eyes off of Verity. "Not if we have anything to say about it."

"I don't... this was a mistake. I can't... I can't even think. My brain..." She could feel herself tunnel visioning.

Holly rolled up the sleeve of her cardigan, and offered her arm over the line. "Here. It'll keep you going for the time being."

Verity stared at it. Pale, and plump, and with that fiery liquid pulsing through it with every beat of her heart. She could hear it from across the circle, even if Holly herself couldn't. *Thump thump. Thump thump.* That vital process of life, and Holly was offering it to her...

"I can't," she said, and she closed her eyes, covered her ears, all to block out that heartbeat. "It took me... *years*, to stop. I had to stop drinking blood completely. Every time I went back, I was right back in it."

Holly pulled her cardigan sleeve back down. "I thought quitting smoking was hard. We're gonna help you."

"I don't know if you can," said another voice in the room, and Verity jumped.

There had been another person here, the whole time. A huge, statuesque figure of a woman who had been standing behind them all, and *Verity hadn't noticed her.*

"You're..." she stared at this huge furred woman, picking out the edges of her. Her heart was beating, but there was no life in her veins. She didn't light up the room with her bloodflow like the others did. "You're like me."

The woman cleared her throat, shifting in place with an awkwardness unbefitting a woman of her size. "Yes," she said.

No gold thread tied behind her. No connection to the Dark Scaffold. "You're not a vampire," Verity said.

"Munro has..." Arabella said. "A second chance."

Verity bit her lower lip to stop it trembling. "So it's true. You can save us."

Munro gripped Arabella's hand for support. She couldn't hide the discomfort wracking her.

"We can try," Holly said, firmly.

"If you'll forgive me, you are... a fascinating case study," Roman said. He grinned a crooked smile. "And I have a lot of ideas." He kneaded Arabella and Holly's shoulders. "Ladies, if you don't mind, I'm going to get to work." He grinned. "Feels good to be the one with the specialty for once!" He turned to Holly. "Oh, and, try not to fuck the sexy vampire before I get back."

Holly scoffed, then looked at Verity, turning as red as her hair.

Verity just blinked, still transfixed by Munro, by her nature, by her fortune.

They all started to file out, and Verity let her heavy eyelids droop.

***

Arabella hung in the corner of the room, trying desperately to keep her eyes open. It had gone past noon now, and she'd woken up so early. The vision this morning, the adrenaline, it all seemed to have taken it out of her.

The cadaver of a young man, skin yellowed like old leather, lay open on the operating table like a purse, as Roman picked at him.

She finally spoke. "I don't think she can drink the blood of dead bodies."

"I know," he said absently. "I've got a plan though."

"Where did you find this guy anyway?"

Roman looked up, weighing his answer. "You remember the necromancer from a month ago?"

She looked at his face on the slab, frozen, slack-jawed. She hadn't recognised it without the rictus grin. "Oh God…" she screwed her face up, covering her mouth as though it would make a difference now. "You *kept* the body?"

"It's recycling, honey," Roman said. "Besides, aren't you glad I did now?"

"Not exactly," Bella said. She slumped down in an armchair in the corner of the cold-room as he muttered under his breath, coaxing what little magic had not broken down in the corpse's body.

"I think if I can get enough Good Juice out of his heart, I can make a homunculus she can feed on."

"Isn't that just laundering the problem?" Arabella said. "Homunculi don't last that long."

"Did you see her in there? She has days, at most. She really waited until the most dramatic moment to reach out for help — I have to congratulate the vibe." He took a deep breath, and then ripped the blackened heart from the chest cavity. It made a noise like meat being ripped from the bone by a dog's molars, and Bella shook herself.

"Why do you do all this shit?"

"I tried reading futures, it just wasn't for me," Roman said. "Besides, I'm like *CSI: Trongate* right now. You can tell so much about someone from what's left in their body."

"Okay, I'm gonna go," Bella said quickly, standing up and shaking herself down, wanting to get out of the room before the smell started sticking to her clothes. "Try not to get entrails on the carpet, yeah?"

"I'll do my best!" he shouted after her. "Oh, and bring me a Lilt if you're coming back!" When she didn't respond, he called again, "I'd accept a Lucozade!"

23

chapter 5

Even sleep was tiring for Verity now. She couldn't rest, the pain was too deep in her bones. And if she nodded off too deeply, Breckenridge would come. She had to keep her mind shielded, or lose herself to them again. But she was running out of power.

Sleep was strange in the darkness. A swirling cloud of smoke, full of glass dust that caked her clothes, hurt her lungs. When vampires dream, they are supposed to return to the Scaffold. But she was wandering the wilderness alone.

She was used to it though, by now. Every time she gave up drinking blood, she found herself here. And alone was better than with her grandfather.

So when she saw the shape of another person in the fog, she recoiled instinctively, falling to her knees.

"Oh, it's you," the figure said. It was the selkie woman. She stepped out of the fog and reached down to help Verity back to her feet. "How are you here?"

"I come here—"

"—every night," they finished it together, and then there was silence as they both looked at each other. So this Munro really was like her.

"How long have I been asleep?" Verity said. She thought about her body, withering in the witches' spare room, a million miles away.

"A while, it must be. They're working through the night." A smile cracked her hard exterior. "They're going to bend over backwards to save you."

"So I can trust them?" She didn't know why she bothered asking, she couldn't even trust herself these days.

"Bella is… everything to me," Munro said. "I promise you, if she's in your corner, you'll be amazed at what she can do."

"That's nice," Verity said, though it didn't do much to warm her heart. She watched Munro's body flicker and fade in and out, the same way hers did now. "You're nearly gone."

Munro bit her lower lip. "People have been saying that to me for hundreds of years."

"No, but…" Verity said. "You're *really* nearly gone now… aren't you?"

Munro nodded.

"They don't know."

She shook her head.

"I just want the end to be nice, y'know?" Munro said. "I want to be happy. And then I want to just… disappear one day. They'll be sad, and then they'll get over it, and that'll be that."

Verity chewed on this. It was the opposite for her — she didn't want to die yet, she had lived so little under Breckenridge's thumb. And she had no memory of her human life.

Munro didn't seem to realise she was crying, put her hand to her face and wiped her tears, looked at them on her fingertips like they confused her.

"You should tell them."

"What good would that do?" Munro wiped her wet fingers on her furs, smiling despite herself.

"You strike me as the type who keeps things bottled up."

"It has been said," Munro said. "It is actually nice to have someone to talk to who's… going through a similar thing."

"Tell them. They can help."

"There's nothing to help. I'm old. I'm tired. And the last five years have been... the best of my life," Munro said. "I'm ready. And if I tell them..." She grunted, like she was trying to lift a car. "It's like the second people think you're not going to be around anymore, they start sucking away all your responsibilities. They try to be nice, they go all gentle and start doing things for you and don't want you to do anything. They try to take your burden... but it just makes it feel like you may as well already be dead. Like no-one needs you at all, and until now they've been pretending."

"That does sound awful," Verity said. She couldn't picture it though. She'd never had any responsibilities worth having — stand up straight, simper for the family, be quiet, be seen and not heard, don't ask questions.

"You're right though," Munro sighed. "If only because I can't keep it secret much longer." She raised her hand, still flickering like a guttering candle. "It's started pulling other life force in, like a whirlpool. I can feel it. It's not affecting the witches, they're too strong. But... strangers. They walk past the Archive and they shiver. I don't know what'll happen soon."

"Then we *are* the same," Verity said, her face dropping. "Leeching off other people."

"No. I'm no leech," Munro said. She tensed, but like she was too tired to argue. "I'll choose death. Before it gets too bad."

Verity was trying to be there for Munro, this strange woman, like her in so many ways. Trying to show her kindness. But all she could think about was the knot in her stomach that even the Witches' Miracle had had strings, that it had started caving in on itself.

"Oh," Munro blinked. "I'm waking up." She smiled. "I'll see you in the morning. Thank you, it's been nice to talk about it."

"A pleasure to meet you," Verity said.

And then she was alone again in the dark.

chapter 6

The first beams of cold sunlight crept through the curtains like an intruder. Arabella pulled the covers tighter around herself, making Munro stir, across the bed from her.

She smiled, and cuddled into Munro's back, running her fingers along her long black hair, tracing the outline of her shoulder, her back, her shoulder blade.

Miracle upon miracle had led to this moment. That they had met at all was unlikely, that Munro had been freed from her servitude under the Witch Queen was impossible. And now, on top of everything, Munro should have died. Four years ago, in Elf-hame. They'd twisted the laws of the universe to keep her here, for a time. No-one knew how long the spell would hold. But every second, Bella luxuriated in it like a warm bath. Every morning when they rose together and took on the world.

She wanted to wake up next to this woman every day for the rest of her life.

She peppered small kisses on the crook of Munro's neck, and Munro took a deep inhale that signified that she'd been roused from slumber.

Turning, with her eyes still closed, Munro stretched her arms out and pulled Bella into an embrace. "Good morning, my love," she said, bleary and sleepy.

Arabella smiled, leaning into the embrace and squeezing her tight. "Morning."

She went to kiss her, but Munro put a hand up, wetting her lips. "I've got morning breath."

"I don't care," Arabella laughed.

Finally Munro opened her eyes. Dark and sparkling, they crinkled as she smiled. The hand she'd raised turned, on autopilot, to stroke Bella's face. She kissed her jawline, up to her ear, as if in compromise.

"Let's just stay in bed all day today," Arabella said, stretching like a cat.

"I thought you had that vampire situation," Munro said.

"I can do that any time," Arabella lied, and she leaned into her drowsiness, and they dozed for another hour in each other's arms.

***

Eventually, their stomachs rumbled enough that it forced them to get up. Arabella padded through the frozen-cold flat with the duvet wrapped around her, while Munro threw her seal skin over her shoulders.

She poked her head in the kitchen. No-one here. "Has Holly already gone out?" she asked.

"I think she stayed with the girl. She didn't come home," Munro said, still walking through from the bedroom. Her hearing was better than humans. "What's in the fridge?"

Bella opened it. "Three eggs, and two very old limes." She plucked the net bag and held the shrivelled raisin limes in the air. "I thought I threw these out." She did so now, before she forgot again.

"We could fry 'em," Munro said.

"The limes?" Arabella smirked. She turned, and saw Munro standing in the door. She burst out laughing.

"What?" Munro blinked.

"Nothing, I just—" Arabella said. Standing, filling the threshold of the door, Munro looked the spitting image of one of those novels with the erotic windswept love interest, barely clad but for animal fur, her wild eyes and hair, the thick, powerful legs free to the elements... and the fuzzy pink slippers she'd put on to protect her tootsies from the cold floorboards. "I like your footwear."

Munro blushed, uncharacteristically. "They're not mine, I just found them in the porch." She shuffled in the door. "This flat is freezing, okay?"

Filled with a sudden rising urge, Arabella crossed the room, took Munro by the fur coat, and kissed her.

Then, after a moment, she pulled back. "You brushed your teeth!" she said, outraged.

"I knew you'd do that eventually."

"I hadn't brushed mine yet!"

Munro laughed. "I don't care."

"You traitor!"

Munro wrapped her arms round Bella's waist and dipped her into another kiss. Arabella protested for a second, and then melted like a dod of butter on a hot pan.

***

They ended up going out for breakfast, picking up bagels on the way to the Archive. It was bitter cold outside, which was ideal because Arabella had been waiting for the chance to wear the cloaks and capes she'd spent the year making. Carrying the bag, she nursed the paper cup of latte in her hand.

"This is a bit of a trek every day," Munro said.

Arabella laughed. "I thought you were a hunter-gatherer. You must have walked way more than this."

"Ran! Swam! But, I also never went the same way twice," Munro said.

"You bored?"

Munro wrapped herself round the arm Arabella was using to hold the bagels. "With you, my darling?" she said, in a mock voice. "Never!"

Arabella snuck a quick look to check no-one was watching, then they kissed.

It was nice, Arabella thought. Their relationship had been like a firework, but now... it was the sun. Warm, constant. Life-giving. Like a glass of wine with friends at the end of a stressful day. It had stabilised into a feeling that Arabella knew had changed her as a person.

They arrived at the Archive, which was already opened, orange light warm and inviting through the windows of the dingy shopfront exterior. Above the door, a black placard with silver calligraphy: *The Archive of Merchant City*. Half of it was in Iona's handwriting, the other half in someone else's. It was old, too... aged by the elements.

She opened the door, and was welcomed inside by the incense.

"Good morning," Iona said absently. She was sitting at the main desk for once, going through a small leather notebook on her desk filled with old fountain pen scratchings. She looked like she'd been up all night, eyes darkened by heavy purple bags. "Coffee's just done."

Arabella raised her paper cup. "Sorry, couldn't wait." She put it down so she could start unwrapping the ten layers of clothes — it was supernaturally warm in here.

"Am I still okay to work on my painting?" Munro said to Iona. She'd nicked the guest room to set up this big easel.

"Oh yes, I had to move it into Roman's room, we needed the guest room for... you know." Iona shrank at the mention of the vampire in their walls. "It's very beautiful, by the way! Though I'm not sure I understand it..."

"Good, it's doing it's job," Munro said, and she sped off. "Oh!" she shouted, rushing back as if she'd forgotten something. She kissed Bella on the cheek one last time. "Love you."

Arabella blushed as Munro tore off again.

"Young love, eh?" Iona said, still looking down at the notebook.

"It's lovely to see around here for once."

"Thanks," Arabella said. She moved to the table and drained her latte, looking down at the paper cup, then at the coffee pot. "...Why not? I've earned it." She chucked the cup in the recycling and got a mug for her second coffee of the day.

"How are things going, by the way, with Munro's..." Iona paused. "Situation?" She had that tone in her voice that she was trying to sound like she was just making inconsequential small talk, but Bella knew her too well.

"Um... Fine," Bella said. "I think. Why?"

Iona made a thoughtful noise. "Don't know. Witch's intuition, maybe. I would've expected some side-effects by now."

Munro had been brought back from the dead, centuries ago, held to the world by grief and spite by the Queen of the Witches, Nicnevin. The Coven had convinced Nicnevin to let her go, and the spell ran out. But they'd hidden that from the universe, kept it from noticing her time was up. They'd known at some point the charm would wear off, that the rounding error would be corrected. But they had no idea how long she had.

"Well, none yet," Arabella said. "That's a good thing, right?"

"Maybe," Iona said. "Honestly, I don't know. I've never seen magic used quite like that until now."

"And if it starts to run out, we can just... cast it again right?"

"Quite the opposite, my dear," Iona said. She closed her notebook to give Bella her full attention. "Munro is an unresolved coin flip. We so much as look at her lifespan with magic, she'll topple before we can get the words out."

A cold feeling rose through Arabella's chest. She wasn't used to situations she couldn't resolve with magic.

Iona squeezed her hand. "Enjoy every day, petal," she said. "You don't want to have any regrets."

Arabella took a deep breath, bracing herself. "You've lost people. Important people."

Iona nodded.

"How do you deal with it?"

Iona sucked her lower lip. "You don't."

Arabella felt a cold spike in her stomach.

"It's like a broken leg that sets wrong. Some days you carry it badly, some days you carry it well. But you never forget it's there. Not for a moment, not for the rest of your life."

The room was so quiet Bella's ears rang. She opened her mouth to speak, when Munro came back in. "Who touched my paints!" she shouted, furious.

The words caught in Arabella's mouth, she laughed. "Probably Roman?"

"I'm gonna kill him. He's dead... He's gone too far this time," Munro said, under her breath.

The bell above the door tinkled as the door opened and Roman entered. "Bloody hell, it's baltic outside!" he shouted.

"*You!*" Munro hissed. She pounced.

Arabella and Iona laughed, watching her chase him through the door.

chapter 7

The Archive creaked, its floorboards stretching under Verity's steps, like an old cat looking up as its owner walks past.

She tiptoed off the bed, first one foot, then the next. She could hear laughter outside. Witches laughing didn't sound like she'd imagined — they just sounded like any other people.

She stepped over the magic circle, which had long since burned out, and cracked the door.

"Hello?" she said, a meek voice into the lion's den.

The laughing continued. No-one had heard.

She cleared her throat. "Hello?" she said again, louder.

The laughter stopped abruptly, and the next thing Verity knew, Iona was in the doorway, wielding her broomstick like a spear. "What are you doing outside the circle?" she asked.

"I heard voices…" Verity said. "Don't worry, I'm not a danger to you. I've been off the wagon long enough, it would take a lot to tempt me." She gently moved the broomstick handle out of her face.

"You're awake!" Holly said.

Verity nodded, looking over Iona's shoulder.

"Do you drink coffee? Water?"

She nodded again. "Either would be good."

"Gimme a second." Holly disappeared off to the side, popping a biscuit in her mouth to free her hand.

Verity was used to this — the cravings were at their worst when she woke up, but if she could fight through them, she would be able to ignore them by sundown.

Her limbs were still weak, so flimsy that when Holly handed her the cup of coffee she almost dropped it. She guided it down onto the messy coffee table, and sat for a second, trying to catch her breath. Her head swam.

She could feel them all looking at her, but she couldn't look up. Holly's aura filled her field of vision. It was blinding. Eventually, she snuck a glance, unable to stop herself.

She could see the worry in Holly's face through the astral flames that clung to her. But she could also see that heartbeat. The drumbeat in her throat that made Verity's body coil.

The room was so silent now. "I'm sorry for interrupting," she said quietly.

"It's fine!" Bella assured her, raising her hands as she was about to touch her shoulder — but she didn't, in the end. Verity felt radioactive.

The doorbell went, giving them all an excuse to stop staring at her. Iona answered it, to a girl in hysterics. She was wearing a private school uniform, her hair matted and her makeup running.

"It's the girls in my class," she warbled around a mouth that was so overwrought that she could barely breathe, let alone get the words out. "They're after me, they've turned on me, they're in my head, I need your help! I can't—"

"It's okay, it's okay." Iona guided her to the kitchenette and had her sit down in a chair.

Suddenly it felt like Verity was sitting in a war hospital, lying on a stretcher, triaged amongst all the other supernaturally besieged of Glasgow town.

"I tried an unbinding, but it didn't work, it just made them mad, I—"

"It's okay. You're safe." Iona squeezed her hand. "Take a second, breathe. It's going to be okay."

Bella was lighting candles on the coffee table around all the mess, off in the corner with Verity. "Teenagers," she said under her breath with a smile. "Goddess, to be that age again. Why were we at each others' throats *so much*?"

Verity didn't remember being that age. Didn't even remember when it would've been.

Iona stepped up to get something.

Left now to catch her breath, the crying girl's gaze fell on Verity, and they stared at each other across the room. Two people both having the worst day of their lives.

"Do you have any allergies?" Roman asked the girl quietly.

"Paracctamol," she whispered, still looking at Verity. Her tears had burned out like an old candle and she was catching her breath.

"Here," he said, handing her a green clay mug with no handle.

"What is it?"

"Tea," Roman said. "You need to rehydrate." He waggled his fingers at her tear ducts.

She looked down into the mug, like that was the last thing on her mind. "I'm not safe, I'm n—"

"You're safe here." He scoffed. "These walls? No coven in a thousand years could pierce our protections."

She took a sip.

"Catch your breath. And then tell us everything," Iona said, returning. All of the witches were hovering around her now, perched on the furniture like attentive ravens.

Verity suddenly felt like she was stepping in on someone's therapy session. As the girl began to explain her high school problems, her clique, their dabbling in magic... Verity picked up the coffee cup, and excused herself from the room. A vampire can be unheard when she wants to be, but still she spotted Holly look up, and see her go.

***

The bed was still warm from her getting up. She'd only made a few steps in the end. She collapsed back into the pillows and linen and tried to catch her breath.

A quiet knock on the door made her jump.

"Holly!" she gasped. "You shouldn't... be able to sneak up on me like that."

"Being sneaky and subtle isn't historically one of my strengths," Holly said. The fire of her aura filled the entire doorway.

"No... I expect not," Verity said. She leaned on the bed for structure, and forced herself to look at the witch.

The magic in her was far stronger than the other witches, even her High Priestess. "Why do you look like that?"

"Look like what?" Holly said, sticking out her chin. "I dress the way I want to dress, I look the way I want to look."

"No," Verity said, turning her head to look at her from all sides. "Not your wrapping. Underneath."

Holly smirked, covering her nipples with her hands. "Are you looking at me naked right now?"

Verity scoffed. "You are incorrigible! You're like a child to me, believe me I'm not looking at you that way."

"If you say so." Holly grinned. "So what do you mean, *underneath*?"

"Your... aura. It's different with witches than it is for normal humans."

"That makes sense."

"But yours..." Even as Verity said it, it flared and billowed with Holly's every breath, like an open flame. With her every will, her every movement, her every twitch of emotion. A smirk, an eyebrow, an errant look...

"Ah, the *spiciness* you mentioned?" Holly said.

Verity nodded.

"Bella did say I was different." Holly sat down next to Verity. Verity expected to feel the sheets kindle and burst into flame, feel the wall of heat sear her, but there was nothing. Just Holly. Like it was all in her head. "I lost my magic once," Holly said. "Had it pushed down into my subconscious. And when I dragged myself back into the light, it was stronger for it."

"Hm," Verity said. "I keep hoping something like that will happen with me." She raised her legs up onto the bed, wrapped her arms around them, felt the boniness of her limbs. She could see what she looked like. A stork-like bird crumpled, a vestige of the power she'd had before. "If I keep pushing, maybe there's another form on the other side. Maybe the vampires are all wrong."

Holly looked at her feet, the fire around her smouldering, receding.

"That's not going to happen, is it? I'm just gonna die like this."

"We don't know that," Holly said. "We've cheated death before."

Verity could sense the others in the house. The High Priestess, Iona. The kind one, Bella. And the boy-thing, Roman. She knew Munro was in there, but she couldn't smell her, couldn't sense her. A soul-less object, like she was.

"I don't know if I want that." She swallowed. "We're corpses, Holly," Verity said. "I know it doesn't look like it, but we're beyond the pale. You're so powerful, you *must* be able to feel it. We twist entropy around our fingers, we deny the natural world our bodies. But is this... shambling, better than death?" She'd spoken too much, the weakness in her lungs crested her like a wave.

"If you're up and talking, that's good enough for me," Holly said.

The lethargy swept Verity under, and she passed out onto Holly's shoulder.

***

The dream space was becoming familiar to Verity. Every time she closed her eyes, she was here. The murky ink was like a lake this time, and she treaded water. The golden thread, Ariadne's string, spun behind her deep into the depths below.

Breckenridge stood over her now, the water bearing his weight. He reached a hand down. "Must we keep doing this? We still love you."

"Your love is plastic, Grandfather."

"Yes!" His eyes glinted in the darkness, his fangs catching the reflection from the lake. He bent to one knee, holding both his hands out to welcome her home. "It lasts forever."

"It's fake. And rotten. And it's destroying the planet." Her limbs ached as she scooped water. Watching him hover effortlessly made her feel pathetic.

"Fake?" His perfumed smile didn't break. He spoke like he was talking to a child. "My dear... it's you who's being fake. You're denying your very nature."

"Fake." She spat it again, before he could twist her words. She gulped water and spluttered to spit it out. "You're *fake*. You don't care about us, except in how we're an extension of you."

Breckenridge coiled like a snake, and finally stepped back from trying to help her. "Well. I'm sure your mother will be upset to hear you say that."

Her arms gave out, and only her legs kept her from sinking. Her thighs burned, and a part of her brain was starting to give up.

"Well then. I did my best," he said, and turned away from her. "If you want to drown in your own body like an animal, I can't stop you."

Her head dunked, the water filling her nose, her vision blurring, and she kicked, breaking the surface again, knowing it was for the last time.

Breckenridge began to walk away, a black bat-like shape in the darkness, until eventually she couldn't see him at all.

This was it. She was going to die. She would never wake up from this one. She took one last gulp of air, and let her legs give up.

The ocean went on forever. The endless abyss of space lit only by the bioluminescent umbilical cord of her connection to the Dark Scaffold. Even that was beginning to fade as she did, flickering like the dregs of a dying candle.

She closed her eyes, let the water fill her. There was no panic. Her heart hadn't beat for hundreds of years after all. It still distressed her, her ribcage as still as a corpse. When she lived with other vampires, she could almost ignore it. But now, being around humans, she could feel it constantly. She was a dead thing.

For a moment, she was still. And it felt right. She could just make out some distant memories of a time long ago, memories that belonged to another woman, with another name, with blood coursing through her veins. All of those memories which had died and decomposed when her brain had stopped the first time.

"Verity."

She almost assumed it was Breckenridge, the voice was sharp and insistent in her head.

The darkness began to break. A fiery shape in the water before her, first candlelight, then a bush, and then a human.

"Verity, wake up," the voice said, disembodied.

The heat of the flame was impossible to bear, it bubbled and boiled the water around her, Verity started

And opened her eyes.

She'd fallen asleep on Holly's shoulder. "Verity, are you okay?"

Verity looked up, dazed, blood-tired. No-one else had ever been able to enter Breckenridge's mind space. "I need to stick to you like glue, it seems..."

chapter 8

Munro was used to it by now.

It started small.

The voices in the room would start to sound like she was underwater. She had learned panicking only made it worse. She gripped the kitchen table while the coven talked, their voices fading into background noise. She closed her eyes, breathed. In, out. In, out. Felt the varnish of the wood. Still here. Still here.

She stood, as quietly as she could. She just had to get to a bathroom. She moved fast, hoping no-one would stop to ask her anything — though if they did, she probably wouldn't hear. She stumbled down the corridor, head spinning, tumbling into the bathroom, reaching for the door, the deadbolt, but before she could grip her fingers around it, she started to fall—

I am on the beach, the sun has decided to peak round the clouds. Haar stands over me, his wee face screwed up with impatience.

I grin. "You can get your ball back when you're big enough to swim out and get it."

"Mummm!" He's got the reddest hair of anyone in the family and he's stamping his wee feet up and down until I'm laughing. I jump up and grab him by the leg and pull him up like the catch of the day.

"See! That'll be you if you get caught in a current!" I'm waving him about by his leg now. He's laughing, upside-down, all his problems forgotten in an instant.

This is a horrible feeling. Experiencing every moment, every single feeling as it was on the day. But you can't change a thing. Your body just reacts. You're just a viewer.

Haar wriggles so he's got his wee hands around my fist. With an almighty wrench, he pulls my grip free and falls to the ground.

"Oh my God!" I gasp, feeling the shock to my nervous system. I drop to check him for bruises. "Are you okay?" But of course I know he is, this happened almost a hundred years ago.

He jumps up onto all fours, grinning with his sharp wee teeth. He snickers. "Freedom!" Then he starts running around me on all fours like a spider.

I chase him over the hill, screaming threats of tickling, leading him away from the beach—

Now I am in a fitting room, trying on a suit. We're going to a wedding, one of the witches' friends. I am nervous, they haven't taken me to a family event before. Bella comes in wielding two different ties, but stops in the door. She turns bright red and looks at her feet. "Oh for goodness' sake, you can't do that!"

"Do what?" I ask. I can feel heat rising to my cheeks. Maybe it doesn't fit, this was a terrible idea.

"I am so annoyed how good you look right now!"

I roll my eyes. "Okay genius." I start to take the suit jacket off, to find something less formal, when she grabs one of my fingers.

"I'm serious!" Bella said. She's still bright red, still can't look me in the eye.

I grin, and wrap my arms around her waist. "Look at me."

"I can't, I'll die, I'll literally go blind."

I tip her chin up, and we kiss, Bella's hand scrambling blindly to close the changing room curtain—

Someone is knocking on the door.

Someone is—

"Hello?" There's a voice on the other side of the door. For a moment, Munro thinks—

For a moment, Munro thought it was Bella, she was just—

Getting no reply, the person tried the door handle, just as Munro gripped it. "Just a second!" she called, getting her bearings.

"Oh, sorry Munro!" the voice said, and Munro could process it was Holly now. She wiped her eyes, looked at her hands.

Still there. She was still there.

She made a fist, just so she could feel her fingernails dig into her palm.

Sometime soon, she was going to fall into one of these trances, her entire life would flash before her eyes, and that would be her. Gone.

But not today, she hoped.

chapter 9

Arabella stormed into Roman's workroom with a vial of inky black fluid and put it on the little metal trolley by the operating table. He had removed the corpse's heart, and was holding it in huge black rubber gloves. He looked up at her, and then at the vial. He was wearing goggles that made him look like he had big bug eyes. "Aw, beezer! Did you get my Lilt?"

She blinked. "No."

He tutted, before huffing a huge toke from a censer on the trolley. He held the incense in his lungs for a moment, then breathed it into the tubing of the heart. It inflated, like some ghoulish balloon.

He recoiled like he was going to throw up, but when he pulled away, the heart began to beat by itself in his hands. "Almost ready! How we feeling?" His voice was thick with the smoke.

"Shit."

"Yeah you look like shit, girl," Roman said. "After this is over, let's get a roll and fritter and fall asleep in front of the telly."

She didn't smile.

"That bad?" he said. "Oof. What's up?"

"Nothing, it can wait." Arabella brushed herself down, and forced a smile that was probably not very convincing.

"We've got two hours until this heart goes back to being dead, and I don't have another one. Can you go get our friend?"

***

Iona hovered on the threshold of Roman's room like there was a barrier in the way.

"Come in or don't, Iona," Arabella snapped. She could count the number of times she had raised her voice to Iona on one hand, and the retaliating guilt was immediate. She tried to ignore it.

It took a long time for Iona to make up her mind. "If you're going to do this, if you're *really* going to do this… you're going to do it without my help. It's against my code."

"Well, if you're not gonna help then get out the doorway," Roman said. "I need clear corridors, please!" He squeezed past her carrying a hessian sack in the vague shape of a human baby, and disappeared down the hallway.

Now out in the corridor, Iona deflated. "I can't stop you doing this, can I?"

"No, I expect not," Bella said. "Not unless you want to tie us down until she dies of natural causes."

Iona looked at her feet. "I'll be in the other room. If you end up biting off more than you can chew, come get me." She looked up to see Holly guiding Verity down the narrow corridor towards Roman's operating theatre. Verity walked with the tiny, unsteady steps of an old woman.

Iona made a noise like she was trying to stop herself from saying something horrible. "Good luck," she eventually fell back on, but it was clipped and short. And then she left.

"How're you doing?" Arabella took Verity's other arm as she hobbled into the room.

"Not great," she huffed, curling in on herself in pain. "Tell me you have something for me."

"It's a little experimental, but we think so," Roman said. He put the beating heart in the sack, and dragged his finger across the edges until it sewed itself shut with magic. It was covered in huge, thick stitches like a baseball, and once it was closed it began to wriggle like a louse.

"What is that?" Verity peered over from the operating chair.

"It's what you're going to be feeding on instead of humans," Roman said. He lifted the goggles up onto his forehead so he could see to inspect the stitching.

"It's a homunculus," Bella said. "It's not really a living thing, but it is technically alive."

Verity watched it wriggle on the table — a limbless, faceless thing. "It's like me."

"We're gonna sew it to your chest," Roman grinned, his eyes veritably sparkling, his face creased by the goggle marks.

"*Roman.*"

"Oh. Sorry." He calmed himself, taking a deep breath, and then repeated, incredibly soberly, "We're going to sew it to your chest."

Verity smirked. "I'm too old to be squeamish, don't worry. Though it is..." She stared at the little fake thing. "Unsettling."

Bella resisted the urge to pace. "We don't know what it's going to do. But you have hours at best." She gulped. "Honestly, I'm amazed you're still fighting the hunger."

Verity lay back on the operating theatre, taken by a dizzy turn. "If it would lift the curse, I'd tear every one of you apart. But it will never be happy. I'll never be able to stop."

"Nice to know wur value." Roman lifted the homunculus sack up. "I don't suppose anyone wants to sing the opening to the Lion King?" A sound escaped the bag, like gas settling in a pipe. Bella blinked, for a second the bunching of the sack around Roman's hands made the thing look like it had little arms and legs.

"Where's Holly?" Verity asked suddenly. "I need Holly." Her head was lolling now, disoriented.

"Went to get her stuff. I'll... go get her?" Arabella and Roman shared a confused look, and then she left Roman to continue the prep work.

She was surprised to find Holly sitting on the couch in the main room, doing a tarot spread on the coffee table. It was Bella's deck, the beaten old deck that Roman had given her years ago that smelled like chip fat and incense.

"You okay?"

"I can't get the answer I want." Holly collected up the cards and shuffled them.

"That's... not how that works at all," Bella laughed. It was very Holly to just keep rolling dice until you got all sixes.

Holly lay back in her chair and stared at the ceiling. "I know. I have a bad feeling about this."

"Me too," Bella said. "I feel like we might be going over the line on this one."

Holly sucked air through her teeth. "We're doing the right thing, yeah?"

"I think so. Though... it seems like we solve a lot of our problems with necromancy these days."

"It'll be fine," Holly said.

Bella nodded.

"No, I was telling myself." She sat the cards down on the coffee table and rapped her fingers off of it. Then, like she was trying to take it by surprise, she snatched a single card from the top of the deck. "Aha!" She turned it round — Three of Wands.

Bella rolled her eyes. "It doesn't count if you keep doing it until you get the answer you want."

Holly waved the card in her face. "We build the future we want. We make it happen. We're witches." She sat the Three of Wands down on the table. A woman in a gold-trimmed wedding gown faced away into the middle distance on the card, leaning on one of three trees. The gold trim of the dress had once been engraved with tooling, in the deck's better days, but had been slowly eroded by the thumbprints of a thousand tarot-readers.

Bella rubbed the bridge of her nose. This was why she tried to treat the cards like a sounding board rather than a divination tool. "She's asking for you in there by the way."

"Oh." Holly stood up.

"What's that all about?"

"She's having these mental dreams, I think her..." She snapped her fingers. "Not coven. Vampire-y coven."

"Brood? I want to say brood."

"Whatever. I think her family are in her head. And apparently my magic holds them off."

"That's... strange. How does that work?"

Holly shrugged. "Aren't you the one who always told me not to question *how* it works, just trust that it does?"

Bella smiled. "You know, I remember teaching you how to cleanse a room. Now you're talking back."

"They grow up so fast," Holly said.

Bella gave her best friend a little side-on hug and a squeeze. It was a grounding hug, just a little touch to remind each other they were still there. It brought a smile to Bella's face before she could even fight it. "Let's go sew a dead man's heart onto a vampire."

***

The operating theatre reeked of formaldehyde, and it was burning Verity's nose. The queasiness was making her heightened senses sharp as a razor's edge. She would have thrown up, but there was of course, nothing in her stomach.

She focused on her breathing, since she couldn't do much more. In, out. In, out. On the cold of the metal table. Next to her, the baby homunculus began to cry — or whatever approximated a cry from a thing with no mouth.

"How's it going, hen?" Roman asked lightly while he got out tools. She'd expected surgical instruments, scalpels and drills. But it was needle and thread, and the censer, and a wooden twig warped with age. "We'll be putting you under in a minute," he said. Bella had scolded his bedside manner, but his casual air was actually quite comforting. Like he'd done this a million times before, like he wasn't worried about it at all.

"Do I have to be asleep for it?"

He nodded, screwing his face up apologetically. "Yeah, sorry. It's going to bond to your subconscious, so you need to be... y'know." He pinched the wick of a large black candle and it ignited in his fingers. "Unconscious."

"Where's Holly?"

"She's coming." He smiled. "Don't worry, she'll be here when we start."

"My ears are burning." And like a ray of sunshine, Holly marched through the open door, Bella in her wake.

Verity sighed in relief, lying back on the table. "They're going to knock me out," she said, looking up at the ceiling. "He'll come for me."

"If he does, he'll get socked in the mouth." Holly smiled. The three of them got to work, drawing in chalk on the floor around her table. She focused on her breathing again. In, out. In, out. Trying not to think about how her organs were starting to fail.

"Could you unbutton this for us?" Bella asked, giving a gentle tug on the collar of her blouse.

Verity fiddled with the buttons, but the dexterity in her fingers had gone. "Sorry. I..." She trailed off as the nausea crested.

"Am I okay to do it for you?" Bella asked. She'd gone cold now, clinical. It really did feel like being in a hospital. Verity hadn't been in a hospital since the Great War.

She nodded, and Bella began to open up her shirt. Verity lay back, breathing deeply, and her eyes fell on the homunculus again. She felt a kinship with it in this moment, getting opened up, a bag of stitches. Maybe they could work together, these two not-alive things.

The coven of witches began to congregate around the table.

"Tits out for the gods," Roman said.

Verity laughed before Bella could scold him, then retched as her diaphragm protested. "Can we get this over with?"

"Count down from ten for us," Bella said gently. Verity reached a hand out and grabbed Holly's, squeezed it tight. She didn't realise how cold and clammy her hand was until Holly's felt like hot coals in her hands.

"Ten. Nine."

They began to chant.

"Grant her rest, grant her sleep,
Swimming under oceans deep."

"Eight. Seven."

"Cradled by the night, pass from..."

And she was in the dark.

chapter 10

For a moment, in the Dark Place, she thought she was alone. Somewhere, in the distance, a baby was crying. She was treading water again.

She followed the cry, her sodden clothes weighing her down as she swam.

The homunculus was floating on the surface, like a piece of driftwood. The piercing sound of its crying went deep into her heart.

It really was a sack, she realised, when she actually got there. A hessian thing in the vague shape of a maggot, vestigial seams that looked almost like legs at the corners as they wriggled.

"It's okay, it's okay," she said quietly, but she didn't even know if it had the capacity to hear her. She reached out with a hand, and it was surprisingly warm to the touch. It grabbed her hand with its body and held on like a kid grabbing their parent on a high ledge.

It was holding her up, she realised. She didn't have to kick anymore. She was rising out of the water, until she was standing on the surface like Breckenridge had. She cradled the homunculus in her arms and rocked it gently like a baby.

She could feel the heat radiating off of it now. "Hello," she said. "We're going to become good friends, I hope." She stroked it. It screwed its featureless face up.

She shifted its weight onto her other arm, her good arm, and when she looked back at the hand that had been holding it, she could see that its threads, its stitching, had worked its way into her arm, tying them together. It didn't hurt, even as it poked into the flesh.

"What is this?"

Breckenridge. His voice sent a shiver down her spine. She turned, and there he was, as usual.

She hid the homunculus, held it behind her back as she looked up at him defiantly.

He rolled his eyes, and already he started to probe her mind, his fingers running over the seams of her brain, coaxing her thoughts out...

And just when the chill of his presence began to run across her subconscious like a virus, she felt... a warmth.

Flame.

She smiled, as a fire began to burn behind her, a flare in the shape of a bird that resolved into a person. "Leave her alone."

Holly.

Breckenridge looked her up and down. "What on earth are you doing in here? This isn't your space, witch."

"You opened the door, I just walked through," Holly said. She looked to Verity. "I'm above you right now, in the operating theatre. We're all behind you."

He waved his hand through the air, like Verity had seen him do a million times before. Reaching his fingers into her mind, planting a compulsion, a placation, a command.

But the fire that burned around Holly was starting to spread, the very lake itself was catching like an oil spill.

He looked at her, confused when her face didn't change.

"Oh. Oh buddy," Holly said.

Breckenridge was looking around, almost disoriented. "I don't... I don't understand."

"I've had people jumbling around in my head before," Holly said. "And I'm strong enough now to make sure that'll never happen again."

"But you can't—"

"Oh it's already happened," Holly said. "Oh, you poor old man. You just put your finger in an electrical outlet. It's just taking a second for your pain receptors to catch up."

The room began to burn, and Breckenridge began to scream as Holly filled his vision—

The illusion broke, and for a moment, Verity could see through the Dark Place into the real world. Their old home, up in Park Circus, with its high ceilings and pristine brick roads. He was in his study, lying on his chaise-longue, and she watched as he sat bolt-upright suddenly. His head ripped open into two pieces, hanging suspended, lolling against his shoulders like a falling tree. The enormous gaping wound where his brain used to be was on fire, visible to the world.

Holly stood for a moment. Finally, pleased.

The two halves of his head, smiled. "Oh... Now *that*, is interesting," he said, in their heads. Already his neck was beginning to knit itself back together, the immortal vampire healing doing its dark work.

For a moment, Verity had almost imagined maybe Holly could actually kill him.

He reached his hand out, as his vertebrae snapped back into place, his chin, his lips, his nose healing, reforming, but his eyes locked solely on Holly.

Holly threw her arms up, and a ring of fire lit around them. A protective spell. Already Verity could feel his fingers teasing the edges, feeling for weak points, seams.

"I am *really* glad that worked," Holly said, turning back to Verity.

"I..." Words failed Verity. "I've never seen anyone resist Breckenridge's telepathy."

Holly shifted her weight from one foot to the other. "Let's just say it's kind of a sore spot for me."

"Thank you. For all of this."

"It's not just me," Holly said. "We've got your back, all of us. Bella and Roman are still up there, and we're gonna make sure you wake up okay."

The homunculus started to cry again. The twine had continued to wrap around her like vines. She had a sudden wave of claustrophobia, but she fought it.

"I better get back," Holly said.

"Wait, but what about…?" She gestured to the ring of fire. He was still out there.

"I'll hold him back from up there. As long as it takes."

"But—"

She put a hand on Verity's cheek. "It's going to be okay."

Verity smiled. She knew, in this space, that Holly didn't know that. But she felt the conviction, like steel. She smiled. "I'll see you around."

Holly vanished in a wisp of smoke.

Verity lay down, felt the fire warm her, a light in the dark. A tiny, flickering flame. She breathed, and felt the thread encase her like a chrysalis.

***

She wasn't sure how long she'd been asleep for. It had been the first time in decades since she'd dreamt without Breckenridge in her head. When her eyes opened, she was almost surprised to see the same candlelit room she'd passed out in.

Her whole mouth felt dry. She wet her lips, and tried to sit up, but there was a weight on her chest.

She looked down. The homunculus dozed quietly, grafted onto her chest with thread so thick it looked more like rope.

It looked… disgusting, she thought. An abomination. But it was hers. She stroked the head of the homunculus bag idly, looking around.

Roman was asleep on a fold-out bed in the corner, Holly dozing in a chair. They'd waited by her bedside.

For now, it looked like everything was going to be okay.

***

Bella had thought she would've slept fitfully, with everything going on, and so much on her mind. But she'd been so tired, she hit the pillow and passed out immediately.

She turned, wanting to nuzzle Munro and steal some of her heat, keeping her eyes squeezed shut to keep the morning out.

Her hands found Munro's furs, pulled them in, and then a groggy confusion washed over her. She opened her eyes.

The bed was empty. Munro's furs were there, the bed undisturbed, like her body had been snatched away while they'd slept.

The adrenaline panic shot through her. "Munro?" she said, first quietly, and then, when there was no answer, shouting. "Munro!"

And, between blinks, Munro appeared on the bed, as though she'd always been there. Naked without her furs, the weight on the bed didn't even shift. Like she'd been there the whole time.

"Morning," she said, half-asleep.

Arabella clutched the furs like they were going to run away. "You're fading again."

Munro's face dropped. But not the face of someone surprised. The face of someone who'd been found out.

chapter 11

"Munro?" Arabella flicked the desk lamp on.

"I'm fine. I'm okay. Just go back to bed."

"Munro, what's happening?" She looked over Munro's shoulder, and saw it.

Most of Munro's hand was gone. Three fingers and half the palm, just faded to nothing.

"Oh, Goddess…"

"Oh no," Munro said, looking up. "Listen, I didn't want you to worry, I—"

"How long has this been happening?"

Munro smarted against the pain of the missing fingers.

"Munro."

"Yep, just a sec…" Munro hissed, squeezing her wrist. She rode the crest of the pain, and then her fingers started to reappear from the aether.

After several, excruciating seconds, the entire hand was back, and Munro was heaving like she'd run a marathon.

"How long has this been happening?" Arabella's voice was low now, resigned. The trick they'd played on death. Death had caught up.

"Few weeks…" Munro said. "I didn't want to worry you."

"No," Arabella said. "We're not doing this."

"I don't think we have a choice, my love."

"No." She spoke the word into the air like a red rubber stamp. She could feel the anger bubbling inside her like a cauldron. "It's barely been any time at all. We're not doing this. It's not fair. We're going to—"

"Bella, you're panicking. It's okay." Munro put a hand on Arabella's shoulder but she shrugged it off.

"No! No! Are you fucking kidding? After all this, all we've done to keep you here, and now your time is up? We're supposed to just accept that?"

"I—"

"We broke spacetime and you're already supposed to just shuffle off into the night?"

"I just—"

"No, we're doing something about this. You're not just going to disappear like Marty McFly, I—"

"I don't know who that is!" Munro shouted, exasperatedly, finally able to get a word in edgeways.

Arabella's dam burst, and she started blubbering. Loud, wet, sobs as she grabbed Munro like a life raft. "I don't want you to go. I don't. I don't want you to go. You can't go."

"Listen," Munro said, clutching her. "I know you love to talk, and plan, and take the initiative, and you never give up. I love that. But I'm not good at it. Talking about it. So I need you to... just listen."

Arabella wiped her nose with the sleeve of her dressing gown. "Okay."

"The average selkie lives a human lifespan. I am *two hundred years old*, Bella. I've had close calls... hundreds of times, and literally cheated death twice. I'm... I'm done. I'm happy with my life's work."

Arabella took a second to digest what Munro was saying. "You're happy with just... fading away?"

"I was given a second chance, and it was cocked up for me. And then the universe gave me a third chance. Most people only get one chance. I'm happy."

"Is..." Arabella's stomach was doing backflips. "Wait, what do we do now?"

"The same thing we were already doing," Munro said. "Enjoy the borrowed time." She grinned. "Somehow, the air tastes better when it's illegal."

"I don't like this," Arabella said. "No. No. It's just magic. There must be something I can do."

Munro looked down, averting her eyes.

"I promise baby, I will spend my entire life hiding you from the Reaper if I have to."

"That's what Nicnevin used to say..."

She may as well have slapped her across the mouth. Bella was lost for words.

chapter 12

Verity felt queasy. She'd been so used to feeling hungry, the lack almost felt dangerous. Like getting a tooth out. She was numb but aware she should be in agony.

The homunculus wailed on her chest, and she stroked the back of its head absently.

Roman had a corpse lying on the operating table. "I get it, you know," he said absently. He was wearing lace gloves as he pushed the person's throat from one side to another, drawing marking lines on their neck like a plastic surgeon. He'd done this before.

He looked up, and deep into Verity's eyes. "You got given a pretty shit hand."

"I don't think I got given a hand at all."

He smiled. "Well, I'll see if we can't give you a blackjack."

She looked confused.

He blinked. "I don't... play cards. Does that make sense? Is blackjack a thing? I only play Scabby Queen."

She snorted, then moved to cover it. He grinned, revealing his snaggly teeth, before reaching for a glass of white wine by the operating table and drinking it carefully so as not to smudge his lipstick.

"Should you really be drinking while you're doing that?"

"Non-alcoholic, babes." He put the wine down and opened a sleeve of Hobnobs on the operating table next to them. "I just do it for the aesthetic." Biscuit in mouth, he plucked a metal stylus from in his hair, and started to scratch at the slate operating table like he was marking it.

"What are you doing?"

"Time bubble," he said with his mouth full.

"Wh— time bubble?"

He swallowed. "Rotting corpses give me the bolk. So" —he gestured— "time bubble."

"Witches can make time bubbles."

"Witches can do anything!" Roman said. "You just need the willpower."

"And you don't have to hurt anyone?" Verity stood up. The corpse on the table was a young guy. Maybe just over twenty. She could see herself in him.

"Nah, see, it's fine," Roman said. "Taking a lot of energy, but he's frozen! It's where I got the heart from. We'll use all of him, eventually."

"So even with this," Verity said, gesturing to the homunculus baby that lay across her chest, "a man still had to die for me to live."

Roman see-sawed his hand. "Eh. He was already dead, to be fair. More like an organ donation. And trust me" —his face took on a darker tone— "he was a heartless bastard in life anyway."

She looked down. The corpse on the table had a plate behind its teeth to stop its lower jaw from collapsing.

Roman ate another Hobnob, and swayed on his feet.

"Are you okay?"

"Mhm!" he gave a thumbs-up but his eyes were still wobbling. "I uh, had to prop the heart up with my own blood. I'll be fine. It was a one-off."

"Wait, so I'm still drinking your blood?"

Roman sighed beleagueredly and took his gloves off, wiping his sweaty hands on the sleeves of his poet shirt. "God, you are hard work, Verity. No, the little demon baby needed some blood. He needs something to pump and this corpse's blood is stagnant. Now he's attached to you. It's not the same."

"Feels the same."

"Well, I've done it now. Relax, I consent! And think of the return on investment!" Roman snapped his fingers. "Alright Jonathan, back to whatever hellhole you came from."

As if a VHS tape was playing in reverse, the rotting body on the table shifted, magical ink markings vanishing in reverse order before he lifted off the table onto his feet, reversing gravity, reversing entropy. He moonwalked backwards out the room.

"Jonathan? You know the corpse?"

"He's my nemesis."

"You have a nemesis."

"Right, listen, it's completely normal to have a nemesis!" Roman said. "And he's a wee prick as well, you don't even know him, there was this one—"

Holly poked her head in. "Roman... why did Jonathan just walk backwards out of your room?"

"You keep your neck in!"

"You better be minding the Code, or Bella'll be pissed."

A sudden burst of safety bloomed in Verity's chest. "Holly!" She coughed, realising how loud that had been, and collected herself.

Holly smiled — "Heya," — before turning her ire on Roman. "Do No Harm, Roman!"

"Yeah, and Take No Shit! And I'm sick of his shit!"

"He's *dead*. He's not giving anyone any shit anymore!"

"He thinks he's better than me! He'll get his, Holly! Mark my fucking words, he'll get his!"

Verity tried to stand up, but her head swam, the blood pumping through her and the homunculus rushing from her head. Roman made a clumsy attempt to catch her, missed, and Verity grabbed the side of a table.

Holly pinched the bridge of her nose. "Why do I leave you in charge of anything, Roman?"

"A bitch gets results!" Roman said. "Those results may be a D in Intermediate Maths but I get them!" He helped Verity to sit back down. "What the fuck's going on today, Holly? Why are you on my arse?"

Verity clutched at the homunculus before remembering it was just a sack of entrails and blood. She took a deep breath as her peripheral vision came back. She shouldn't be thinking of it like a baby, she should be thinking of it like an oxygen tank.

"Here, let me see," Roman said, removing the lace gloves and stepping up to eye the stitching. "Connection still looks fine."

"You might need to watch yourself for a few days," Holly said.

The homunculus made a gurgling noise on her chest, like an empty stomach, like a child stirring in its sleep.

"Yeah..." Verity said. "Yeah."

She fought the urge to scratch the homunculus off of her.

chapter 13

The sunlight was antagonistic as it streamed through the blinds in the morning. Arabella sat up, no more rested than when she'd gone to bed.

The planner brain had activated. It had always been how she dealt with stress.

She grabbed her suitcase from the top of the wardrobe and started throwing clothes in it, packing everything tightly into cubes. She had managed to get about a week's worth of clothes all set, and was heading to the toiletries when Munro finally woke up.

"Are the British coming?" She blinked at the open suitcase.

"I'm packing so we can go on holiday, dafty," Arabella said.

"What, now?" Munro said. She sat up. "What's the rush?"

"You are *literally* disappearing, Munro. I'm sorry, I wasted so much time, I—"

"Hey." Munro stood up out of bed and hugged her in one fluid motion. "Not a single day of this has been a waste."

Arabella deflated. "No, I know, I—" She sighed. "I just want to make sure you have no regrets."

"I would not change a moment," Munro said.

Arabella smiled — for a moment Munro was like anaesthetic. She leaned in and kissed her, just in the corner of the mouth. "I love you." In that moment, as the words crossed their mouths, she remembered again. And she knew she wouldn't get to say it many more times. "I love you, I love you, I love you."

"I love you too." Munro squeezed her, then stepped out to go shower.

Arabella stood there for a second, gathering her feelings and trying to remember where she was. "Toiletries!" she shouted, rushing off before Munro locked the bathroom door, trying to ignore the spiky, ugly, selfish feeling in her gut that remained despite their conversation.

She stepped into the room as Munro ran the hot water and slipped out of her seal furs. "I think I might go for a walk this morning if that's okay. I feel weird."

"Do you want me to come with you?"

"I need to clear my head."

"Okay, that makes sense. Do you wanna stop by the Archive when you're ready? I'll head there."

Munro nodded. She folded her arms over her chest like she was suddenly cold, standing there naked on the bathmat before her partner. The hiss of the shower intensified behind them.

Arabella gave her another peck on the cheek. "I'll give you some space." And she took the wash bag, and left.

***

Bella finally staggered over the door of the Archive. Her brain was like cotton wool, barely aware of what was going on around her. Twice she'd been caught at the traffic lights, staring at the green man.

Munro had wanted some time alone. Now? Why? Didn't she realise she only had a precious little time left?

No.

No.

Stop that.

She gripped her head. She was completely drifting.

Of course Munro wanted time to process. How long had she been going through this by herself? Sleeping by Bella every night, knowing it might be the last time, and Bella was just snoring like an idiot?

For the first time in her life standing in the foyer of the Archive, she didn't want to be here.

There was no-one about, but noises of activity in the rooms down the back. She needed to disappear, she needed to—

Bathroom.

She shuffled down the room, trying to move quickly but make as little noise as possible. Right on cue however, Holly burst out of Iona's study, waving a book in her face.

"Bella, you've got no idea what some of these necromancers got up to, I— Bella?"

Bella knew her lip was quivering, could feel her throat ache and her chin pucker like a golf ball, but there was nothing she could do to stop it.

"Bella, is everything okay?" Holly dropped the antique book on the floor like scrap paper.

"Munro's dying."

Holly's face dropped. She started to well up. "Aw hen, I'm so sorry."

And that, for some reason, was what did it.

Bella burst like a dam. She grabbed Holly like she was going to fall through the floor, wailed like a banshee, and felt Holly's tight grip just hold her. Holly, her best friend, her rock. Helpless. Both of them.

"What am I going to do?" She just kept saying it over and over again, pleading with the universe for an answer that never came.

She was aware of Holly whisking her into the room, of sitting her on the couch, and then a cup of tea was in her hands and she was just sobbing into it.

Eventually, she became aware of the world around her, and she knew that some time had passed, because the tea was cold. But Holly was still just sitting there, rubbing her back, holding her hand.

She wiped her nose with her sleeve, and wiped her eyes with her other sleeve. "Thank you. For sitting with me."

"I'm sorry," Holly said again. Her cheeks and eyes were puffy, and red as her hair.

"God it's like we're kids again. Shut in a wee room, greeting."

"At least the room is nicer." Holly smiled.

Arabella nodded, looking around the room. She could see the glowing rune lines along the walls, Holly must have sealed it with a quick silence spell. "You know, you've become some witch."

"Learned from the best," Holly said. "When did you find out about...?"

"This morning," Bella said. "She wants some time to think about stuff. Like, before she goes. Oh Goddess, she's going to go."

"We just have to make her comfortable."

"Yeah." She was fighting bursting into tears again. There was that spiky feeling again. Like Nicnevin herself had shoved a knife in her abdomen.

"Well, you had a choice of eight billion people and you picked a two hundred-year old undead selkie." Holly had never been able to fight the urge to crack a joke, even with her eyes swollen like fresh bruises from crying. "What was it you said? You want someone who will ruin your life?"

Arabella laughed, snot streaming down her nose. She wiped it again. "In fairness to me, have you seen her biceps?"

Holly cackled. Arabella was laughing and crying at the same time in a way that was making her brain whirr like she was about to have a panic attack.

"We'll get through this. We knew this was coming. It'll be okay."

"No... it won't though," Arabella said. "Will it?"

Holly was silent. "No. I don't know why I said that, I'm sorry."

"She could disappear any day now. The spell didn't work."

"Oh, come on now," Holly said. "It did its work. You've still got time together. You can't think like that."

Bella squeezed Holly's hand so tight her knuckles threatened to pop. But Holly just squeezed back. "We're gonna get through this. We're gonna get through it."

But no matter how many times Holly said it, Bella knew she was wrong. There were some things about the world that words couldn't manifest.

***

Arabella awoke on the couch, unaware she'd fallen asleep. Her face was wet with drool and tears, and the pillow under her was sodden.

Holly had multiple books splayed out in front of her, compiling notes from them.

"What are you doing?" Arabella asked, her voice still muggy with sleep.

"Oh, you're up," Holly said. "Sorry. I'm working on something for Verity."

Arabella wiped her eyes. She'd never felt so tired. She could've gone back to sleep, slept for a year. Eventually, she twigged. "Oh. Right. Of course."

There was a chap on the door. Holly got up to answer it.

"O— Alright, Munro?" she said. If Bella had felt a bit better, she might have laughed. Holly always defaulted to talking like a middle-aged dad when she was awkward. She didn't look up to see if she'd shaken Munro's hand. She hoped she had. Munro had always found that funny.

"Hi, Hol," Munro said. "Is Bella in?"

"Aye, sorry, sorry." The door creaked as Holly opened it all the way, and Bella threw a glamour on her face to hide the tears.

"Hi babe," Bella said, smiling. "How was your walk?"

Munro shrugged. "It was... outside."

"I'm gonna give you two some space," Holly said. She reached out like she was going to pet Munro on the shoulder, then didn't. "Cool. Cool. Alright," she said, stepping out, closing the door behind her.

"How are you feeling?" Bella asked.

"Besides 'on death's door'?" Munro laughed.

"... Yeah," Bella said.

Munro looked at her feet. "Yeah. Fine. Business as usual."

"It's not, though, is it...?"

Munro stroked Bella cheek. "I don't know. I'd quite like to treat it that way."

Bella smiled. "Sure. Of course. Whatever you need." She looked into her eyes, smiled. Beaming confidence into the abyss. She furrowed her brow. "Munro?"

"I'm fine," Munro said. Her eyes were fogging over, the colour in her irises, her pupils bleaching. "I'm just... just gonna go to the bathroom." She let go, staggering—

Bella held her tight. "It's okay. Whatever's happening, you're not alone. I've got you."

"No, I—" Munro gasped, an intake of air like she was about to be plunged underwater, and then she zoned out completely.

Bella watched her stare into space. "Munro? Munro, can you hear me?"

Munro didn't respond.

How long had she been going through this alone?

***

The skies above are stormy, and I am far from home. My lungs burn. I break the surface of the water, just long enough to get a breath, and then I am back under. The wind and the rain threaten to peel the skin from my bones. I know, even then, that there is no way I will find you in one piece. But still I search.

I will look for you until I am nothing but bone and dust.

—

Lily has her father's eyes. She has been passed around the room like a loaf of bread, and finally she is in my arms. "Hello, little one," I say, and I stroke her cheek with the back of my finger. She breathes quietly, eyes closed. She is supernaturally soft, her wee nose smaller than a button. She smells of milk and cotton. I rock her.

"What do you think, Granny or Granma?" Haar says.

"Ohhh, I don't mind," I coo. "Do you mind? I don't mind at all."

Baby Lily screws her face up, cries.

"Oh no!" I rub her back. Aww, babies. Every discomfort brand new, a unique cruelty in the universe.

Lily farts, and promptly falls back asleep.

Everyone laughs

—

The rain is lashing us, but we're already so wet it means nothing.

That little baby is now a young woman, hiding behind her parents. She won't look at me. Her father has his hand on the axe in his belt. Please. As if he would bring it against his own mother.

I swallow. "Haar, don't do this."

He isn't looking at her either. He's staring into the distance, not making eye contact. "Munro Selkiefolk, you are banished, and will not return to our shore."

"And what if I do?" I ask. God, I used to love an argument. "What will you do, Haar? Kill me?"

He makes eye contact with me, for the first time that day. "If I have to."

I am struck dumb.

It still cuts, all these years later.

I never do find out whether he had the balls to attack me for returning. After he said that, I didn't see the point in finding out.

I turn, and see Nicnevin standing on the horizon, a lone figure, an imposing statue in the mist. I wish she would pull a string to stop the rain, but I'm grateful it hides the tears

—

I am winded, looking up at the murky shadows above. I can't breathe. I reach for the spear in my chest, and for a moment I fear the worst.

I look down.

The tip has punctured the plate, and is jammed in there tight. It didn't make it through the chainmail. I heave for breath, fighting my winded lungs, my diaphragm, but make time to say a silent prayer to whoever upstairs took pity on me.

I snap the shaft of the spear off as I get to my feet, look for my love.

"Nicnevin!" I shout, and she is hundreds of feet in the air, her arms tendrils of seaweed that lift enemy combatants like the tide sweeping everything, anything out to sea. A creature with the head of a wolf and the body of a tiger leaps at her but I hurl the spear.

"Munro." I feel a hand holding mine in the muck, and she looked at it as the shield in her hand started to fade. She was in the room. The Archive. She was still here.

"Bella?" she asked. She didn't recognise the faces, two of them, just guessed from context. One held her hand. They almost didn't look like people's faces, just strange shapes of skin, full of holes.

And then whatever synapse needed to connect did, and the picture formed. "Bella," she said. She pulled her into a hug.

Holly stood in the door — hadn't she left? How long had she been out? — looking at them in concern. "That was... wild."

"What happened?" Munro said.

"That's never happened to you before?"

"No, it happens a lot. I just... I don't know what it looks like from the outside."

"It's okay," Bella said. "You don't have to worry." She was squeezing Munro's hands like she'd been outside in the freezing cold and she was trying to bring the life back into them.

"It looked like..." Holly said, trailing off, looking out beyond the door. "I guess if I had to put words on it... I would say it looked something like that..." She nodded beyond their gaze. "What the hell?"

Roman's voice came tunnelling through the Archive, propelled by magic. *"Holly!"* He sounded like he was outside, in the plaza.

"I'll be right back," Holly said, jumping up and leaving, her cardigan swishing behind her in the doorway.

***

Bella couldn't think, her heart was pounding. Munro had been flickering, fading in and out like a bad radio signal.

"Come on, let's go," Munro said, lumbering after Holly. As if none of that had happened. She didn't, she couldn't — she just needed time to think!

She forced herself out of the room, staggering after her. Roman and Holly were shouting at each other but her brain was so fuzzy she could barely make it out.

It was a man. He was flickering the same way Munro had been.

"Hi there, is this number seven aye? Hi there, is this number seven aye? Hi there, is this number seven aye?" he said. Over and over and over again.

Roman was transfixed, trying not to touch him in case it was catching. "What the..."

Eventually, the pattern collapsed. "Hi there, is this number s—" He seemed to shiver, and fell to the ground in a heap.

Iona and Roman hovered over him. He lay on the concrete in the plaza, as if he'd been dead for hours.

"He's deid!" Roman shouted.

"Yes I can fucking see that, Roman!" Holly said, falling to the corpse's side and casting her hands over him, a metaphysical frisk. "Who is he?"

"He was just walking past when I saw him keel over!"

"It's like his life force was sucked right out of him," Holly said.

"That's what I said," Iona said.

"The vampires?" Holly asked.

Iona shook her head. "In broad daylight?"

By this point, Bella got close enough to see. He was just some guy. Mid-forties, hairline starting to give up the ghost. He had big horn-rimmed glasses and a superhero t-shirt on under his hi-vis vest. His face was frozen, like he'd seen the face of God and the shock had killed him.

"Are you okay?" Roman said, looking up at Bella. Her face must have still been puffy.

"Fine," she lied.

He raised an eyebrow.

Iona dropped to her knees by the man. "Oh, poor boy." She tidied him up a bit, gave him a bit of dignity.

"What do we do?" Roman said. "I've never had to deal with a dead member of the public that wasn't... eaten by a monster or something."

"We phone the emergency services, Roman." Iona rolled her eyes. "Whatever happened to him, he has a family that deserve some peace. Holly," she nodded. "Would you mind, petal?" Then she looked down at the man. "...Maybe just for good measure." She tapped his chest, and the corpse jittered. "There. Now it looks like his heart gave out."

"But what *did* happen?" Holly said.

"Something snuffed his life out. I suspect by accident, or they would've hidden their tracks." She looked up, through them all, at Munro, who was just making her way out to see what all the commotion was.

Bella's heart froze.

Having to announce the worst thing to ever happen to you, to everyone you know, it just didn't seem fair.

***

Iona shut the door to her study as Bella and Munro entered. Who knew what Holly was telling Roman outside. "Okay, I'm going to ask a blunt question — did you kill that man out there?"

"What? No!" Munro said.

Iona lifted her hands, and a single emerald thread appeared around Munro's head. It trailed like a comet, in perfect concentric circles. "Well there it is."

"There's what?" Bella said. She could feel her temper flaring, she had other things to be worrying about.

"His life force. That's where it went. His world line decayed, it'll be gone by the morning."

"Can we put it back?" Munro asked.

"No," Iona said. "I take it then that..."

Munro grit her teeth, the silence cutting her.

"I see," Iona said. "Your window of grace is closing. You are now a danger to the people around you."

Munro nodded.

"Wait, what?" Bella said. "What are you saying?"

"Her weight is pressing on the fabric of the ley lines, the map of all of our lives. That fabric is beginning to unravel around her, it's sucking people in."

"I mean it's not sucked us in."

"No. I suspect witches are strong enough to withstand it. For now. But the longer you leave it, the worse it'll get."

Munro wiped a tear from her eye. Bella hung on her, but then realised it might be smothering her, and fell back to holding her hand.

Bella's voice was breaking as she asked, "Is there nothing we can do? No-one who can help?"

Iona chewed her lip. "We've said it the whole time, when the spell starts to fail, that's all the grace we have."

"That *we* have," Bella said. "Surely there's someone who knows more about this than we do."

"There's Nicnevin," Munro said. "No-one knows more than necromancy than she does. And she said, that's it."

"Well, maybe she'll change her mind," Bella said. "Have a flash of inspiration."

"Bella," Munro grumbled.

"What?" Bella said. "We should at least ask!"

Munro looked to Iona, as if for help.

"I can't see what harm it would do," Iona said. She collected herself. "And, since I didn't get a chance to say it until now, I'm sorry to hear this is finally happening, Munro. We all hoped you'd get longer than this." A sheen betrayed the tears in her eyes in the dark room.

Munro opened her mouth as if to protest, before sighing. "Thank you, Iona."

Bella was bubbling over. It seemed like Munro's ideal situation would be to disappear without anyone even knowing she was gone.

"The only problem is, I don't think we have a way of contacting Nicnevin," Iona said. "She's a bit above our paygrade."

"Don't worry, I have a way," Munro said.

It was only then Bella realised that they were about to essentially phone up Munro's ex.

chapter 14

Bella tried not to act like she was watching Munro set up the call. "I'm surprised you still remember the configuration…" she said, when she couldn't help herself.

"I used it for a long time," Munro said. "I also remember the one I used to talk to you too, if it helps."

Bella smirked. "It does, thank you."

Nicnevin's network stretched far and wide, through the trees of the Glasgow Outwith and into the rest of Elf-hame. Any place where water flowed, and stopped, was hers.

In hindsight, using it to talk to Munro under Nicnevin's nose had been… incredibly cavalier. The things new love did to your brain.

Munro smiled, planting a kiss on Bella's cheekbone as she stood up. "Love you."

"Love you too," Bella said. "Do you need help with getting it going?"

"I shouldn't do. I think I should just be able to ask her to open the connection and she can do it."

"Calling reverse charges, I like it," Bella said.

Munro sat in the circle, put her hand on the floor and closed her eyes. The candles flickered in time with her breath.

"Nicnevin?" she asked. Her voice echoed.

"*Munro?*" came the response, ringing around the room like a ghost. "*Well I never!*" The unexpected sound of her voice was like a nail file on

Bella's teeth.

"Yeah, it's me."

"By the tides, I haven't seen you since... well. Since you broke my heart."

Munro squirmed. Bella boiled. She didn't have to sound so smug about it.

"Sorry," Munro said.

"Honey, I am so over it? Hang on—" she cut herself off, and there was the sound of fussing. Smoke began to billow from the candles, and there, in the smoke, was her face. *"Hey gorgeous."* She winked. *"So! What can I do for... oh."*

She'd spotted Bella and Iona in the background.

"Your Grace," Iona said.

Bella just nodded.

Nicnevin smiled. *"How good to see you again. I must say, you look far better outside of a jar than trapped in one, Ms. Howell."*

"I'm glad you feel that way, ma'am," Iona said.

"Hm. Quite." She had evidently decided to ignore Bella standing there. *"So. What can I do for you?"*

"I wasn't going to call but... they insisted," Munro said. "It's... that spell. It's wearing off."

At this, Nicnevin looked up, her full attention. If she was acting, she was good enough to fool even Arabella.

For a moment, the image disappeared, as if she'd hidden herself. When she returned, she was the image of poise. *"Oh no, Munro, I'm so sorry."*

She hadn't known.

For some reason this made Bella breathe a sigh of relief. So the Arch-Witch wasn't all-knowing after all.

"It is what it is." Munro shifted her shoulders as if there was a weight on them, and tried to avoid eye contact.

"Munro..." Nicnevin just looked at her for a second.

"It's Bella's idea," Munro gestured over to Bella. Nicnevin looked over, as Bella scrambled to not look like she'd been eavesdropping, like a spider spotted in the bath. "I'm... causing problems for the locals."

"Oh well, of course. Your world line is so frayed, I wouldn't be surprised if it started tugging on everyone you walked by. A simple mortal would unravel in a moment."

Munro steeled herself. "Is there anything we can do?"

"Go somewhere where there's no mortals," Nicnevin said, as if it was obvious. *"Until that happens, I'm afraid..."* She let it hang.

"Leave?" Bella said. "She can't leave!"

"I don't really know that there's much else you can do about it, I'm afraid. Every time you slip, you form a gap in the ley line. Non-magical people are just more susceptible to falling in."

"We have to go... back to Elf-hame?" Bella said.

"We? No way. You're not leaving your family behind," Munro said. "Plus, I could be putting you at risk as well."

Bella's heart leapt, her stomach dropping out. "Hang on just a second—"

"You could stay at my place, if you like," Nicnevin said warmly.

"Hang on just a fucking second!" Bella shouted.

"I don't think that's a good idea, Nevin..."

"Oh don't be silly. You could bring your wee... thing, if you wanted," Nicnevin nodded to Bella. *"Hell, you could bring your whole coven. It's not like I'm hurting for space, you've seen my house."*

Munro hemmed and hawed. "I couldn't—"

A moment of relief for Bella. Munro wasn't going for it.

"Nonsense, silly. If you stay here, I might be able to try and find a more lasting solution for your problem," she said it oh-so-flippantly. *"Besides, I can't have you shuffling off without making you my steamed kipper one last time."*

Munro paused. "I forgot about your steamed kipper."

Damn your stomach, woman!

"I'll go ask the others what they think," Munro said. "Thanks for the offer, Nicnevin."

"Not a problem at all! If you make your way to Reminiscence, I'll get you from there." Nicnevin said. She looked down, like she was checking something. *"Where the hell is that driver?"*

The smoke started to dissipate. Munro turned to walk back over to Bella. She was smirking. Smirking!

The image of Nicnevin reappeared for a moment. *"Oh, and Munro!"*

"Mm." Munro looked back, noncommittally, the smile still sitting on her lips.

"I really am sorry."

She looked sincere, but Bella was starting to think this was all a ruse again.

Munro nodded. "Mm," she repeated, before stepping away. The candles flared, and went out.

"That was nice," Bella said. So fake it smelled like cling film. "We're not going to go though, right?"

Munro shrugged. "Not if you don't feel comfortable with it."

Bella spluttered. "Why wouldn't I feel comfortable with it?"

Munro stroked her cheek. "It's fine. We don't have to."

Bella shook herself, trying to remind herself she wasn't the centre of the universe. "Munro. If you want to go, we'll go. I just want you to be safe."

Munro smiled at her. "Okay."

The pit in Bella's stomach yawned wider. "It'll be fine." She couldn't tell if she was lying. But honestly, if it meant keeping Munro she would burn the world to make it true. Everything was going to be fine.

***

Arabella chapped the door to Roman's room. Now that she had a task, all she could think about was completing it. It was strange, how she'd packed this morning as if she knew they'd have to go *somewhere*.

"I just talked to Iona," she said to Holly. "We're taking a trip into Elf-hame." She seemed all business now. Verity tried to keep to herself. "I was asked to ask if anyone else would like to come."

"I'm going," Holly said, before Arabella could even get the words out.

"But you have..." Arabella looked briefly at Verity before she could stop herself. "Responsibilities here."

Holly squirmed.

"Go," Verity said. "It seems important."

"We can't just let you stay here by yourself," Roman rolled his eyes. "What if you go through my porn?"

Verity blinked. "Um, I promise I won't go through your porn."

"He's joking," Holly said. "To be honest though, it might be good for you. There's no way your grandfather would be able to reach you in the Glasgow Outwith."

Verity blinked. She hadn't considered this. Vampires weren't, on the whole, welcome in Elf-hame — it was part of why she was so hesitant to agree.

"And the constant mists mean you'd probably be able to go out during the day."

She swallowed. That would be nice.

"I don't... Maybe..." She would be lying if she said it wasn't the way Holly was looking at her that was convincing her.

"Good, I'll g—" Arabella started, before she was cut off by Roman's gangly arms wrapping round her head in a clumsy hug. "Roman..."

He rubbed her shoulders vigorously. "You seem like you need a hug," he said.

She leaned into the hug, exhaling deeply. "Thanks Roman. I did."

Roman sighed happily, and it vibrated through Bella's chest. Then he added, "Also, I haven't eaten since I gave blood to the homunculus."

"Are you going to pass out?"

"Don't know. Please catch me if I dip."

chapter 15

"Just like old times, eh!" Roman hoisted his little rucksack over his shoulder. He was still looking a bit peaky from his bloodletting. Verity stood by the door with a small suitcase of clothes Holly had hastily bought on the high street with the money out the Archive's tip jar.

They were a strange-looking bunch, Verity thought. Their varying ages and styles and body shapes — Iona with her long formal dresses and her smart suitcase; Holly with nothing but the clothes on her back in bright red colours like a warning light; Roman trekking a huge camping duffel bag but otherwise looking completely unprepared for being outside in his skirt and his mesh top. The devil potato baby on Verity's chest was just another detail in their bizarre tapestry.

The only person who looked more uncomfortable than Verity did was Munro. She hung in the background like a shadow, hiding in the furs she wore over her like a shawl. It was strange, this enormous, muscled woman who seemed to take up no space in Verity's vampire senses. Like other vampires, she couldn't smell her — but unlike other vampires she had no tie to the Dark Scaffold, caused no instinctive tingle of the presence of family.

Holly was making small talk that Verity couldn't make out. She couldn't concentrate. And without the sound of the bloodlust rising constantly, with the homunculus purring contentedly on her chest, the tingling of the voice in her head was gone. The one that told her how to open her fangs and unhinge her jaw, the one that had hungered in her belly for centuries and was now listlessly sleeping...

That voice looked at Munro and said, 'you're like me'.

***

They couldn't Go-a-Wander to get to Elf-hame this time, not with Verity — a vampire would just be left behind. Besides, Bella had a quicker way and speed was, after all, of the essence.

They got on a train. Didn't matter which one, any would do — it just needed sealable doors and a space with no one else around. They were lucky it was the time of year when the sun went down by four in the afternoon, so they didn't need to work out how to get Verity into the train station.

The group of them took up two tables like one of those big boisterous families with all the screaming kids, and Roman sat painting his nails while Holly continued her scribblings.

Verity was looking deeply uncomfortable, and Bella's urge to say something, to be the Mum Friend, was like a kettle whistling in the back of her head. But Munro was sitting across from her, staring out the window at the station, looking so... vacant.

Bella nudged Munro's toe. Then again.

"Mm?" Munro looked at her, her train of thought disrupted.

"You okay?"

"I'm fine." It had a sharp finality to it that Munro never had. Munro was aloof, but she was never brusque. Not with her anyway.

"I've got the DVD player if you want—"

"I'm good." It didn't sound rude, as such. Not like Munro was annoyed at her. But for some reason it felt like it.

"Okay," she said. She tried to sound nonchalant, and then immediately worried it came across as chipper. Shit. Fuck.

Roman nudged her. "Can you pass my juice?" he asked, like they were just on a school trip. She really had to tell him soon.

She passed him the Lucozade Sport and watched him fiddle with the cap for a minute trying to get it open without messing up his top coat, before she snatched it off him and did it for him.

"Jeez, Bella, what bee flew up your arsehole…" he raised an eyebrow at her. "You alright?"

"I'm fine."

He looked at Bella, then at Munro, then tanned the rest of his Lucozade.

***

Once the train was in motion, Arabella got up and made sure the doors between the carriages were closed. She usually did this trip by herself, where she could just throw a blanket over her head before the train conductor came past. But the theory was the same either way.

Door, closed. Curtains, drawn as much as possible. You had to not see where you were, but feel that you were in motion. Arabella had to do it fast before the rocking of the train set her car sickness off.

She arrived back at the table to find Iona already throwing out her wee rug so she could do the spell.

"I'll take it from here, petal. You sit down," Iona offered with a smile, lit only by the slit of dim light through the drawn curtains, refracting off her black hair and her features.

Bella sat down, and looked at Munro, who was still looking out the window as if the curtain wasn't in the way.

Iona started with deep breathing, synchronised with the rock of the train. There was a knack to it, staying in sync when it would rock at random, crossing a hill, entering a tunnel. Iona had done this before it seemed.

The whole train lurched, and Bella felt her lungs overfill, her heart rise up like a lift going down too quickly — and then they were between worlds.

The carriage could be any carriage, on any train in Britain. There was no way of telling. And therefore, in some ways, it was every carriage on *every* train.

She watched Iona slide her slender fingers through the air, willing the superposition to collapse into the state she wanted. There was only one train in Elf-hame, so aiming wasn't particularly difficult, and she hadn't actually met anyone who had crashed two trains together, or fizzled into the cosmic soup, or annihilated their atoms — but she'd heard enough horror stories that it scared her every time.

Holly was watching this all with rapt fascination, of course — it occurred to Bella Holly had only been to Elf-hame that one time, when they'd Gone-a-Wander. She wondered how long it would be before Holly worked out she could use this to get her friends fare dodges.

But again, again, her eyes fell on Munro. And the spell was as strong as ever. Every time she looked at that selkie's eyes it was like falling into a deep pool you could never escape from. Munro's emotions, unspoken, travelled along her like electricity. Her joy, unbridled. Her sorrow, vast and endless and numinous.

Right now, Munro was too calm. Something lurked, unsettling and unseen in that bottomless sorrow. Arabella watched, and a lump formed in her throat knowing that soon she would have no-one to worry about.

The clipped, pan loaf voice of the tannoy spoke, and the soup of possibilities collapsed, fixed in stone. "We will shortly be beginning our descent into Reminiscence," she said, not in disjointed robot speech, but in the cadence of an airline pilot. "Local weather is looking around 9 degrees, with chances of sunshine in a few months. We ask you not to unfasten your seatbelts while the seatbelt signs are turned on. We thank you for travelling with us and hope to see you again."

Iona snapped her fingers, and all the curtains opened. Outside the windows, blankets of Elf-hame fog wrapped around the carriage, like an octopus' tentacles, grasping, testing. The carriage started to rattle like a jackhammer. Roman's Lucozade and bottle of top coat jangled towards the edge of the table. He snatched at the top coat bottle, and the Lucozade clattered to the ground, where Iona picked it up.

"Cheers," Roman said sheepishly.

The train came to a stop, and they rummaged off the carriage onto a stout-looking platform of grey tarmac, brick, and a baroque rusted awning of glass and iron. Behind them, there was a bang that made Holly jump, and the train coiled up like a spring, and disappeared.

There was a ticket turnstile, and Munro intuitively reached out to a thumb-pad on which sat a spinning needle. It pricked her thumb, and a rich globule of red dripped down it before the turnstile hummed.

Nothing happened.

Munro stood awkwardly for a moment, staring at her still-bleeding finger like it had betrayed her. A queue was starting to form before Arabella realised why it hadn't worked.

Trying not to look Munro in the eye, she overtook her and pricked her own finger. The same happened, but the gate grew hot and hazy like a summer day, before it disappeared entirely before them.

They all shuffled through, Arabella looking at her feet the entire time.

Munro stared at her bleeding finger all the way out of the train station.

"Welcome to Reminiscence," Iona said. They exited the front gates and stood in a little town square by the sea front. Statues of cats adorned plinths between the buildings — tall, austere structures that were blackened with soot. "I hear it was the 1990 Elf-hame City of Culture." She said it like she had been appointed the role of a stand-up comedian for the day. It didn't land.

"Where is this?" Holly asked. "Like, on our map. Is it the fey version of one of they seaside towns?"

"I told you, Elf-hame can't be mapped at all, it's not a 1:1," Iona said. "It's all just reflections, ideas, social constructs."

"Unlike the material world," Munro finally piped up, disgruntled. "You know, everything there is completely real, and you don't make anything up."

Iona floundered at the sarcasm, looking at Bella for reassurance. Bella fumbled, before Iona said, "Well that's a very good point! This is your neck of the woods after all. Why don't you tell us about it?" She was putting on her too-nice polite voice, and it was making Arabella's stomach cramp in cringe. Roman seemed to have just now picked up that something was wrong.

Munro rubbed her finger. The pinprick hadn't sealed, so it was just getting messier over time. Arabella leaned against her arm, reached down and sealed it with magic, running her hands over Munro's fingers as the blood fizzled away.

Munro didn't respond, just kept looking at it. Then she cleared her throat and looked at Roman. "I was born here. I lived here for a century. I moved out of here."

"Succinct," Roman said. He looked at a bench plastered by a firing squad of bird shit. "Well, it has character!" he said, before adding under his breath, "'Serial killer' is a very popular character." He turned to Bella. "Why are we here again? I prefer our shithole."

Bella tried to pretend she didn't see him. But then she looked up and saw something that made her completely forget he was there. "Oh, you have got to be kidding me."

Standing by the bin having a cigarette in her swimwear, propping her arm on the roof of a bus shelter she dwarfed, and holding up a paper sign saying "WITCHES" on it, was the Arch-Witch Nicnevin.

chapter 16

Bella was speechless.

Her mouth gawped open and closed like a fish.

The Witch Queen of Elf-Hame, all nine feet of her, was wearing a sheer mesh robe over a swimsuit as she stubbed the cigarette out on the roof of the bus shelter. The Patron Saint of the Buried at Sea. Munro's ex-lover, the Arch-Witch Nicnevin. Her teal skin dappled like the ocean viewed from underneath, and when she looked down and saw Bella, she smiled like a carnivore.

"Bella, *darling*, how are you?" She hunched over and pushed down her sunglasses to get eye contact with Bella. Like the pose on a magazine cover.

Arabella cleared her throat, trying not to look at the Arch-Witch's cleavage, accentuated as it was. "Fine, Nicnevin, how're you?" Jealousy had never been in Bella's character, so she wasn't exactly sure how to hide it. Even growing up before transitioning, she had never been 'jealous' of other girls, not really — it was difficult to feel jealous when something was so out of reach.

"Absolutely fantastic," Nicnevin said, reaching for a cocktail which appeared out of thin air and drinking it through a straw so as not to smudge her lippy. "And you've brought all your little friends with you! What a pleasant surprise."

Holly joined Bella, carting bags behind her, blinking when she saw Nicnevin. "Wow, your Highness. Looking good."

"When am I not?" Nicnevin smiled. She reached out with large, manicured fingers and felt the wool on the hem of Holly's cardigan. "I like your new look. You've gone local."

"Well... when in Elf-hame, as they say."

"Hm, don't they just," Nicnevin said, like she was barely listening. She pushed a few strands of Holly's hair behind her ear.

"So, this is why you said to meet at Reminiscence..." Munro said.

"I was here sunbathing, you know how hard it is to find the summer here."

Bella was on fire. She had never felt like this in her life. She was on fire. She was literally on fire, screaming at the top of her lungs, and everyone was just standing there like this was normal.

"Looking forward to staying at Chez Nevin!" Holly piped up.

You traitorous bitch, Holly Winter!

"Great! I'll go get the car brought around." Nicnevin turned and walked away. She took a long time leaving for a woman with five-foot long legs.

Holly whistled, eyes glued.

"Holly!" Arabella hissed, pushing her.

"What?" Holly said, still watching Nicnevin walk away.

"Roll your fucking tongue in!" she hissed, pulling Holly away from the group.

When they'd gotten out of earshot, she hissed under her breath. "She's fucking with me. She's decided to fuck with me. This was a terrible idea."

"Oh, Bella, relax. There's n—"

"You are literally drooling like a dog right now, Holly."

Holly finally broke her gaze to look at Arabella and scoffed. "Oh my God, you *are*! You're really jealous!"

"... No," Arabella said. Her voice cracked like an egg on the pavement.

Holly cackled. "Oh my god, I never thought I'd live to see the day, Bella succumbing to a petty emotion like jealousy like the rest of us."

Bella fizzed. "Listen, I don't trust her."

"She helped save Munro's life."

"She's playing a long game," Bella said. "She's gonna steal her." She knew even as she said it, it sounded ridiculous.

Holly cleared her throat. "So, it wouldn't be bad if *I* shagged her?"

Bella's icy glare put an end to that thought.

"Fine, fine. Fuckin' hell, you don't half make this difficult." Holly fussed about picking up Roman's extra bags.

Bella stared into space. Was she just jealous? Didn't they have more important things to be dealing with right now?

Holly continued to grumble. "I just wanted to know what that's like, fuck sake... She's as big as a building, that's wild. I wonder if she'd lift me against a wall like that meme..."

Bella shook herself. "Sorry, Holly, I missed that."

"Just talking to myself. As fuckin' per," Holly rolled her eyes, finally hoisting up the assembled bags.

"You know I can take some of those right?"

"How else am I going to impress your bird's ex-girlfriend into shagging me if not by lifting all the bags?"

Arabella took a deep, panicked breath.

"I'm kidding, relax," Holly smiled. She turned and pushed through the door. "Besides!" she shouted over her shoulder. "I can just ask Munro what it's like!" And she ran away before Bella could respond, carrying all the bags like Gimli the Dwarf running across a field.

***

The carriage that came to pick them all up dazzled in the afternoon mist. The entire party of witches looked incredibly shabby by comparison.

"Oh, a straggler!" Nicnevin said, peering down at Verity. "You have the vampire's curse?"

Verity looked up at her, just shaking like a terrified puppy.

"This is Nicnevin, kind of like a Queen of the Witches," Holly said.

"I know who she is," Verity said. Breckenridge had trained them to fear Elf-hame witches most of all. There were records of the Archfey and Breckenridge's grandparents in the earliest treaties between Elf-hame and the waking world.

"Charmed," Nicnevin said, extending her hand.

"You're being very nice today," Munro said quietly.

"Oh, I've got a whole new outlook on life! Best thing you ever did for me, leaving me a greetin' wreck on the floor," Nicnevin said with a smirk.

They clambered into the carriage, and it began to move, pulled as it was by seemingly nothing at all.

"I've been here before," Holly offered, when Verity had no idea what to say, watching out the window as houses started to go by. Wooden huts, streets lined with trees made from fibre-optic cabling. "Once. Though not by carriage."

"Where did you go?"

"The government. We took the bus," Holly said, spacing as she remembered.

"What were you there for?"

"It's kind of a long story," Holly said.

Arabella looked away, pretending not to hear. She leaned her head on Munro's shoulder, as she looked out the window.

She should be fine with this. This was fine. She was fine. Everything was fine. She had no reason to be annoyed about this.

And yet, when Nicnevin laughed and pointed out of the window at some passing frivolity, she could feel her blood begin to boil. This woman meant trouble, she fucking knew it. She knew it in her bones.

And even as the logical part of her knew she had more important things to worry about, that this was trivial nonsense, that she was wasting Munro's final days... trying to pretend these feelings weren't there felt like trying to tell the ocean not to be wet.

And so, she watched like a hawk all the way up the road, and she waited for this bit of the trip to be over. If Nicnevin turned out to not have the solution she had dangled in front of them, Bella would kill her herself.

chapter 17

Nicnevin's home was enormous. Rustic stone castle walls, with three acres of land on either side — wildflowers and lilies growing with abandon, almost bursting their banks onto the road. They drove over a bridge at the foot of the property, with a little burn where ducks were wetting their feet. The carriage moved through trellis arcs with ivy and roses that seemed to be made of glass, lit from within by lights that travelled up and down them.

As they got closer, the manor home itself came into view. Huge windows looked out onto the grounds, overgrown with those same glass flowers. Bella couldn't tell if they were grown or made. Either side of the road were lined with statues of kelpies, swimming with their huge fishtails. They were so detailed, and looked so scared, eyes large and lolling with fear, tongues flailing, that Bella wondered if they were real petrified animals. She sank into her chair, feeling like she was being led into a trap.

The house chimney plumed wood smoke into the air to welcome them as the carriage stopped and they all disembarked.

"I forgot you didn't actually live in the Seelie Court, Nicnevin," Holly said, looking up first at the house, then at their hostess. Suddenly the eight-foot-tall doors made sense. "It feels a bit like thinking about your teachers going home at night."

Nicnevin laughed again, and it was a knife on the violin strings of Arabella's nerves. "Well, sometimes it does feel that way, I'll give you that. It feels like the more time passes, the more there is to do…"

She snapped her fingers, and the main door opened. "Make yourselves at home," she said, waving her hands. Their luggage lifted off the ground, out of their hands, and into the house before them. "I hope you don't mind, I have to make a call." She plucked a long black strand of her own hair, pulled it taut between her fingers, and then spoke into it. "Glaistig?" she said out loud, and the hair seemed to vibrate like it was carrying her voice. "Yes, my darling, it's Nevin. Listen, I'm…" She trailed off as she walked off into the grass to speak among the topiaries.

Arabella realised she was the only one still standing there and staggered in after them.

The house was spacious, but cluttered. It was like a warped reflection of the Archive with its books and a wafting smell of cedar, but Arabella couldn't get comfortable. She followed the floating luggage through an open kitchen into a corridor when Holly stopped in front of her.

"Are you okay?" Arabella asked.

Holly was standing in a doorway, staring sombrely into the room. Bella looked inside and stopped herself.

A bedroom. Bed still made as they'd last seen it, though unslept in for decades. A little chest of drawers by it. Unadorned, unpretentious, as its owner wished.

The weight of it sat on Arabella's chest.

"This was the room she died in the first time," Arabella said out loud. She'd not been there, of course. But she'd seen it. Everyone in the courtroom that day had, thanks to Holly. She'd watched Munro's point-of-view as she'd expired on this bed, from sheer old age. And then Nicnevin had stopped her leaving. The very spell that was now beginning to lose its grip on her despite their duct-tape.

Maybe Nicnevin *was* over Munro now. After all, she couldn't stop her dying anymore. Bella cringed at the selfishness. It had been twenty-four hours since she'd found out and she'd spent most of that time thinking about herself.

What had Connie always said? *'Feel your feelings, expecially the inconvenient ones'.* She'd always said *'expecially'.* Arabella smiled, and Holly squeezed her hand. *'The inconvenient feelings are the ones we need to pay the most attention to.'*

Arabella leaned her head on Holly's shoulder. "I'm glad you're here."

"I'm glad I'm here too." Holly's soft shoulder pillowed her face, her voice vibrated against her cheek.

They found Verity standing by the bags, staring off into space. "You okay?" Holly asked.

She just continued to stare.

"Verity."

Verity jumped. "Yes. Sorry. Yes. What?"

"How're you doing? I know you have a lot going on."

"Baby." She poked it. "I'm carrying a baby around."

Holly nodded. "I'm sorry. It is pretty baby-like."

"Cup of tea?" Arabella asked.

"Maybe we could get you a black pudding or something." Holly nudged her and grinned.

Verity smiled. "Actually, I think tea would be nice."

"I'm gonna go to the bathroom, I'll be one second."

It was then Nicnevin chose to walk through the front door, kicking off her sandals and throwing her sunglasses in a bowl. "Right! Wine?"

Arabella looked at the little watch on the inside of her wrist. "Nicnevin, it's still technically the afternoon."

"It's also a Saturday." Nicnevin crossed the room to a wine rack and picked a bottle of white, so cold it was wet to the touch. "Come on, live a little."

When Arabella's first urge was to assume the bottle had been poisoned, she realised she may have been overly wound up.

She forced herself to smile. "Sure."

***

Verity stepped out onto the grass while the others messed around in the kitchen.

It was her first time being alone.

No Breckenridge whispering in her mind.

The witches off in the other room.

And the hunger quietened.

Just her, and the homunculus, listening to nothing.

She couldn't decide if it pleased her or scared her.

With nothing to drown it out, all she had was the whispers of her victims rattling around in her head.

She smoothed out her skirt to sit down on the grass, felt the glass bulbs of the daisies brush her fingers as she did.

And she sat, with her own thoughts.

It took about a minute for her to realise she didn't have any thoughts. Nothing. She looked into the glass, and saw it reflect the sky behind her, with nothing to show she was even there. Vampires did not have reflections.

Without his whispering, telling her who she was... was she nothing at all?

She raised her hand so she could see it. Squeezed her thumbs, her fingers, just to prove they were there. Committed them to memory.

She wondered what her face looked like.

Suddenly, she wasn't alone. The wind picked up, the trees murmuring as they rustled, and it was like they surrounded her.

She braced herself, when the moment was broken by Nicnevin half-throwing half-placing a wine cooler down next to her. Verity jumped out of her skin.

"Be a doll and grab some glasses, would you?" she said. She was paying more attention to other other hand, tangled in golden strings that glittered in the afternoon fog.

Verity nodded, but it took her a minute to get up.

***

The sun was just beginning to set, and the mists took on a pink tone over the hills of House Nicnevin as the group sat in the grass on the hill. Behind them, the manor cast a long shadow into the night.

Arabella eyed her wine glass, letting the vanishing light refract through it. Well, if it was poisoned it was very slow acting. A lot of the tension she hadn't been aware of in her shoulders was gone. The conversation had been sparkling, but she'd not said much, and now everything had fallen a bit hush, other than Roman, who was still babbling on mostly to himself as Nicnevin nodded.

Verity stood up. "It's been a lovely evening, you all. I'm going to go to bed if that's okay."

"Night," Arabella said, and her words were a little slurred for her liking.

Nicnevin was lying in a deck lounger, and she seemed rapt at what Roman was saying, something about cosmic truth. It was probably about mushrooms — he was usually talking about mushrooms when he got like this. Every so often she'd interject with a point that made Roman stop and go "huh", before his eyes would sparkle and he'd frantically pull a notebook from... somewhere.

"It's getting chilly out," Nicnevin said, pulling the flimsy mesh shawl around her tighter. "Should we move this inside?"

"Huh?" Roman said, looking around. "Oh, shit, yeah. Hang on." He seemed to be sketching a glyph down, trying to get his pen to shade like it was charcoal.

"Where is everyone?" Bella asked. She said 'everyone', but she meant Munro. She wasn't sure why it felt weird to ask.

"She's inside." Nicnevin looked at Bella, and smiled, white teeth, dark lipstick, emerald eyes.

Oh shit. Was mind-reading on Nicnevin's endless list of magical powers? Did she know Bella was onto her?

Was she onto her?

Roman snorted, threw down his notebook, and patted the pockets on his jacket. "Right, I'm rolling a ciggy before I come in, I'll get yous in there." He started teasing out tobacco on his skirt for a rollie.

Nicnevin picked up the almost-empty bottle of wine, and the two other empties between her knuckles, and stood, taking in a deep breath. She towered over them all, stretching like she'd done a long day at the office.

"Coming?"

The wine bottles vanished into the aether, so she could offer her hand to Arabella. Bella took it, getting to her feet.

She was... very beautiful, Arabella admitted. It made the envy worse. The pettiness worse. She had everything. She was a billboard model come to life, at scale. She was clever, and whip-smart, and had everything. And Munro had thrown it all away, to live in a pokey little flat with her scrawny bird body and her shabby bohemian friends.

Wait. No. That wasn't what she thought. That wasn't fair. She loved her friends. Hell, she even loved herself — and she'd worked very hard for that.

She had a weird suspicion that there *had* been something in the wine, a feeling she couldn't shake.

"Well, goodnight, my dear," Nicnevin said, at the foot of the stairs. Her cheeks were rosy with wine.

"Goodnight."

She'd been drinking it as well. Arabella was just being paranoid. Surely. Surely.

Arabella smiled and turned the corner into the room where Munro lay, already asleep in the bed. She slipped her shoes and socks and her bra off and sidled in without bothering to change into other clothes. She didn't have the energy. She cuddled into the warmth of Munro's back, felt the movement of her breathing against her cheek, and started to fall asleep.

She could hear crying. Somewhere in the house.

An uncomfortable feeling in her stomach. She couldn't tell if she was imagining it in her half-awake state. She listened to the crying until the sound stopped, or she fell asleep, or both.

***

Verity sat on the porch, waiting for the homunculus to fall asleep. She didn't know if it did sleep, but she figured now was the time.

Nicnevin entered the kitchen from the other side, and Verity could just about make her out from where she was sitting.

"Evening!"

"Evening, dear," Nicnevin said, taking her wine glass to the sink with languid steps. "It's so good to meet you, by the way."

"Thank you," Verity said. "I never thought I'd be breaking bread with the Arch-Queen of the Witches."

"I never thought I'd see a vampire living off a dead man's heart." Nicnevin came to the front door and sat next to Verity.

"I don't know what I'm doing here," Verity said.

"Enjoying a glass of wine with beautiful people," Nicnevin said, and her eyes sparkled. "Isn't that enough?"

"I mean... maybe I shouldn't still be here."

"You sound like Munro," Nicnevin said, and the room went dark for a second as clouds passed overhead. "Always chasing death. I didn't understand it."

"You're one of the few people who wouldn't."

"It is our lot in life, as eternal beings." Nicnevin plucked a tangerine from mid-air, and began to peel it. "We will continue to live, long after humankind has forgotten us, but forever changed by their tiny ministrations." She popped a slice in her mouth, chewed it slowly. "I used to think it was a blessing."

"You don't anymore?"

She swallowed the slice, smiled through clearing a pip from her teeth with her tongue. "Wisdom of old age."

The homunculus on Verity's chest began to wail. It sounded more like an old dog than the baby she'd been thinking of it as. She rubbed its head.

Nicnevin whistled. "Those witches really did a number on you, eh?"

"Mm." Verity still felt the lack of pain in her limbs, her muscles, like an actual feeling. A bliss of absence.

"What will you do now?" Nicnevin said. "With this extra life you've been given?"

"I..." She hadn't thought that far ahead. "I don't know." She had no family anymore. No home. She was a lone abomination, there had never been another like her.

"I think you might want to work that out. It's a terrible thing to live with no purpose."

Verity looked down at the little faux-life stitched to her chest. What would its sacrifice get her?

"Well!" Nicnevin smiled. "I'm going to go read before bed." She stroked Verity's cheek with long, delicate fingers. "My God. Say one thing for vampires, but they have fantastic complexions."

And then she vanished in a puff of smoke.

Verity stood on the edge of the room for a few minutes, feeling that absence of pain. The lack of Breckenridge's voice whispering in her head. And the horrible thing was... she hated it being gone. Like without it, she didn't know who she was.

chapter 18

Arabella woke to an empty bed and panicked. "Munro!" she shouted.

The bed looked disturbed this time, and Munro's furs hung over the back of a chair like a discarded jacket. She jumped up, clutched the pendant still around her neck, reached out with her mind.

"Find my darling, find my heart,
Show the distance we're apart—"

Before she could finish the spell, Munro popped her head back in the door. She was wearing an ill-fitted nightie that stopped at her knees, and she had a toothbrush in her mouth.

Arabella grabbed her like a life raft. "Sorry," she said quietly, ashamedly.

"No, it's okay." She hugged her until eventually she said, "Can I go spit the toothpaste out?"

Arabella laughed into Munro's neck. "Yeah. Sorry. Sorry."

Munro detached herself to go to the bathroom.

Bella stood, clutching the pendant again, steadying her breath. Stupid. Stupid.

And then she yelped as something from behind lifted her into the air.

"Dummy," Munro said, as Bella turned to face her in her arms. They leaned into each other and just held their faces together. Sharing their presence.

"Love you," Bella mumbled.

"Love you too."

Bella idly fiddled with the tag on the back of Munro's nightie.

"I'm hungry," Munro said. "Let's go raid Nicnevin's kitchen."

"This is surreal," Bella said.

"I'm trying to go with it."

"You're doing very well. Way better than I am," Bella said, as Munro set her down. They held each other's hands, and went to greet the day, Bella trying not to think about how Munro still seemed to be taking this all in stride.

***

"Good morning, Granny!" There was a man in the kitchen frying anchovies and eggs in a pan. He was almost as tall as Munro, and just as wide, with the same dark grey lashes and a mischievous smile. "Long time no see!"

Munro cleared her throat, stiffening. "Good morning, Burn."

He tapped one of the anchovies with calloused fingers to tip it over, then sucked on his fingertip to cool it. "Ow!" He wiped it on his selkie furs. "You don't sound happy to see me! I brought eggs and everything."

"Did Nicnevin ask you to come?"

"Oh, it's not just me!" That goblin grin of his hadn't left for a moment. He pointed out the front door. "They're all out on the grass. I'm running late."

Munro nodded, calculating. "I suppose I should go say hi."

Arabella poked out from behind Munro and extended her hand to shake. "Hi, I'm Bella. Nice to meet you."

Burn nodded, with a grunt, still smiling like there was a secret joke Bella wasn't aware of. She retracted her hand when he didn't take it.

There was a pop as a bubble of oil in the pan burst. Bella started. She laughed, overcompensating. "Sorry! Jumpy today."

"You coming?" Munro asked.

"Where?"

"To meet the family."

***

"Granny?" Bella said under her breath, grabbing Munro's arm as they walked across the grass and the wildflowers. "You're his grandmother?"

"No," Munro said. She sighed, feeling the weight on her shoulders. "I'm his *great*-grandmother."

"Oh, *shit!"* Bella said under her breath.

"I know."

"You're a gilf. You're a great-gilf!"

A strangled noise escaped Munro. She was trying not to smile. "I'm gonna kill you."

"Murdered by a great-gilf! Who'd have thought?"

"Stop it," Munro laughed. "I can't be laughing when we meet—"

"Grandmother," a selkie woman who could easily have been Munro in an old photograph interrupted. The same strong shoulders, the same powerful bridge of the nose, the same way she tensed her jaw like she was thinking about other things.

"What are you doing here, Lily?" Munro sighed.

"We heard the news."

"Did Nicnevin tell you?"

"Word travels fast," Lily said. "I'm pretty sure everyone from here to Harris has heard by now."

Munro stiffened. "I don't like being the subject of gossip."

"You're important, grandmother. Everyone wants to know." Lily only now seemed to notice Bella was there. "Ah. You must be Arabelle."

"Arabella," Bella corrected, smiling. Lily gave her a hug that was warmer than she expected, and Bella watched Munro roll her eyes while Lily's gaze was broken. "Lovely to meet you."

"*So* good to meet you." She gripped Bella's shoulders like she was trying to impart years of affection in one go, held for the maximum amount of time before it would become weird.

Bella smiled like a china doll, suddenly piecing it together. "It's a shame it's taken so long."

"You know the way life is. Gets in the way."

Bella held her smile.

"Come! Burn should be right out with the nibbles, we're going to have a barbecue and a bonfire. It'll be fantastic!"

Bella looked at Munro, who tutted. "Sure."

They were led over the hill, to a den of selkies coaxing a pile of sticks into burning.

Within fifteen minutes Nicnevin showed up, wielding deck chairs and with a metal box full of ice and wine. Goddess, that woman liked a drink. "Good morning!"

"Morning," Bella said. She suddenly felt underdressed. Nicnevin had a full face of makeup and was wearing one of her ballgowns. Well, it wasn't like Bella would risk wearing her glad rags in a field, they'd probably get ruined.

Nicnevin folded a chair out for Bella, patted it to come sit next to her. "You seem very un-chipper today, it's not like you," she said, as Bella sat down.

"My partner is dying," Bella said. Saying it out loud at last felt strangely good, like putting your tongue in a tooth cavity.

Nicnevin nodded, letting it sit.

"What are these people doing here?" Bella said. The anger was rising in her. "Munro's never even mentioned them — if they were important, why are they only showing up now?" They watched a little selkie boy playing down by the burn at the bottom of the hill, splashing and playing and imagining war.

"It's... complicated," Nicnevin said. "You've not been around dying people before, have you?"

Bella's hair stood on end. She was being called naive, though Nicnevin managed to sound so neutral Bella couldn't have called her on it. "Only once. It wasn't like this."

"Most of the things that happen around dying people aren't really for the person dying. People reach out because they feel bad, and because they know if they don't, they'll feel bad forever." She watched the little boy duck his head under the water and blow bubbles. "Funerals aren't for the people who passed. They're for the people who have to carry on. It's just a shame in Munro's case, she has to watch it all happen."

"You shouldn't have invited them," Bella said. Munro was padding about like a grumpy bear, even as Burn was bringing the pan of still-sizzling anchovies and a plate of eggs out to the congregation. Bella could smell the salty oil from here.

Nicnevin smiled devilishly. "These people have been Munro's family since before your parents were born, child."

Bella swivelled, looking at Nicnevin, her smug face and her prying eyes and her body posed just so on the deck chair. "What's that supposed to mean?"

"It means, you are not the main character of reality dear. None of us are."

Bella sucked air through her teeth. "You know..." She made one last attempt to hold her tongue, but the seal broke. "You have a fucking cheek to lecture me, Nicnevin. I still remember what it felt like when you trapped me in that jail cell like an animal."

She'd expected Nicnevin to get angry then, the famous temper of the Arch-Queen of Witches. But she didn't. She just smiled like Bella was a recalcitrant child, and that stung even more. Stung enough that she didn't think twice about how Nicnevin had washed away entire villages into the sea for less.

Perhaps holding all the cards took the bite out of insults.

"I *am* sorry," she said. "I don't know if I ever apologised for that ugliness." She leaned over the chair and put her hand on Bella's shoulder, dwarfing her.

Bella shook her off.

"It's okay. We're all together now," Nicnevin said.

"I don't want us all to be together," Bella said. "I want Munro to live." It sounded childish, even as it left her mouth she could tell. "If she can't do that, I want her to enjoy what time we have left, not sit making the family that abandoned her feel better."

"I understand," Nicnevin said. Bella balled up her fists. She felt a sudden need to scream. She could see Nicnevin winding her fingers around everything. She had a plan, she always had a plan! What was she up to?

"I have to go," Bella said, choked. "Bathroom." She got up and stumbled away before anyone could stop her.

chapter 19

Verity sat on the edge of the group, watched them all eat fish and laugh and avoid her gaze. Selkiefolk were a superstitious lot, and it didn't take much superstition to be nervous around a vampire.

She was fine. It did feel strange to be not in the company of people she knew, but she was a big girl. And it was a lovely day outside. She closed her eyes, enjoyed the smell of late morning air. She had forgotten what day smelled like.

The witches were right. The mists in Elf-hame protected her from the sun's purifying light. Her family used to talk like they would take this place like a swarm of locusts if it wasn't for that pesky deal with the Archfey. But she knew even then, there were no humans in Elf-hame. Without human blood, they'd never be able to stay for long.

Iona was knitting, one eye watching Roman flirting with Burn by the fire.

Nicnevin grinned. "You look like a nervous mother."

"I am a stepmother, of sorts," Iona said. "To all these wayward children. And the others before them."

"They're not the first?"

"Oh no," Iona said. "Though they may be the last. It was always my wife's vice more than mine." She worried at her knitting like she was trying to undo a knot, like there was something stuck in the fibres trying to get out. "She was always bringing home strays. We have to pass on the knowledge."

"You know, you're quite the hypocrite," Nicnevin said. "Telling Munro she can't live forever, and yet here you are. You're almost as old as I am, it seems."

"Not quite, Your Highness," Iona said. "Not quite. Though I suppose you're right in a way. I could argue with you it's different, that I'm just stretching the life I have. But that would be a question of semantics. And a witch should never lower herself to dealing with semantics." She freed one hand from her knitting to get her mug of tea.

"Morning, everyone!" Holly arrived, a beam of sunshine in her dungarees and a pair of welly boots. Again, Verity felt a flash of that phoenix flame, the atoms in her cells telling her to go to her. In the light of day, in the light of the first day Verity had seen in a very long time... she was wary of it. It was the reaction of chemicals, not to be trusted.

She watched Holly move around the room, introducing herself to the selkies one at a time with a strong handshake. She had the energy of a dad, both business-like and informal at the same time.

When she reached the last one, Burn, she looked up at Verity on the edge of the group. "Verity, come on over!"

Verity felt like a child being trotted out at a wedding, but she came nonetheless. She smiled. "Hello," she said to Burn. The smell of wood smoke was so strong by the fire she could feel it sinking into her clothes already.

"Miss," Burn said. He looked a little nervous at the sight of her, but he was trying to hide it.

"It's nice to meet you."

"Likewise," Burn said. Roman was hanging off him like a cloud of midges, but he was doing a good job ignoring it — he probably got a lot of that kind of attention.

"What you making?" Holly asked, looking down at the iron grill on the ground as he made a bed in the fire for it to sit on.

"We've got two sides of bream and a big tuna." He gauged the size of it with his hands.

"Selkies, man. Love your fish, eh?" Holly grinned.

"The sea provides," he said with faux reverence. They laughed. "Not a fish person?"

"I'll eat bloody anything," Holly said. "I just didn't think yous would take the time to cook it, Munro makes you sound like hunter-gatherers."

"Aw, it's a special occasion," Burn said, lifting the grill and putting it on the fire. "It does taste better with the kiss of the flame." He jostled it until it sat flat. "I'm gonna go get the food, I'll be back."

The second he was gone, Holly said, "God, I already ate some of they anchovies. I'm gonna go home more salt than human."

"What else is new?" Roman said.

"Here, are you gonna give him space to breathe?" Holly said.

"I'm not saying anything!"

"Aye, that makes it even weirder. It's like you're hoping he'll walk into you. You know he's Munro's great-grandson right?"

Roman blinked. "Are you wanting me to ask for her blessing?"

Holly huffed. "Come on, man."

"I can turn the charm on if you think that'd be less weird!"

"I think it's just," Verity tried to think of a way to say it tactfully. "With everything going on with Munro right now…"

Roman screwed his face up. "What's going on with Munro?"

Verity's stomach dropped.

"Oh, You—"

Holly rubbed her eyes. "Don't make a lot of noise about it. Munro's spell's wearing off."

Roman stopped. It took a second to sink in. "She's…"

"Come on, man, hold it together," Holly said, looking around to see if any of them were watching.

"Stop that," Verity said to Holly.

Roman was welling up, fighting his bottom lip. "That's... she's..."

"I know," Verity said.

He reached into Holly for a hug and quietly sobbed into her shoulder. She rubbed his back. "It's okay, buddy. It's alright."

Burn returned with a fish almost as big as Verity was. He looked at the scene, and then at his feet, going about his prep and trying not to give it air.

Holly nodded to Burn over Roman's shoulder as if to say, 'see you later, mate', and the three of them shuffled over to a quiet corner.

"Sorry," Roman said. "Sorry." He wiped his eyes, and then looked at the tears on his fingers, wiping them on his top like an inconvenience. "Fuck!"

"Are you okay?"

"No, I'm not okay!" he said. "I'm gonna go for a smoke."

"Alright," Holly said quietly. They watched him leave, and then Holly exhaled.

"What did he think we were here for?"

"He doesn't really ask questions about this sort of stuff — especially when it involves a holiday."

They stood in silence for a second, watching Roman disappear down the hill into the brush.

"I feel like a spare part. I shouldn't be here," Verity said.

"Our coven's all spare parts, that's kind of the point," Holly said. She smiled. "Besides, we asked you to come. We want you here. *I* want you here."

Verity looked at Holly. Could she feel what Verity was feeling? It wasn't love, she didn't think so. She was old enough to have felt love many times and it had never been so... immediate. So unfounded.

"I... hope I can be of help to you all during this. You've done a lot for me. And I owe Munro — I only knew to come to you all because I'd heard about her."

The homunculus on her chest started to cry.

"Shh!" she hushed it, rubbing its head.

"I wouldn't say it in front of Roman," Holly said. "But that thing is really gross."

"Yeah..." Verity said. "Imagine how it feels having it attached to you."

"Maybe I'm just jealous of it," Holly joked, before she could stop herself.

"You are an incorrigible young woman, Holly Winter," Verity said.

Holly grinned. "My maw always used to say, if you don't ask you get nothing. It's like Munro always said. We just gotta enjoy what we have while we have it."

There was a pause.

Verity looked up, and Holly was staring into her eyes.

Her heart pounded in her ears.

Holly leaned forward and gave Verity a peck on the cheek.

Waves of goosebumps travelled up Verity. "Um, I. Um."

"Sorry. Maybe wasn't the time."

"No!" Verity said, pacifying. "It was... just unexpected."

"You're a beautiful woman, Verity."

"You're..." Verity took Holly in. Even in her dungarees, her muddy wellies. She carried herself with such power, strength, self-righteousness. "You're beautiful too." She blushed.

Holly quirked a grin. "I'll see you around."

Verity nodded, and Holly stepped away to go help Burn with the food.

***

Wandering away from the festivities, Verity followed the trampled grass path Roman had left on his way to get away from them all. She didn't like the idea of them leaving him alone.

109

He wasn't smoking when she arrived. He looked like he'd started the process, the filters and tobacco out on the grass, but he was busied with something else. Moving stones around, arranging them like a puzzle. He would step back, shake his head, and swap their positions.

"Hi," she said, as quietly as she could, but he still jumped.

"Oh. Hi." Seeing Roman with tears down his face was so pitiable. It was like seeing a sequined robe left in a corner, all the lint and dust bunnies clinging to it magnetically.

"What are you doing?"

"Good vibes," Roman said, reapplying himself to his strange work.

"I wanted to say thank you," she said, trying to give him something else to think about. "I don't think I got the chance before."

"Oh," he said, like he was barely thinking about it, so fascinating were his rocks. "Don't mention it." He moved a big one to the east, picking up the small one that was in its place and centred it north.

She stepped out into the little clearing and finally got a good look around them. Beyond Nicnevin's property, the grass was spun out of glass, like the cabling she'd seen on the way here. Tiny glass crocuses of different colours jingled like bells as she moved. They went on as far as she could see, until they vanished into the mists. It was only then she realised just how much magical effort Nicnevin had spent making her house appear 'mundane'. Like one of those big houses where the grass was cut to exactly half an inch every week and fed with chemicals to keep it green all year round.

Roman didn't seem phased by any of this. How many times had they all come here?

"I don't think you can do much to extend her life," she said, when he was growing more and more frustrated with the arrangement.

He looked up at her, finally catching his gaze. The tear tracks were drying in, but he looked confused. Almost offended. "I'm not trying to extend her life. I'm trying to bring her peace."

Verity squirmed. "Sorry."

"No, it's fine, it's just—" He sat back, and gave her his full attention. "I'm sorry. I mean, you're going through it as well."

Verity shrugged. "If it wasn't for you, I'd be dead already."

"Oh, I'm sure they would've worked something out."

"It was a big deal, you don't have to be modest about it."

Roman smirked. "I think that might be the first time anyone's ever said that to me." He wrapped his arms around his legs; this far from the fire the mists were chilly. "I told the others as if it was a joke, how you waited until the last possible minute before asking for help."

Verity squirmed. She didn't like being analysed. She'd spent her whole life being analysed.

He squinted. "What's your deal, missus? Did some piece of you want to die in that house?"

"No," Verity said firmly. "No. Never."

She waited for him to respond, to fill the silence. He didn't. He just watched her. It was excruciating.

"I didn't know where to go," she said. "I didn't have anywhere else. And they had told me they were the only people who would... care for me." She swallowed. "Everyone hates vampires. Breckenridge treated me badly, but he was... a known quantity."

Something in Roman tensed like a cat. "What a bastard. A decrepit old bastard."

She still found herself flinching as he said it, as if Breckenridge was right over her shoulder, listening.

"Enough about me though," Verity laughed, waving her hand. "I came out here to find you!"

He reached out and put a hand on hers, breaching the touch barrier. "I talk about myself enough."

She understood, in that moment, why the others liked him so much. She had thought he was nice, but kind of an idiot. 'Full of sound and fury, signifying nothing.' But he really was watching, in his own way.

"I think, if he hadn't kicked me out, I would've just died locked in that room," Verity said. It stung her eyes. "So, when he says he kicked me out to save me, he's... he's right. And it makes me wonder if he's right about everything else too."

Roman chewed on it, squeezing her hand while he thought of how to respond. "I can't... begin to understand what you've gone through. But what he was doing wasn't love. He can't just lock you in a room until you comply." She could tell even as he said it, he was frustrated by the fact he couldn't get his point across the way he meant it. "It must have taken a lot of courage to stick to your convictions while even your own body is telling you no." He smiled. "You kind of remind me of Holly in that way."

"I didn't stick to anything," Verity said. "I didn't have much of a choice." That had always been her problem. She'd always been a disappointment to the others, she had no spine. She couldn't make the hard decisions. "By the time he locked me in my room, I couldn't even bring myself to break the skin. I couldn't have drunk blood if I'd wanted to." Now, with the homunculus flooding her with oxygen, endorphins, energy, it felt like a lifetime ago. She'd barely been lucid. It was only now she realised just how little she'd been able to think over the last months between the hunger and Breckenridge's hovering.

"How so?"

"They'd lost all patience with me. They found a young guy, maybe mid-20s? And Breckenridge had him—" her breath hitched, at saying the words out loud.

"It's okay," Roman said. "I want to hear, but you don't have to talk about anything you don't want to."

Verity shook her head. "They hadn't even hypnotised him. He'd been pinned against the chaise longue, and he was looking up at me. His eyes were so wide, he was like an animal in a trap."

The words were bringing the memories back. The voices still so real. *'There. I can't make it any easier for you, girl. I even picked one I thought you'd like.'*

"I protested. The man — I think he thought this was the one chance he was going to get to try and escape. He shouted... something. I can't remember. And Breckenridge" —she wrung her hands, trying to make a movement rather than say it— "he ripped out his tongue."

'You better hurry, if he bleeds out it'll all be for nothing and I'll need to find another one.'

"I was crying. The man was crying..." she trailed off.

His mouth, empty and filling with blood.

She sobbed. "He tried to force me, like a dog to a bowl. But I couldn't even get my fangs to come out."

"It's okay," Roman said. He'd found a tissue somewhere, and handed it to her. She wiped her face, her cheeks, her nose.

"After about twenty minutes, the guy died. And that was when he locked me in my room."

"And this happened... a few weeks ago?"

"Maybe a month," Verity said. She could still hear it echoing. *'Wasteful! You wasteful girl!'*

That anger in Roman was back. "You did nothing wrong. It's not your fault."

"I didn't know how to fix it."

"There was nothing to fix, they weren't listening to you. I'd have killed him, if I were you."

Verity laughed, a wet bubble at the absurdity of the image. "Even if I'd wanted to, I couldn't. He's more powerful than any of us."

"Would you want to? If you could."

"...Yes," Verity admitted. When she allowed herself to think about it, she wanted nothing more than for him to look up at her like that young man had, afraid and cold, and powerless. Not even for revenge.

Just because it was the only way she could think to make him understand how she felt. "Yes. I think I would."

Roman shivered. He reached for his cigarette papers. "We've killed monsters before. If you say the word, they will." His hands were shaking.

"Do you think it's the right thing to do?"

Roman scoffed. He wasn't looking at her any more, busying his hands with his cigarette. "The right thing to do…" he said. "Definitely. But it terrifies me. Maybe I'm the real coward."

"I don't even know *how* to kill him. He's not like the other vampires."

"But you would do it?" Roman asked.

"Without question." She had talked herself into it by now, and the more she thought about it, the more inevitable it seemed.

He smiled. "You *are* just like Holly. It's weird. You're the complete opposite of her, but there's something similar about you."

Verity blushed.

Roman cackled. "Look at you, like a wee school girl."

"Shut up," Verity shoved him.

"Thank you for distracting me," Roman said. "I couldn't find the focus for the spell." He dangled the cigarette between his lips to free his hands, so he could move the stones on the ground again.

"What does it do?" she asked again.

"I'm going to trap all the bad feeling in the circle, and then it'll wither away like a flame with no air," Roman said. "At least that's the idea. I don't…" He rubbed his chest. "I don't do well with conflict. I know it about myself. I can talk my way out of anything, but when that doesn't work, I don't have anything else I can do except run away. And I can't run away now. So I'm just gonna give everyone a little reprieve, maybe it'll make the weekend a bit nicer."

"That sounds nice."

"Wouldn't help you with your grandfather, would it?"

"No," she said. "But I ran away. And that worked. For now, at least."

He smiled. "I'm glad you're here. You're sound."

She coiled. It had been a lonely life in that house. Unasked-for compliments were simply not the done thing. It almost hurt. "I'll let you get back to what you were doing."

"Thanks," Roman said. "I'll see you around."

She nodded, and turned to leave.

Just as she was about to break into the glass fibre brush, he interrupted her. "Oh, Verity."

"Hm?" She turned back.

"I know you think you didn't make the decision to leave. But you did. Every time you chose to disobey him, you did." He smiled. "And we're glad you did."

She left, before her eyes started stinging again.

chapter 20

Bella watched Lily trying to draw teeth making small talk with Munro. She sipped a can of Coke, trying to work out whether she should step in and help or not.

While she was deliberating, Nicnevin slid in. She passed Munro a goblet of wine and smiled to Lily. "Sorry, work's absolutely killing me at the moment. They should leave me alone for a minute now."

Lily grimaced. "I was just telling Munro about the bridge over the loch. The troll's had triplets!"

"Oh, wow!" Nicnevin said. She clasped her chest in shock. "That's amazing news! It feels like it was only year before last he was pregnant!"

"Four years. Flies by, doesn't it."

"That it does," Nicnevin said. She put her hand on Munro's arm. "Feels like only yesterday you were telling me he was planning to conceive."

Bella lurched into the conversation, squeezing between the two towering figures of Munro and Nicnevin. "Hello."

Nicnevin retracted her hand like Munro was on fire. "Hello, dear," she said, with that simpering sweetness that Bella didn't buy for a second. *What was she up to?*

"Insh!" Lily called down to the little boy paddling in the water. "Don't go any further than that!"

Insh barked like a seal.

"Is he still not talking yet?" Nicnevin said.

"He's a bit slow, but he'll get there," Lily said. "Teachers don't know what to do with him, he's got so much energy."

Munro swallowed. "It took me a long time to speak as well."

Lily turned, surprised. "I didn't know that!"

Munro shrugged.

"Maybe that's why you're so quiet," Nicnevin said, a little too familiarly for Bella's liking.

Munro shrugged again. "I'm starving..." she said, rubbing her stomach.

"Burn, where are we with the bream?" Nicnevin said.

"Five minutes!" Burn said. He and Holly were standing by the fire, nursing big glasses of something that looked like beer.

"I could get you a snack or something?" Arabella said.

"I'm fine, don't fuss," Munro moved like Bella was a fly buzzing about her.

"Okay," she said. She was fucking it up, she didn't know what to do.

Nicnevin produced another glass of wine seemingly from nowhere, and handed it to Bella. Bella took it, and stared at the clear-gold liquid.

There was something in the wine. She just knew it, in her *gut*. Nicnevin was playing some game and she just couldn't work it out.

Everyone around them was just chatting away like this was any old day. Laughing, joking...

The flames continued to chew on her.

"Excuse me," she said quietly. She put the glass down, and went back into the house.

She was going to get to the bottom of this.

***

Nicnevin's office was so well-kept, Arabella wondered if she actually did any work in it.

117

She wasn't even a hundred percent sure what she was looking for, as she rummaged through the bookcases, the drawers.

There was a lot of stuff about contracts but it was mostly just correspondence — fey deals were all verbal, it was the point. But nothing about Munro, nothing about her, no sign of—

"A diary."

The motherlode.

Nicnevin's Book of Shadows.

It was thick, its pages swelling with the words written inside. Odds and ends of ephemera and loose paper tried to escape the leather bindings, but they were locked.

Though... not with any magic that was beyond Arabella.

She stopped, instinctively. This was a terrible idea. For her to do to anyone — but, Nicnevin? Her wrath would obliterate Bella on the spot.

Well, she thought. *It's better than being on fire.*

She snapped her fingers, and the lock opened. She flipped through the pages, skimming them for names.

Most of it was just boring work-related stuff, spats and friendships with other fey houses that she didn't recognise.

But then—

Munro isn't going to make it. I'm not sure how to feel. From the moment Arabella asked me to save her life, I knew this would happen. It's what she wants, and I have to be happy for her, but it's so difficult.

Yes, yes, we're all very saddened, Bella thought. She wondered suddenly if this was actually left as a false flag, if Nicnevin had wanted her to find this.

It was followed by a number of drawings, diagrams, alchemical formulae that read more like brush strokes — incomprehensible up close, but she couldn't back up enough to see the whole picture. She could barely read it, let alone understand it.

At times though, it dropped into more mundane magic. The kind of magic she or Holly would do. Written scribbles, surrounded by sigil magic and flowers pressed into the pages.

'I cast a seal of protection,
On you, my love,
My seal of protection.
You have swam far, and farther still,
But you have so far left to go.'

Arabella did not have to be a genius to know who 'her seal' was. Her vision tunnelled as the rage shot through her like rocket fuel, and her first instinct was to rip the diary to shreds right then and there.

This was about Munro. All of this was about Munro.

She *did* have a method to help her, and she was withholding it.

She continued to leaf, trying to figure it out. It was interspersed with other info — unimportant info, dates, planning, good God could this woman not invest in a partition...

She flipped to the most recent entry. The ink was barely dry, bright red. Bella could see the dark spots where the ink pooled against the nib on the corners.

Ninety-nine percent of me knows this is ridiculous. I know. I know. But the one percent, that little lizard survival instinct is opening the trapdoor in my stomach and now my guts feel like they're tumbling about.

Logically, I know that not all of my exes are going to be widows. Obviously, I know that. Obviously.

And yet, on some level, I clearly expect to be all things, to all people, at all times, forever.

If Munro had asked to take me back, I would say no. I don't want to be with her anymore, that story is over.

And yet, seeing someone else in that role just makes my entire body shiver. I hate it. I hate thinking about it. Why do I hate thinking about it? Things are good, this is the perfect outcome.

"I knew it!" she hissed. "I knew it, I knew it!" she poked the pages.

"That homewrecker!" She could barely read she was so angry, skimming over the entry.

It ended: *I feel like I'm on fire.*

The word 'fire' was underlined three times.

I feel like I'm on fire, and I can't even scream, and everyone is just walking around me like everything is normal.

The gnawing feeling that I know it would be easier if she was ugly isn't a good look either.

I am doing so well, why do I feel so inadequate?

Bella... stopped. Confused.

And then the door opened.

Bella flailed, pushing the diary away from her in a futile attempt to distance herself from it.

Nicnevin stared at the book sitting open on the table like a murder weapon, mouth hanging open.

Bella's nerves, already on edge, were fraying. "Nicnevin, I'm sorry, I didn't know what it w—"

Nicnevin let out a ragged gasp as she clutched her face, scarlet rushing to her teal cheeks. "I'm going to die. I'm just going to die."

Arabella rushed to her as she fell forward onto her knees, the ground thudding under her. "No, I promise, it's fine, I—"

"The embarrassment. Oh saints." Her entire body was turning scarlet now, her cheeks freckling like sunspots. She was hyperventilating. She finally looked at Bella, like she'd spotted an oncoming train.

"Nicnevin, I am so sorry. I am *so* sorry."

"Kill me. Just fucking kill me. I'd rather die than feel this shame. You saw everything."

"No, I—" Bella said.

"You read it! You read it! Why did I *write it down*? I'm such an idiot!" She'd never seen Nicnevin like this. Her sea-dappled skin had completely changed colour, she was coral pink.

"I'm sorry," Bella said. "I—" The shame bubbling up inside her was overpowering this new perspective.

Nicnevin raised her hand, and Bella spotted it in an instant — the Arch-Witch's favourite spell, the memory wipe.

Bella panicked, and clasped Nicnevin's fingers in her open hand, stopping them. "No. I can't let you do that."

"I can't let you walk around knowing I feel like that," Nicnevin hissed.

"What, that you had a way to help Munro and you were sitting on it?"

"W… what?" Nicnevin said. Her face was still ruddy.

"It said in there. Spells of protection. Huge works with the ley lines."

Nicnevin looked genuinely confused. "I had to try. When I found out, I had to see if there was something else I could do. Wait, why is *this* what you care about?"

"You could save her. And you're choosing not to."

"N— no. I don't even know if that stuff will work. I—" Nicnevin said.

"Liar," Bella spat.

Nicnevin looked at her, deep in the eye, as her embarrassment, her confusion, started to be replaced. By rage of her own.

"You tiny little worm. You would call *me* a liar?" Nicnevin said. Her hair began to billow around her as though it were underwater. "You, maggot, would sneak into *my* study, read my Book of Shadows — a witch's cardinal sin — and deign to call *me* a liar?"

Bella knew her life was in imminent danger. But she couldn't help herself. This horrible succubus that locked her in a fucking cage and would steal Munro forever if she could. "I hope they put 'liar' on your fucking gravestone, Nicnevin." And then she stood up, and made to walk away.

"Where the hell are you going?"

"Away. I can't fucking look at you right now." Bella walked out the door.

"You— what?" Nicnevin said. "Where the hell are you going?" She chased her, and Bella had to speed up. She took three steps for every one of Nicnevin's huge gait. "Come back here! What the fuck?"

"I can't deal with this," Bella said, the fury still bubbling over inside her. She could feel the words coming out, the avoidance, the pushing it down, but she couldn't tell why. She knew it wasn't resolving anything, she sounded like...

Oh God, she sounded like her mother.

Quiet, angry arguments that would bubble over into screaming matches, and then trying to end the conversation once you got the last word.

It made her even angrier. Fuck that. She wasn't doing that. It wasn't the same. She opened the door into the light and stomped up, suddenly realising everyone was still standing on the grass having small talk.

***

Munro raised an eyebrow as Arabella arrived back at the barbecue, Nicnevin close behind. "Everything okay?"

Bella's cheeks were burning, she must have looked like she'd run a marathon. "Fine! Fine, my love," she said. Nicnevin stepped out behind her, looking like she'd stopped time and redone her face. It had returned to the normal teal colour.

"Nevin?" Munro's brow furrowed further.

Nicnevin smiled dreamily. "Absolutely dandy." She let her gaze fall on Bella afterwards, in a way that could only be read as incidental by anyone else.

She heard Nicnevin's voice echo in her head. *Listen, you little twerp. This is Munro's day, and I'm not going to ruin it. But we will have fucking words later.*

Bella swallowed.

Munro shrugged. "Alright." Munro was a little too good at not asking about these things.

The fish was steaming on a plate in the sand. It looked like they'd missed the first helping. Nicnevin picked a piece with her fingers and chewed it, pulling the bones from between her lips.

"We should've made tatties," Munro said.

Bella felt like if she ate anything she was going to throw up. She already hadn't been hungry properly for days with everything going on. But now she had Nicnevin's threat hanging over her as well.

She settled for leaning against Munro. "You okay?"

Munro tried to smile. "No."

"I know." Bella lay her head on Munro's shoulder.

Munro whispered under her breath. "I wish they would just fuckin' go. This was a terrible idea, I don't know why she invited them."

"Try and enjoy it. It'll not be long."

Their whispering was interrupted as Lily shouted, "Insh? What's wrong?"

The wee boy was stumbling into the camp, snot dribbling down his face, his selkie furs dishevelled and muddy.

"What happened?" Lily asked.

Insh looked back down the hill, and pointed. He was about to cry, it was cresting.

"You okay?" Lily asked, and then he burst.

It was that way only weans know how to cry. The lip starts going and the throat aches under the weight of their sadness, their chins pucker up, and then it arrives. This low, mournful sound.

"What's happened? What's the matter?" Lily scooped him up and rocked him.

He just kept pointing and wailing. When Lily tried to go look, he flailed in her arms and screamed like she was carrying him to the executioner's axe.

"I'll look after him," Bella said, stepping up towards them before she could stop herself.

"Sure," Lily said. She looked shaken, and put the boy down. He made a half-hearted attempt to keep a hold of her, before collapsing in a heap.

"Hey…" Bella said to him soothingly. "It's okay. You're safe here. Look, we're all here to help."

He looked up at her. He'd stopped wailing but she sensed he was just catching his breath.

"Insh, is it?"

He nodded.

He was that age where his adult teeth had come in but they were still too big for his head, so all his expressions were the wrong shape. Bella remembered being that age, right before her dysphoria had really started to make itself known.

At the bottom of the hill, Lily screamed.

The adults all leapt up, Bella grabbing Insh by the hand, craning to see.

Lily was on the ground, she'd fallen back, and was scuttling away. Roman was unconscious by the side of the river, and hovering above them both was a figure. A shadow. It flickered and shimmered like the shadow between trees. For a second Bella thought she was imagining it.

"Grampa!" Insh shouted, pointing. "Grampa!"

Lily was stumbling over her words, shaken. "Dad? Dad, is that you?"

Iona started down the hill like a paramedic. "Bella, Holly, with me."

Bella motioned to Munro, who took Insh's hand, and the three of them marched down the hill towards the apparition.

Bella approached Roman, checking he wasn't bleeding anywhere.

"Oh, Roman, what have you done..." He seemed fine, and she could sense his spirit hadn't been cast out of his body. She looked up at the ghost.

Iona summoned her broomstick and planted it in the ground. "Wandering spirit, we mean you no harm."

"I think it means us harm, not the other way round," Holly said. Her hands burst into flame. "Want me to char-grill it?"

"No," Nicnevin said. Her voice, unexpected, put a chill down Bella's spine. She could tell Munro everything, at any time. "This isn't like the mortal world. If you burn it down it'll just come back." She'd lifted her skirt and was plodding down towards them all. "I'll never get it out."

It hadn't said anything yet. Bella could feel it watching them, absorbing them.

"Dad..." Lily said. "Why are you here?"

"It's not your father," Nicnevin said. "It just thinks it is."

It was starting to take shape now, an elderly selkie man, struggling under the weight of his furs. The scowl lines on his face were mountainous, his eyes yellowed and bloodshot.

Bella pressed her forehead to Roman's.

"I need my brother, need my friend,
Now before the story ends,
Give me precious hours to spend,
Whatever you broke, it's time to mend."

Nothing happened. She was too distracted.

Time for the more direct approach. She put a hand on his chest. *"Wake up!"* she hissed, and he started, gasping, suddenly awake, adrenaline shot through him.

"Bella! There's a, there's a..."

"I know," Bella said.

"I was *stupid, stupid!*"

"What happened?"

"It was just a little... a nothing! For Munro. I was just trying to—"

"Oh, you silly boy." Nicnevin smiled. "You're in Elf-hame, Roman. You can't just collect bad energies in one place and expect them not to come to life. You just lit a match on dry-grass."

The ghost shuffled towards them. Holly lit a circle of fire around him, trapping him. "We have to contain it, then scatter it."

Verity was looking at the floating selkie man as she stepped forward out of the brush.

"Grampa!" Insh shouted. "Grampa!"

"Will someone shut that kid up?" Roman said under his breath.

Bella gave him a look and he paled, suddenly realising he wasn't in a position to be snarky.

Holly waved her hands, shrinking the circle around him tighter. The ghost cried out. *"Mother..."*

"I'm not your mother, mate," Holly said.

"No," Munro said, stepping past her and into the path of the fire. "I am."

chapter 21

"Hello, Haar. It's been a long time," Munro said.

Verity watched from the sidelines, holding the cold homunculus with one hand, and Insh's warm hand in the other.

Munro was struggling to say anything. Twice she looked like she was going to speak, but then gave up and groaned.

"It's not your son, Munro," Nicnevin said.

"Feels like it," Munro said placidly.

"You abandoned *us… your own flesh and blood,"* the ghost spat.

"Yes I did," Munro said.

"No, you didn't!" Nicnevin shouted.

"Yes she did," Lily said quietly, looking down. She still hadn't gotten up off the floor.

Bella and Roman were scampering towards Iona, muttering among themselves.

"I didn't bring the stuff," Roman said. "I didn't realise we'd have to do a fuckin' exorcism in the middle of a family barbecue."

"Do what witches do, Roman," Iona said. "Make do."

He took a deep breath. "You guys hold him, I'll be back."

"What do you mean by that?" Nicnevin snapped at Lily, incensed. "You were the ones who kicked her out!"

"Nicnevin, we like you. But you're not one of us. Don't pretend you didn't know getting involved with Granny would get her kicked out."

Clouds began to form overhead as Nicnevin tensed and her hair billowed. "That's not fair. You can't control the way she feels."

"But you can," the ghost of Haar whispered, like he'd been waiting to say it.

"Stop it," Iona said to Lily and Nicnevin. "We're all wading through this thing's aura, it's *making* us fight."

"It's not revealing anything that wasn't already here," Nicnevin scowled.

"You're not helping, your Highness," Iona said.

"Hell hath no fury like a milf scorned," Holly laughed, the glint of the fire reflecting in her eyes.

"Holly!" Iona hissed. "Decorum."

"Are we all just going to go around the room telling each other to calm down now?" Arabella said.

It was then that Verity stepped up to the flame. She wanted a better look at the ghost. She'd never seen one in the flesh. Its form flickered and spat in the fire like hot, bubbling oil. It looked at her, and then it looked like Breckenridge.

"Why don't we just kill it?" she said. She had the power now. She wasn't tied to him anymore.

"It's not him, Verity," Holly said. "Not really."

"I know." Seeing him, even like this, brought it into focus. Her fear had fizzled away, but her rage burned bright. "But it would feel good anyway."

"Verity, step away from the flame, we have to—"

"Yes, my dear," the ghost said, with Breckenridge's cashmere tones. *"Do as the girl says. You wouldn't want to hurt yourself."*

Verity swiped through the fire, catching nothing. The ghost was like smoke, and it danced around her fingers.

Munro put a hand on Verity's shoulder and interposed herself between them. "Sorry, but I think this one is mine."

"It's no-one's, stop engaging with it!" Iona said.

"It was made out of all the hateful thoughts of everyone around us," Munro said. "I think that makes it mine."

"Munro..." Arabella said, but Munro put a hand up to stop her.

Munro swallowed, looking the ghost of Haar up and down as he formed in the smoke. "I'm sorry, son," she said, to the dead man who looked far older than her. "I'm sorry I put you in that position."

"*You* abandoned *us.*"

"Yes."

"*You* abandoned *us.*"

A tear rolled down Munro's cheek. "Yes, I did."

"*You* abandoned us." He said it again, with the exact intonation he'd said the first two times.

Munro screwed her face up in confusion. "Yes."

"*You* abandoned *us.*"

Munro looked at Arabella for guidance. "I... I don't understand. Why is he just repeating himself?"

"Because it's *not him,*" Iona said. "It's just reflecting our own feelings back at us."

Holly swayed. "I'm actually, kind of struggling to hold him, so if you could stop giving him fuel that would be great."

"*You* abandoned *us.*"

"I don't know what you want from me, Haar. I never knew," Munro said. "You didn't have to take the family from me."

"Great." Holly said under her breath. "Thanks."

"It was so hard for him," Lily said. She reached up like she wanted to touch him, but she couldn't get near the flame of Holly's ward. "Dad... you did your best."

"His best wasn't good enough," Nicnevin said flatly.

"How dare you? He died trying to hold my family together," Lily said.

"Guys..." Holly winced. "Please..."

"It's not their fault," Iona said.

"Lily," Munro said. "I want you to listen to me because I'm only going to say this once."

Verity watched the entire room come to a standstill. It was like being back in Park Circus, the pregnant pause of words unspoken for a century.

"My son," Munro said, "was a bastard. In every sense of the word." She swallowed. "I loved him, dearly. But he was not a good man. Part of that is my fault, and I will take it to the grave."

Lily stood up. "You old harpy. I tried to make you happy. I tried to reach out, and still you disrespect his memory! At least he had the spine to die with his family."

Holly fell to one knee, her hands struggling to carry the weight of the magic. Bella sat next to her, cross-legged on the floor. "I've got you, pal," she said. "Roman'll be back." She raised her hands and the fire began to flit, becoming a swarm of burning pixies, their powers combined. "Hold on."

Munro looked to her partner, then back at Lily. She wiped the tear from her cheek. "I don't know what you want from me, Lily. To pretend none of this ever happened?"

"I want to know that when you're in the ground, we did everything we could to keep you," Lily said. "It was your choice to leave."

Insh had worked his way up to them. He reached up and took Munro's mitt in his little hand, and the two of them just stared at each other.

"Come back, Insh," Lily said, reaching out for her son. "She doesn't want anything to do with us."

"Why would you say that?" Munro said. "You're poison. All of you." She kneeled to the boy. "I'm sorry, son."

"Granny," he said, and hugged her. She rubbed his back, then pulled back.

"Go to your mammy," she said. "Thank you, Insh."

Insh toddled back to Lily, who scooped him up and turned him away from her.

"I know it's not been easy for you, Lily. It wasn't easy for me either. I don't like the idea that once I'm gone, you'll carry this with you for the rest of your life."

"Maybe you should've done something about it then."

There was a noise in the brush, and Roman emerged carrying a boombox over his shoulder and a litre bag of salt under his arm. "It was all I could find!"

"Roman," Holly smiled. "Thank fuck." She passed out on the grass. Bella, under the sudden weight of holding the spell by herself, screamed, as the flame flashed and dissipated, and she was thrown onto her back.

"Holly! Bella!" Iona shouted. She stamped the broomstick again, and a shockwave hit the ghost, stunning it for a moment.

"I've got it," Nicnevin said, forming a fog bank around it. It wriggled and wrestled, trying to get out. She tapped Holly with her foot. "Get up, Holly Winter," Nicnevin said. "I've seen you do far greater magics than that."

Holly stirred. "What happened?"

Roman pressed play on the boombox. "We gotta lift the vibes in here!" Pop music blared from the speakers. "Dance, everyone!"

"He's right," Iona said. "It's feeding on us, even now."

"It's not hard, hen," the ghost said, taking the shape of a woman Verity had never seen before. She was plump, and cardiganed, and wearing a smile with malice that didn't suit her face. "You're carrying around more than any of them."

Iona drew a ragged breath. "Oh, fuck you." She began to dance, and the ghost's form shivered like wind against the surface of a lake.

***

It was as awkward as Verity could've ever imagined.

The witches danced around the ring of fire, all in their own way. Bella with languid swaying and lots of finger movements, Iona like she was reliving the practiced steps of a school dance, Nicnevin twirling and twisting, Holly making a one-person moshpit. They all seemed to be listening to different music.

"Come on!" Roman called, gesturing to Verity and the selkies. He was all limbs.

Verity held the homunculus tight to her chest. "I... I don't know how."

"What do you mean, you don't know how?" Roman said. He took one of her hands, then the other, and guided her, swaying. She bobbed, a buoy.

Suddenly, with them forcing the energy up, she could feel it. The air they'd been marinating in. It was heavy, headachey, like carbon monoxide.

Iona lifted her broomstick, swept around them like she was clearing the space. The song on the boombox changed.

Verity smiled, against her will. It was so silly.

The ghost reached for them, before the fog snatched it back.

Once Verity was dancing, Roman let go, like she was riding a bike by herself, and he eyed Burn. He crooked a finger, beckoning him into the space.

Burn laughed quietly, digging his hands into his pockets.

"Come on, handsome," Roman said. "You don't want me to tell everyone you were scared?"

Burn considered it, but then someone put a hand on his arm, and he looked up.

It was Lily, face still tracked with tears, carrying Insh in her other arm. She motioned back to the house.

Burn averted his gaze, then nodded.

When they left, Roman groaned. "That was my chance!"

"That's my great-grandson," Munro said.

"I'll just have to make do with you then!" Roman said, and he leapt onto Munro's back. Munro laughed, despite herself, and they danced, danced into the night until the fire burned down, and the air was clear, and the ghost had broken down into carbon ashes, a block of used peat.

Bella took a knife from the grill, and cut a lock of her hair. She wrapped some rosemary around it and put it in the ashes of the fire, pressed it into the ashes until it burnt her fingers.

Munro leaned on her, a big cat. It was how people knew Munro was comfortable around someone — if she couldn't say it out loud, she'd just flop.

"Feels better," Bella said, holding her fingers.

"Yeah," Munro said. "For a second, it was like everything was fine. I forgot."

Bella forced a smile. "I didn't."

They hugged.

Verity stopped as the dance wound to a close, and somehow the knot felt worse for its absence. "I don't understand," she looked at the ashes. "What was that, if not a ghost?"

"It *was* a ghost," Roman said. "Ghosts aren't dead people. They're just echoes. When you die, you decompose, and rejoin the earth. Same for your spirit, it just disintegrates. All that's really left of you is the echo in people's heads, their memories of you in life. They really are still alive in here." He tapped his temple. "Your image of them. Whispering to you. Soaking into your walls. It's not necessarily a bad thing."

"It's not the same though, is it..." Verity said. She couldn't remember dying. Couldn't remember what it had been like. She wondered if there had been people walking around at some point, remembering the person that she used to be.

Roman shook his head. "If it was the *same*, death wouldn't be so sad, would it?"

Verity looked down at the homunculus. She wanted to rip it off. She wanted the worms to eat her. She wanted the peace of a sprig of rosemary over her ashes.

No-one would ever grieve the vampires, she thought.

***

Arabella's legs ached from standing so long, and from all the dancing. The house was well-lit when they came in, covered in the muck. It had been like a beacon walking back from the campsite. Lily was sitting up nursing a mug of tea.

"We missed you at the dance!" Roman winked.

"Roman," Iona said.

"I know, I know." Roman waved a hand, and headed off to bed.

"Good evening." Iona nodded to Lily, and then looked to Munro, and gestured for Holly and the others to follow her.

Everyone filed out of the kitchen until it was just Lily, Munro, and Bella. Bella considered leaving, but then Munro took her hand. She elected to just stay quiet and hope no-one asked her a direct question.

Lily looked at Munro like she was waiting for her to leave.

Munro sat down. "I don't want to leave it like that."

"Don't mind me, I'm just 'the poison'."

"Oh, get off your cross, we need the wood," Munro said. "All of this. Why are you torturing yourself? You barely know me."

"Who's fault is that?"

"Your father's."

Lily, a coiled spring in her chest, leaned forwards. "Do not speak ill of my dad again. Do you understand?"

"I was too harsh. No-one can be all things to all people. He did well, raising you. Raising his grandkids. Burn's a good lad."

"I am proud of them," Lily said. She welled up. "Oh, they drive me mad but I am proud of them."

"It's not easy, the family you were born into. The feuds." Munro tried to place her hand on Lily's, a show of solidarity between the two women — but she swatted it away.

"You didn't see how it affected him, watching you go," Lily said. "He was never the same. I loved him. And you broke him."

Munro's hand lowered, reluctantly, to her side. "He broke me too. I loved him. He was bull-headed, but I was proud of him."

Lily looked out of the window. They could just about make out the smouldering embers of the grill in the pitch black over the hill, with no light pollution to hide it. "I just wanted us all to be together at the end. I wanted it to look like we were happy, to remember it that way." Lily retracted her hand. "It was never going to happen, was it?"

Munro shook her head. "You can't change the story at the end."

"I don't want that following my kids about."

"I have no ill will towards you. Haar wanted us to go our separate ways, so I did. And I wanted to abide his wishes, even after he was gone."

Lily simmered, collected herself, until she had the strength to speak. "We'll be gone by the morning."

She made to leave, but Munro stood, the chair scraping the tile floor as she did, and grabbed her in a hug. Lily accepted the hug, but didn't return it.

And then she left.

Munro was silent, processing.

"Why didn't that feel like a resolution?" Bella said.

Munro sniffed, wiped her nose. "Because it wasn't."

Bella wrapped her in a hug as she cried, knowing it was no substitute for the one she'd needed.

chapter 22

"Nicnevin?" Bella chapped the door to Nicnevin's study. It was later in the night, and the rest of the Coven had settled in the kitchen with Burn, laughing and drinking. Nicnevin and Lily had been absent. Now seemed as good a time as any to try and smooth things over with their host.

There was no response, but she could see movement and the flickering of a light under the door. She tried the handle.

"What do you want?" Nicnevin said, as the door stopped, only opening a crack.

"I wanted to talk about what happened earlier today," Bella said.

"You came to apologise?"

"No, I—"

"Then we have nothing to talk about."

Bella made a stronger attempt to push the door open, and it forced open to find Nicnevin sitting behind her desk, writing in her Book of Shadows. Her mascara had dried on her cheeks, and her hand was clenched around her fountain pen like she was trying to throttle the life out of it.

"Oh, sorry, do you want to read future entries as well?"

"Stop it," Bella said. She could feel the anger travelling through her pipes, but she took a deep breath.

"Then apologise."

"No."

"Then we have nothing to talk about."

Bella swallowed. "Your... your plan to help Munro."

"Oh, now you want to hear my plan?" Nicnevin slammed her pen down in the gutter of her diary. "Now that you've read all my innermost thoughts, now that you saw that what I was doing is completely beyond you, *now* you have the fucking audacity to ask me for help."

"Well, why didn't you tell us about it beforehand?" Bella said. "I couldn't trust you—"

"No, you absolutely could have. Because that's the difference between us, Bella. You have everything you could ever want. You have a family who loves you, you have more magic than most, you have the love of a woman who is worth more than life itself. A woman who decided she was unhappy with me, and wanted to leave me. So yes, I was jealous. I think that's normal. I did nothing, nothing, to hurt you."

"Oh, shut the fuck up. Jealous. You, the head of a Fey House, the most powerful necromancer in two realms, a woman with legs longer than my entire body, who could have her pick of anyone—"

"I didn't want anyone," Nicnevin said. "I only wanted her."

"So you admit it! You were trying to get Munro back!"

Nicnevin took a deep, steadying breath, closing her eyes as she calmed herself. "I don't know what you want from me. I don't know how to prove what's in my heart to you. I am not trying to steal her, and she's not mine to steal—"

"That didn't stop you before!"

Nicnevin smarted, eyes still closed. "I made... a mistake. I thought I had atoned."

"You can't just—"

"Let me be clear," Nicnevin interrupted her, as she finally opened her eyes. "You read my Book of Shadows. I would be, legally, and in my mind, morally, well within my right to shatter you like glassware. I have chosen not to do that. Because I care about Munro, and I want her to be happy. She doesn't have long—" Her breath hitched. She inhaled, ragged, and steadied herself, speaking quieter. "She doesn't have long left."

Bella could feel her fire extinguishing, against her will. Even through her tunnel vision, it didn't seem like an act.

"I don't like you, Arabella Morrow. I don't think I am obligated to. But I care about Munro. So I tried to make an effort. I opened my home to you. And you spat in my face. That being said, I am going to overlook that."

She stood up, and as she leaned over the desk the casualwear of earlier in the evening ruffled and fell into a gown, as her mascara tracks hardened into barnacles on her cheeks.

Bella stumbled back.

"I'm going to offer you a deal. I will share what I know of my research into extending Munro's lifespan further with your coven, and you will agree that the information you read about my personal life remains locked in your head forever. If you speak about it, you will die. Instantly. Your life is forfeit."

"You *do* have a way to help her then."

"I do. But you won't like it," Nicnevin said. "Honestly, I only offer you this deal because the alternative is murdering you now, which will upset Munro, or wiping your memory, which your coven has proven does not work long-term."

Bella looked at her outstretched hand. "The only other information I read was you saying you were jealous. You really want to hide it that badly?"

"Of course. It's... wait, do you really not understand how I feel at all?"

"No, honestly," Bella said. "My first thought when I read that... was that you had written that as a lie, knowing I would read it."

Nicnevin's expression darkened. "Either you have no self-esteem, no perspective, or no empathy. Or a mix of all three."

Bella blinked, irritated. "Or you're a woman-stealing harpy who lives to hate me."

Nicnevin started to try to calm herself again, but then changed her mind. "Why am I the one reaching out the olive branch right now? Why am I trying to be nice to you, only for you to continue to spit in my face?"

"I don't know, Nevin, maybe it's cos you've always been 'the bigger woman'."

Nicnevin snorted, despite herself. "Okay. That was funny."

"No. You don't get to laugh at my jokes. That was supposed to be offensive."

"You're terrible at being offensive then."

"Thank you."

The two of them sat in silence, not looking at each other.

Eventually, Bella broke the silence. "You promise to help Munro?"

A crack in Nicnevin's armour. "Always. I made a pact on a battlefield a long time ago." She steeled herself. "Always."

"And you're not going to... monkey paw me by making this extremely literal or finding some loophole in the wording?"

"I'm a witch, Bella, not some crossroads demon," Nicnevin said. "All witches have is their word. Splitting hairs and finding loopholes is for men."

"Then I'll do it." She spat on her hand.

Nicnevin spat on hers, and said a spell as the saliva dripped onto the floor:

"Money, glamour, power, fame,
Hold the honour, hide the shame.
In return, a seed to sow,
We work together to save Munro."

They clasped forearms as best they could with their differing hand sizes.

It was worth it, Bella thought, as she felt the magic tingle in her brain, a length of twine locking the information away, leadening her tongue. It had to be worth it.

Because she knew in that moment, if it was for Munro, she'd even consider the crossroads demon.

***

Munro was unpacking her suitcase when they entered. She looked up, putting down the unfolded pair of trousers. Her heart dropped. Bella and Nicnevin coming to her at the same time felt like an intervention.

"Both of you entering my bedchamber at once?" she said, trying to lighten the mood. "This is either my worst nightmare or my wildest dream."

They didn't smile. Bella looked worried. Munro wrung her palms, rocking from side to side. She couldn't look at them.

Bella approached. "Hi, love."

"This is why I don't make jokes," Munro said. "If no-one laughs it just hurts your self-esteem."

"We wanted to talk to y—"

"Let me guess," Munro said. She was rattling now, like a pup. "You two have some cockamamie plan to do even more experimental things with my world line, to add an arbitrary amount of time to my life."

They were silent.

Munro sat down on the bed, deflating. They didn't understand. The whiplash. Always with these witches. She has three months to live. She'll live forever. She has days. She's fine now.

She buried her face in her hands and groaned in frustration.

"I know," Bella said. She sat next to her and rubbed her shoulder in soft circles.

Munro shrank away, she didn't want to be touched right now. She gathered herself, and said, "What is it this time?"

"Hm," Nicnevin said. "I didn't think you'd be interested."

"What can I say Nevin," Munro sighed. "I always went looking to get punched." She hoped that was it. That she was just a fighter. That she could ignore the urge to lie down and never get up. Because the alternative, knowing that she was breathing against her will, terrified her more than anything else.

"Show her what you showed me," Bella said to Nicnevin, her voice clipped in that way it did when she was angry. Munro looked at Bella, tried to work it out. Had they been arguing?

Nicnevin waved a hand, and light began to play across her dappled blue-green skin, like the surface of water viewed from below. A tapestry of threads in a million colours. They spun out of all three of them like a web, tracing them back as they paced the room, round in circles like eddies and out into the world. And others, from everyone who had ever walked through these walls, weaving in and out of each other.

Munro looked, and when she did, she could see the others in the house, each with their own thread, all in a different colour. Everyone except Verity. Verity walked through the threads and they swerved to avoid touching her, parting like oil and water. The only reason Munro could see her at all was the homunculus. The stitches that bound them together flickered like a failing cigarette lighter.

"What are these?" Munro asked.

"They're the world lines," Nicnevin said. "They're what ley lines are made of. The path of every living being in its journey through the world, each one an irreplaceable thread that weaves with the others to form a rope."

Munro looked down at her own.

The others looked bright and burning, but hers was... dim, like Verity's. A pale blue, that flickered with her breath. The twine was starting to unspool, fibres peeled back. There was a thread through it of seaweed that burst out in places, she suspected Nicnevin's first spell to keep her here.

But the line stopped. A few inches from her.

It trailed behind her the same as the others, but it was like it was on a delay. The others tied to their sternums and hers just floated, like it was going to blow away in a breeze.

So that was the weightlessness she'd been feeling. The weariness. She'd been holding on to this thing.

Nicnevin plucked Bella's world line, rainbow-bright. It made a sound like a guitar string. Bella winced — "ow!" — clutching her chest as her world line buzzed and wobbled, and an apparition emerged from the vibration — a spectral Bella. *"Show her what you showed me."* An echo of the recent past, gone as quickly as it arrived, fading back into the tapestry.

"I suspect the visions have started," Nicnevin said.

Munro looked up, attentive for the first time in the conversation. "Yes. When I start to fade, I see—"

"The past. That's you losing your grip. Your... your life flashing before your eyes."

Munro slumped. "So... so I can't change any of it."

Nicnevin shook her head. "Two rules of witchcraft, hon. You can't change the past, and you can't bring back the dead." She crossed her arms. "I mean, really bringing back the dead is just another way of changing the past. You can reanimate a body like a puppet, you can do what I did and hold the person in stasis at the point of death, but a life is a flame. Once it goes out, it's gone. Once a glass of water spills, refilling it doesn't make it the same glass of water."

"That's what you've always said!" Munro said. "So why are you here, telling me there's another bloody life support spell *now*? When you've already done everything!"

"I didn't want to, for the record," Nicnevin said. "It is dangerous, and invasive."

Munro glared at Bella. "So it was you who put her up to this."

"Yes, and I won't apologise for it," Bella said, haughtily. "Nicnevin did the work of finding it, I think it would be stupid to not even consider it."

Munro looked down at her world line, fading and flickering as it was. "I thought you said, if you tried to do any more, it would break."

"I did say that," Nicnevin sighed. "If we touch your world line, it snaps. The last miracle we pulled off resolves, the superposition collapses and the universe remembers you're supposed to be dead." She rubbed the bridge of her nose. "But... if you were to threaten me with the guillotine... we can't touch your world line, but we could, slow time down around it."

"You can do that?"

"Oh, slowing down time is children's magic, darling. All you have to do to slow down time is get bored."

"No, I mean... to this," she pointed at the frayed world line. She could all but hear it tensing as the twine and seaweed flexed. "It's not even a real thing in space, it's a spiritual construct."

Nicnevin clicked her tongue off the roof of her mouth, turning her thousands of years of acumen to the problem. Munro could almost feel herself being turned over in Nicnevin's head. She tried not to smile despite herself. She had forgotten what it felt like. Every conversation had been like a swordfight. And Munro, young and headstrong, had crossed many blades, but never one that fought like Nicnevin's.

"I... suspect so," Nicnevin said. "I am, as you know, incredibly powerful."

Bella glowered. "Humblebrag."

"Hush," Nicnevin said, and Munro could see the tiny quirk of pleasure it gave her to dismiss Bella like that. By the tides, she wished they could see how alike they were and could get over themselves. Maybe it was because they were so similar, they grated on each other.

"But yes, I do suspect so. I would need to concentrate on it indefinitely, even in my sleep, but that wouldn't be too hard for a witch of my standing. Especially one who acts as psychopomp as often as I do."

"Then why didn't you want to do it?" Munro furrowed her brow. "What's the catch?"

"Your visions," Nicnevin said. "If we slow time down around your world line, it doesn't affect your experience of time, but it affects how long it takes. So the visions would get longer. More vivid. When you relive pain, it will hurt longer."

Munro squinted. "I've never been one to back down before."

Nicnevin coughed. "Also... I would be... privy to them. Anything you see, I'd see as your psychopomp."

"I..." Munro could feel her cheeks reddening. Damn her blood. "I see." She turned to Bella. "And you would be happy with that?"

Bella closed her eyes, and laid her hand on Munro's in her lap. "I'm not happy about it, but Munro if it would buy you another fifteen minutes, I would give anything in the world."

Munro looked her in the eye. Those eyes. She loved everything about Bella. Her righteous anger, the way she saw the entire world like art, the way she laughed when she was nervous, her need to be a smart-Alec... But she would be lying if she said the thing she loved the most wasn't her eyes. Those big sad eyes looked at her and she just melted.

But she couldn't do it just for her. If she was going to do this, it needed to be for herself.

"Can I..." She looked out into the other room, through the walls, watching the world lines of the others going about their evenings. And a sad-looking woman sitting on the porch having a cigarette, illuminated only by the stitches of her homunculus.

Someone else who would understand.

"Can I have some time to think about it?"

chapter 23

Verity jumped as Munro sat down next to her.

"Hell below," she said, putting her hand to her chest by the homunculus while her heart slowed. "It's not common to find someone who can sneak up on me."

"Sorry," Munro said.

Verity looked down at her cigarette, and then to Munro. She offered it.

Munro refused it.

"Not a smoker?"

"Not for a while. Though... the smell of it." She took a deep breath. "I'm just going to hover, if that's okay."

"Go wild," Verity said.

They sat in silence for a good minute. It was excruciating. Verity had half a mind to put her cigarette out and just go inside, but that felt like it would be even more awkward.

Munro poked her head round the door to see if anyone else was coming. "Can I tap one?"

Verity reached down and picked up the carton by her ashtray, the one she had just smoked before lighting this one still smouldering. She passed it over, and Munro grabbed one like it held the golden ticket. She perched it on her lip, produced a match from somewhere in her furs, and struck it against her chin. The flame ignited with a plume, and then died as she lit the cigarette from it.

Verity watched her throw the match away. "That's quite the party trick."

Munro looked her up and down in a way that would've made her feel flattered a hundred years ago. "Terrible habit," she said. "I quit years ago, it's just..."

"Yeah..." Verity said.

"I... the others don't get it," Munro said. "My situation."

"Yeah," Verity said. "They mean well though."

"Yeah..." Munro squatted, resting her weight on the balls of her feet. She stared out into the hills. The sky glistened with aurora, gold and green, and the stars were not pinpricks, but stretched across the sky like the dash of a pen. Far off into the horizon, long, thin silver dragons danced with each other on the wind. "I forgot how nice the view was out here."

"I've been enjoying it myself. It was nicer during the day. But then, it was a novelty I will probably not get used to."

"Mm..." Munro thought. She looked at Verity. "I didn't just come out here to ask you for a cigarette."

· Verity swallowed, suddenly her palms were clammy. "If you're propositioning me, I should say—"

Munro laughed. When she laughed Verity could hear the seal bark in it, imagine her and her family lying on the beach, messing around while they waited for humans to cross them. She had never met a selkie before.

"No," Munro said. "I've never been the 'open relationship' type."

Verity burned. "Sorry. I didn't mean—"

"It's fine. Though I'm flattered," Munro said.

"You are surprisingly agile for a great-grandmother," Verity said.

"Everyone's really got that on the brain, eh..." Munro smirked. She reached around Verity to grab the ashtray and put it between them.

"What did you want to ask me for then?" Verity said, when the conversation returned to silence.

"...I wanted your advice."

"*My* advice?"

"They want to mess with my world line again."

"Your...?" Verity said.

"It's the... life thread. Thing. I don't know. It trails behind you."

"Oh, those lights following us around?" Verity said. "Around ten minutes ago?"

"I didn't think she'd made them visible to everyone..." Munro said. "Shit, they're probably all talking about it now."

"I didn't have any lights."

"You didn't."

"Does that mean I don't have a world line?" she said. "I saw... I used to have a gold thread. It tied me to the Dark Scaffold. To my grandfather."

"Maybe," Munro said, then shook herself. "I don't know. You'll have to ask someone else, I don't know much about it. In the meantime—"

"Yes, sorry," Verity said, though her mind was spinning. There was something to that thread. She was sure of it. It powered Breckenridge, it fed him. Where did it come from? Would it be beyond her to poison him with it?

"I'm not sure whether to let them mess with it," Munro said. "I'm tired."

"So?"

Munro blinked.

"Every morning I got up, running on empty, no blood in my system. Exhausted. Weak. Limp. And I chose to live." Verity rankled, aware she was sounding more caustic than she meant to. But it was something she had been thinking about a lot. She lived as a parasite on other people. But she had never once questioned if she *wanted* to live.

Only worried that she may not be able to do it without hurting anyone.

"I guess that's what I'm asking," Munro said. "Do I choose to try and live? Even if it might not work anyway, even if it hurts me, even if it doesn't give me that much time anyway."

"Hm. Well I'm no expert in palliative care."

Munro opened her mouth to respond, but stopped herself.

Verity gave her time to gather her thoughts.

"I... I guess I just feel a bit powerless," Munro said eventually. "And I don't want to give up control of what little I have left. And I don't want them putting themselves in danger to help me. And if it works, I don't want to be in even more pain."

"It sounds like you've made your mind up," Verity said.

Munro drew the remainder of her cigarette deep into her lungs, relaxed herself, and breathed it out. "Sounds that way, doesn't it."

"So what are you doing asking me?"

"I guess I'm looking for someone to talk me into it."

"If given two options where one is certain death, I'm always going to pick the other one. But... that's just me," Verity said. "Also... it might be painful. But sometimes things that hurt are worth it." As if in demonstration, she took another drag.

Munro grinned broadly. "Oh, I can see why Holly likes you."

Verity felt a flush rise up her neck. "Holly likes me?"

Munro clapped her on the back with her ham hock hand, laughing. "Thanks, Verity. I'll see you tomorrow." She stood up. "I hope."

She left, looking lighter.

Verity continued to smoke her cigarette. Gallows humour was a powerful drug, she thought.

She hoped she had given Munro what she needed to hear. Deep in her heart, she had a thought that she was not being entirely truthful. She believed it, but she also had a deep knowledge that if she was alive, if she was going to make all that sacrifice worth something, she had to do something with it.

Breckenridge had to die. If she could topple the Dark Scaffold, if she could wipe out her grandfather and all his ilk... it would be worth it.

***

Bella and Munro lay on their side. Munro had her eyes shut, but Bella could tell she wasn't asleep yet.

"It's gonna be okay..." Bella said, stroking her hair. She curled up against her, felt her warmth. She was still here. She was safe. "It's gonna be okay..."

"Yeah." Munro didn't sound convinced.

The moon was fully out now, shining through the clouds into their window, bathing them in light. And a voice spoke in their heads.

"It's time."

The shadow of Nicnevin loomed over them from the corner of the room, cast by nothing.

"It's going to be okay," Bella said. "It's going to be okay, it's going to be okay." Munro took a deep, ragged breath, and slumped on the pillow.

The shadow moved its hands, and an emerald symbol began to draw itself in the air, runes and sigils that Bella's mind could barely read.

"What are you doing?"

"Time moves slower... when you're asleep."

Bella got up, stepped round the bed, and approached Munro from the front. Hunched over the bed, she held her face in her hands. She looked so peaceful.

It was alien to see Munro look this peaceful when she slept.

"What can I do?" Bella asked.

"Let me work," Nicnevin whispered.

Green rings encased Munro, circling her, twisting and dancing.

Bella squeezed her hand tight. "Come on, Munro..."

***

There is a crack of thunder as the storm outside rages. The selkies are all inside. Lily is hiding under her blankets, shivering with fear despite the fire. Haar finds this all very funny.

"Hey," I say, lifting the blanket so I can see inside. Lily is curled up in a ball, squeezing a yarn toy her mother made for her. "It's okay." My mothering muscles have atrophied, I can't remember what I used to say to them.

Another flash, which makes her squeal, as the thunder rumbles off in the distance.

"We're safe, it's leaving," I say.

"No!" she shouts, as though I had personally brought the thunder myself, and grabs the blanket from my hand, burrowing into it.

"Okay." I stroke her head. "It's okay..." I sit by the little quivering bundle of blankets, and rest my hand on her head through them.

And then, I remember.

"You know... you can count between the flashes," I say. "If you see the flash, and then count for the sound, you can tell how far away it is."

The bundle stops.

"What do you mean?" comes a little muffled voice from underneath.

"Watch, count with me." And we count until she's stopped thinking about what the lightning is, and is too busy counting it, and I have nodded off...

—

I am lying in a bed, and I am weary. Weary in my bones.

We are supposed to be warriors, and I am dying of old age. I laugh, and it rattles my ribcage like a derelict building. I cough, and everything hurts.

"We are not meant to live forever, your Highness. Not like you..." I say to Nicnevin, who hovers by my bed. Somehow, against all odds, I had

expected my family to be here when I went.

But of course, it was always just her.

I can hear her, saying... something. I am so tired. I can't seem to open my eyes. If I can just see her, one more time. Just once. It might be worth it.

I am... happy.

I open my mouth, to say something. To have some final stamp on my life.

But I don't have the energy.

My vision begins to blotch, inks of purple and yellow and green and colours I have no name for. There is a fear, a deep sense that something is wrong, and there is a crack of lightning as my eyes open and my lungs inflate

—

There is a flash as a bolt of lightning strikes a dead tree.

It is cold.

Colder than I have ever been. The cold needles through my wet fur, the wind beats me and muffles my calls. The rain stings but my skin is numb. I have been out here for hours. I will be out here for hours more.

He is still out here.

I dive again, sealform into the water, under the surface, a hundred feet deep, where the waves roil uselessly above your head like far-off clouds. I look, as long as I can, I hold my breath, and then, when it feels like my lungs will burn, I surface.

I scream.

I cry. The tears are swallowed by the rain. I scream, the thunder takes it.

I will not stop.

I have given the sea everything. It will not take my son. I will search every vein of blue on this Earth for Snow, and if I don't find him alive and well, I will boil the whole thing.

This happened. I am remembering this.
I continue to remember this.
And I do not know how much longer I can bear it.

chapter 24

The sun meandered over the hill, and Verity watched it from the kitchen window, protected by the Elf-hame fogs. She could smell the dew on the grass outside, the air heavy with last night's rainfall. In the distance, the trees shook hands as they greeted each other for the day. Every so often, something would break through the treeline, in a corkscrew or a concertina shape. It took her a few minutes to realise the shapes were buses. Single-decker buses. How bizarre.

The sky behind the fog prismed purple and yellow and blue, like a kaleidoscope. She had a sudden feeling that all of Elf-hame was actually the inside of a giant diamond.

She watched Lily and her boys walking down the pathway towards the road. She would've waved to them, but they didn't look back.

"It's a beautiful view, isn't it?" Nicnevin said. "I wasn't sure about this place when I bought it, until I saw that view."

Verity turned. She'd heard Nicnevin coming down the stairs. "Yes." She looked back. "This is the closest thing I've seen to a real sunrise in centuries."

"I always preferred the night anyway." Nicnevin put the kettle on. "How are you?"

"I know what I have to do," Verity said. "I just don't know if it's possible."

"Ominous," Nicnevin said. "I'm sure you'll find a way. You seem resourceful."

"Thank you for letting me into your home," Verity said. "This weekend has been illuminating."

"Well, I wouldn't have been a very good host, making you stand on the threshold the entire time," Nicnevin said. "I'm glad you enjoyed yourself. It didn't go exactly how I wanted."

"Why *did* you invite Munro's family?"

"I hurt them quite badly when I stole Munro's heart. It seemed like the least I could do."

"Witches seem to have a lot of bad blood."

"All blood is bad blood," Nicnevin said. "I don't think there's a family in the world that doesn't have problems."

Verity scoffed, thinking of her mother and Breckenridge back in that ancient house, stewing. "Seemed like you and Bella sorted things out though."

"I'm glad it looks that way," Nicnevin said, airily enough that it seemed like she hoped Verity wouldn't notice the sarcastic note. Interesting.

"I wanted to ask you a question. Munro told me last night about... world lines. Ley lines. I could see them all through the house."

Nicnevin put a tea kettle on the hob. "Oh, sorry about that by the way. I get so used to living al—"

"I didn't have one."

Nicnevin looked back at her, so sheepish and full of pity that it made her want to crawl out of her own skin. "No. You didn't. Sorry."

"I used to have one."

"As a human, yes."

"No, as a vampire," Verity said.

Nicnevin leaned on the counter, percolating on it. "Your connection to the vampires' False Ladder."

"The Dark Scaffold."

"Whatever you lot call it," Nicnevin said. "It's as you already know.

You have a form of life. But it's not *your* life. You died. The world lines trace people moving wherever they will. That fake line? It just tied you to your grandfather. It kept you under their control."

"So cutting my grandfather's won't kill him?"

"It didn't kill you, I don't see why it would kill him," Nicnevin said. "Though... I happen to know through a little birdy that his was tied into another source of power."

"You know my grandfather?"

Nicnevin curled her nose — "Unfortunately," — as the tea kettle started to whistle and she poured a tea for herself. She didn't offer one to Verity. "The problem with immortals, darling, is that we do in fact all know each other. Live long enough, it's impossible not to run into one another." She held the tea under her nose.

Verity heard the padding footsteps of someone coming down the stairs.

She knew if she didn't ask now, she'd never ask. The question that had been burning in her head since that conversation with Munro. "How would you kill him then?"

Nicnevin put the teacup down on the counter, and put a hand on Verity's shoulder. "I have no idea."

And just as Verity's heart began to sink, she leaned forward as if to kiss her on the cheek, and whispered in her ear, "I do wonder what all those ley lines are doing around his house though."

Verity blinked, stupefied, as Nicnevin stood again, smiling as if she'd said nothing.

So this was how witches fought. Always with words.

Munro appeared at the foot of the stairs, dumping a suitcase. She stopped to catch her breath. "Good morning."

"Morning," Nicnevin said. "You just missed Lily and the kids leaving."

"I know," Munro said. "I was waiting."

Nicnevin nodded.

"This..." Munro circled her chest where the spell had taken. "This thing you did..."

"It'll hold. No more dead postmen. For now, anyway."

Munro let out a sigh of relief. "Every time, you find another way to surprise me."

Nicnevin grinned wickedly. "It keeps me young."

"We'll probably be off soon as well," Munro said. "Thank you for hosting us."

"Please, I offered!" Nicnevin said. "Got no food in, I'm afraid, so I can't send you home with a full stomach."

Munro patted her stomach. "Honestly, I feel like I've done nothing but eat since I got here anyway. I'm gonna go for a swim before the others wake up."

Nicnevin smiled, like she was remembering older times. Munro headed out the door, and Nicnevin exhaled. "It's a long old life, eh?"

"Too long," Verity agreed.

Nicnevin looked at the creature hanging on Verity's chest. "Not too much longer for you though, I think. Hm?"

"No," Verity said. "No, I think not."

***

Bella finished the chalk circle on the patio outside Nicnevin's porch. "All ready for you, Iona."

Iona put down her tea. "Thank you, petal." She took the chalk from Bella and squirreled it away in her bag. "Everyone ready to go?"

Nicnevin sighed, belabouredly. "Ohh, it's gonna be quiet with you gone!"

Bella was not sure what to say. "Thank you. For everything."

Nicnevin stooped, almost comically, to be eye level with Arabella. Bella caught several lungfuls of her perfume at once, floral and overpowering. She still smiled like a predator. "Take care of yourself, darling." And she plopped a wet, pillowy kiss on Arabella's cheek.

Arabella was too taken aback to check if she had a big lipstick mark on her face. Out of instinct, she hugged Nicnevin, arms around her. It felt like putting her hand in a shark's mouth, exposing her neck.

But she'd helped Munro.

Nicnevin rubbed between Bella's shoulder blades until she let go.

Iona formed a cat's cradle in her fingers as Nicnevin backed up out of the chalk circle. It was one of the most powerful spells they had, the spell that would bring them home wherever they were. But this far into Elf-hame, even it needed a little help. The glyphs on the ground lit to a blaze as they channelled Iona's magic.

"Bon voyage!" Nicnevin said.

"See you around!" Holly shouted.

Munro ran and gave Nicnevin a hug so tight it would've crushed a normal-sized person. "See you around, trouble."

Nicnevin welled up. "Not if I see you first."

Munro stepped back, just into the bounds of the spell, and House Nicnevin was whisked away and the familiar, dusty smell of home took them.

Bella felt herself relax a little instantly. The Archive was a comfort all itself. Nothing could get in these walls. Their little temple of safety.

Verity cleared her throat. "Now that we're back... I know what I want to do. Will you help me kill Breckenridge?"

chapter 25

Bella didn't know what to say.

"Yes," Iona said quickly.

"Woah, hold up there." Roman laughed. "I thought you said this guy was more powerful than any of us. And, Iona, that we have some kind of... treaty with them?"

"There'll be no punishment if they're all dead," Iona said. She had that constricted look about her, the fervour she'd had when talking about leaving Verity out in the cold. "If we have one on our side, maybe that's our in. Did you have a plan?"

Verity gulped. "Yes, I think so. I think it's why I'm still here."

Roman scoffed. "You're *still here* because we cut you open and hooked you up with a dead man's heart!"

"It's my purpose, I know it."

"I..." Roman looked to the others. "No? Come on."

"This man has killed thousands of people. Tens of thousands," Verity said. "And his blood is on my hands as well."

Roman looked at Holly and Bella. "I don't want to start a war."

Holly swallowed. "He tried to climb in my head. I don't know if I can make a logical decision after that."

He looked at Bella, pleading. He suddenly looked so small, so afraid. "Let's not do this, eh?"

"I don't know," Bella said. Munro put a hand on her shoulder and she looked back.

Munro. That warbling dark matter in the back of the room. Verity still had to try to even notice she was there. No vampire cord, no heartbeat. A shadow lurking over them.

"What do you think?" Bella said.

"I think, if it was you that asked, no question," Munro smiled. "Besides, you know I love a lesbian revenge story."

Bella welled up. "Are you just looking for a blaze of glory?"

"More a... project to keep me going," Munro said.

"Alright." Bella sucked in a breath, and turned to Iona. "Let's do it. Let's hunt some vampires."

Roman groaned. "Shit."

"How do we do that?" Holly asked Verity. "I blew his head open, and he just knitted it back together."

"Usually you kill a vampire with a wooden stake through the heart," Iona said.

"That won't work with Breckenridge," Verity said. "I've seen him staked. Shot through with silver. Stabbed. Starved. Doused in holy water. He has something else to keep him going."

"So..." Holly said.

"Nicnevin," Verity said. "Something about the ley lines in Park Circus."

"She told you this?" Bella asked.

"She... implied," Verity said.

Bella rolled her eyes. "Of course."

Iona smiled. "Well, it sounds like we have a place to start."

***

Park Circus was the fanciest neighbourhood Arabella had ever been in. A little bubble of mansions at the top of a hill, overlooking the park and the university. Imposing, illustrious sandstone and wide cobbled streets intended for horse and carriage. Bella could feel Holly behind her, rankled, perched like a threatened cat. She tried to take a breath.

Roman whistled through his teeth. "Some'dy's mammy's an heiress," he said to Verity when they walked past a church tower, bleached and pale compared to the other sandstone buildings around. Across the road, a black-brick building buttressed the end of the street.

"It's the inheritance of all vampirekind," Verity said. She looked down at the homunculus strapped to her chest.

"But there's more going on here." He turned to Bella. He was doing a good job of hiding the fact he was scared shitless, she thought. But not that good. "Can you feel that?" he said.

Arabella just nodded. She could.

There was a thrum under their feet. Like the roar of the underground, or the foot traffic of the thoroughfares. This was what they were here to investigate. Get in, get out, without the vampires knowing.

"This is a line too," Iona said. "And it's been used. Recently."

"It makes sense I guess," Holly said, looking up and down the street. "Park Circus is a circle after all. Is there another coven that might be using it?"

Verity said, "That's what Nicnevin told me. Something about the ley lines."

"Vampires shouldn't be able to touch the ley lines..." Iona said, and she lifted a large blue censer on a chain. Swinging it, it clouded the wide-set streets of Park Circus in a fog that followed them, hiding them from view of any people who might decide to wander out. With the Victorian mansions sparkling on the hill and the old street-lamps, it looked like something out of an old penny dreadful. "Keep your wits about you."

This ley line was old. Decayed. Its path had once been as well-tread as any of the others Bella knew, but that was decades ago. Now, it was preserved in glass, like an old whisky. If there was one that a vampire would be able to tap...

The fog smelled of sage and coconut and willow bark, and all the previous things that had been burned in it. It was too overpowering a smell to be directly enjoyable. They walked slowly in its protective cloud, like at mass.

"This is it." Verity stopped at the front door of the dark stone building they'd walked past. It really did look like a church.

"But that's..." Holly trailed off. "If your theory is he's so powerful because he built his house on the ley line, and we can only kill him in that home, then your theory's wrong."

"Aw man, does this mean we don't get to go into the vampire lair?" Roman whispered. "I was so excited to get brutally murdered."

"I don't understand," Verity said. "Nicnevin said..."

"The ley lines don't congregate here. The power here is going somewhere, but it's not here," Bella confirmed. She put her hands on the ground, tried to feel the pulse under the stone, the heartbeat, but it was so faint here...

"If not here, then where?" Verity said.

A voice, quiet as a dormouse, interrupted them. "Verity?"

The door to the not-quite-church was open, and a woman stood on the threshold. She looked younger than them all, barely an adult, with long, curled blonde hair, and a black velvet cloak. Her eyes watered with happiness. "Verity, you've come home." Her accent was thick as treacle, like the Queen's. It seemed to get caught in her teeth on the way out.

"Hello, mother," Verity said. She looked tensed to run.

"I thought you'd starved to death," the woman said. She made a step forward, but then seemed to see the entourage. "You've brought dinner?"

"Friends," Verity said. "They're my friends."

Verity's mother's face crumpled. "Oh, not this again, dear. Must you go around collecting strays?"

"Is Grandfather home?" Verity said.

"Of course." She stepped aside, clearing the doorway. "Come in, all of you."

Verity started walking towards her.

"Verity, wait!" Holly said, reaching out to grab her, but she was too fast. The speed of a predator. Bella only got a glimpse of her face, glassy and vacant, before she was already at the foot of the stairs. Verity was not in control of her actions right now. Hypnotism.

Iona stopped swinging the censer, let it fall by her side. She looked at them, all the colour draining from her face.

Roman looked at them all, his eyes saying 'are we *really* going in there?', but Iona grabbed the censer by the handle.

Verity's mother had left the door open, like they weren't even a second thought.

Holly looked at them all, a fire in her eyes.

"Come on," Bella said. "First sign of trouble, Iona has the teleport." She took Holly's hand.

Roman made a noise like he was passing a difficult shit.

They walked up the stairs after their new friend.

***

The last of them entered the foyer — Arabella had never been in a room that could have this many people standing in the front door before.

Holly cleared her throat. "Nice place you've got here."

She wasn't lying either, the place was a bougie palace. Ceilings like caverns lined with egg-and-dart molding, draped with expensive dark wood furniture, purple and red satins and silks and chiffons. Bella felt like she'd walked through a time warp.

It was so decadent she thought she was going to get a stomach ache.

She could feel it, the electricity in the air around her. All her coven, in fight-or-flight. They were waving their feet over a bear trap.

Roman was the last one in before the door slammed shut. Verity's mother looked him up and down. "Well, aren't you a delicious little pudding?"

Roman hissed at her, like an honest-to-God cat. Holly covered her mouth to stop from laughing.

The vampire turned her nose up. "Charming." She addressed the group. "I'm Alice, by the way. Verity's mother."

Verity held the bottom of the homunculus like she'd been caught with a real baby. She was blinking, dazed, just coming back to herself.

"You'll need to put that out, by the way." Alice gestured to Iona's censer. Reluctantly, Iona lifted it and blew the flame out.

"How many are your brood?" Iona said.

"Oh, just us three now," Alice said. "Why? Are you asking about vacancies?"

Iona grit her teeth. "Funny."

"Well. I hope you didn't invite your... new friends here just to spit barbs at me," Alice said to Verity. "I've missed you dear... I was so worried when all that nastiness happened."

"Nastiness?" Verity said, still looking groggy. She was shaking off the hypnotism. "He threw me off the hill."

"Yes..." Alice said. "Hopefully you've learned from it."

Bella was getting flashbacks of her own mother, and it was turning her stomach. She could see under the Stepford wife smile, feel the anxiety and bottled rage and the desperate need to keep up appearances. There had been nothing more horrifying in the Morrow household than being shown up in front of guests. Guests gossiped. (At least Bella's mum had assumed so.)

Alice started to approach, but stopped when everyone in the room jumped. Then, gently, she stepped away from the group, to Verity. She rested her hand on the homunculus' head. "What is this?" she asked, like Verity had brought a stray cat home.

Verity, to her credit, was not letting her nerves get to her. "It's freedom, mother." She jutted out her chin in a way that made her look fifteen years old instead of centuries.

Bella twinged. She hadn't really thought about how all her programming was still in there even if it wasn't being used. She'd ended up running away for her own freedom. The weight of what Verity was doing suddenly seemed enormous.

Alice blinked, as though Verity had spoken another language. "Whatever do you mean, dear?" She glanced to the Coven, imperceptibly. Bad influences.

"It's a dead thing, a puppet," came a voice from the top of the stairs.

Holly tensed like rope, taking Bella's hand again. This must be him.

Breckenridge was tall, even taller looking down at them from the top of the lavish staircase. His hair was white as a sheet, and curly, and he smiled at them with his lips curled back showing too much gum. His grey-blue eyes looked over each of them in turn like he was perusing a tray of hors d'oeuvres.

He took the steps like he had nowhere to be, and Iona let the censer fall to the ground so she was only holding the chain. Bella half expected her to swing it at him like a flail if he came too close.

"So..." he said, deliciously. "This is the Coven of Merchant City. A pleasure to make your acquaintance." He reached the bottom of the stairs and stood eye-to-eye with them. "Charmed," he said to Iona.

"Father, I—" Alice started.

"Sh-sh-sh-sh," Breckenridge said gently, barely louder than a whisper, putting a finger over his lips. She stopped.

"Oh dear, oh dear," he said, tutting. He swept Alice out of the way like she wasn't even there, approaching Verity for himself. "Just what have you gone and done to yourself now?"

"I'm not using the Dark Scaffold anymore," Verity reiterated.

He laughed. "So instead you've... mutilated yourself."

"I will not feed on the living."

She was on the defensive. All she could do was state her position over and over again, it was hopeless. Bella wanted to stand up, wanted to say something, but she was rooted to the spot.

When Bella had been a kid, no-one had stood up to her parents for her. And now she was here, she could do nothing. She couldn't even move.

"This... thing. We can get rid of it, we can put it behind us." Breckenridge waved his hand. "It's okay, Verity. I'm not angry."

Verity trembled. "I'm angry."

Breckenridge smirked. "This little tantrum has gone on long enough, don't you think?"

"Mate, it's her life." Holly physically interposed herself between them. "She's not coming back. And if you want her, you have to go through us."

"Hell yeah!" Roman said. He stepped up next to Holly, before shooting her a 'I think we're about to be murdered' look.

Breckenridge smiled. "Oh dear, oh dear." He pursed his lips and took a deep breath. "I'm sorry, I'm afraid this is bigger than her. Bigger than me. This is the bedrock of our society. Her actions threaten all of us." He said it in the manner of someone explaining bedtime to children. "I know this makes you uncomfortable, but it is our cross to bear. As immortals, we are Sisyphus ever pushing a rock up a hill. Verity... can't you learn to love the rock?"

He stepped right up to Holly and Roman, reaching a hand over them for Verity, and Iona leapt forward, covering the others with her arms and forcing him back. "Don't you dare. Don't you touch one hair on their heads."

"Come now," Breckenridge crooned. "You have one of ours. I know that *you* don't want her there, Ms. Howell. We don't want her there. Surely we can come to some kind of arrangement." He extended a hand for Iona to shake — pale, thin, fingers open. Confident, feigning timidness. Like a viper camouflaged as a butterfly.

Iona smiled. "Oh no, I don't think so." She looked down at his extended hand like a mouse trap. "Not if my life depended on it. I've met many men like you over the years. I wouldn't shake your hand." She leaned forward to emphasise. "You'd probably steal my watch."

He smiled, unflinching. "You're not wearing a watch."

Iona didn't dignify it with a response.

Breckenridge stiffened. "Well. We vampires do have a canny sense of when we are not welcome, after all." He looked to Verity. "They will reject you, in the end. Them and that beating puppet of theirs." He smiled. "You will see, in the end. You will learn."

Bella was coiled like a snake. This bastard. This sanctimonious bastard. Always the threat of negligence, of violence. And shellacked over it the veneer of love.

Breckenridge placed a hand like a cobweb on Alice's shoulder. "And when you learn, we will always welcome you home." Alice let out a sob, her eyes streaming with tears — an unsettling sight as she tried with incredible might to pretend she was just as calm as Breckenridge. He smiled. "You're *family*, after all."

Oh, fuck this.

Bella's hand burst into flame and she lobbed a fireball at the old bastard.

The fireball exploded, taking a chunk out of Breckenridge's chest.

Time seemed to slow down.

Verity froze in horror. Roman whooped.

Iona, almost before it had connected, drew a symbol on the air and a golden circle sigil lit up on the floorboards.

Breckenridge smiled. Clutched at his chest as already it began to reform — organs, muscle, skin, fabric. And then he looked at Verity. "These are your new friends, my child. Be very careful."

The scene around them dissolved as the teleportation circle

activated and they were standing in the Archive.

***

"What the hell did you do that for?" Verity shouted at Bella.

She was taken aback. Of all the responses, she hadn't expected that one.

"I— I'm sorry, I—" Bella said.

"Now he thinks he's right!"

Oh. She feared the next retribution.

"He's always going to think he's right, Verity," Bella said. "No matter how this ends, you're not going to change his mind."

Verity looked at her, breathing heavier and heavier. And then she screamed at her. Bella did her best not to flinch as the eyes went black, as the fangs extended, as the roar threatened to knock her off her feet.

She turned, and stormed down the room.

Bella turned, suddenly unsure of the ground she stood on. Munro was looking at her. "Am I right?"

Munro just pulled her into a hug.

chapter 26

"That was very out of character for you," Munro said quietly, after Arabella didn't let go of the hug. "I didn't think you had it in you."

"It was something about them…" Arabella said. She felt a tickling of shame in her gut. "It set me off."

Munro stroked the back of Bella's head with her thumb. "It has been a lot this week." And Bella suddenly remembered Munro all over again, about how fleeting this embrace was.

"I don't want you to go."

"I know," Munro said, but it was detached and steely. "I'm gonna go paint."

Bella squeezed Munro's finger as they disentangled. "Okay."

"You should probably apologise to Verity when things calm down," Munro said.

Bella nodded.

As Munro disappeared down the crooked corridor, Bella stood in the foyer, holding her chin in her hand, other arm propped round her side. The room was empty but for Iona redoubling the salt around the door.

"Can I help?" Bella said.

"Vampires can't enter uninvited, and this is a protected space," Iona said, not looking up, seemingly more to herself than to Bella. "But they might send someone else. Or they might try and lure us out. Or maybe they'll just rip it apart at the foundations. Oh, lord and lady…"

"Iona. He didn't seem like he was going to come after us."

"You..." Iona turned around. All the colour had drained from her face; she looked like a ghost. "I cannot believe you did that."

"I'm sorry."

A smile quirked at Iona's lips and she got that crazed look in her eye again. "Don't be. We can wipe them off the map this time. We can win."

"O... kay..." Bella said. She'd known Iona her entire adult life, and she'd never seen her this way. Iona was calm, an island of calm. Pernickety, fastidious, yes. But they'd had poltergeists throw a piano at them. They'd banged on the door of a church and exorcised a demon from a teenager. And she'd not blinked. What the hell was this?

"We can't let them sit and scheme for too long. Immortals plan for the long game. We must strike while the iron is hot, petal."

"I'm gonna go check on Verity."

Iona waved a hand, going back to what she was doing.

Bella had a horrible feeling her family was falling apart.

***

Verity stood from sitting on the floor of the bathroom, and wiped her tears. God, she was behaving like a child. Every time she spoke to him, she was a little girl again. Powerless. Angry. Ashamed. Embarrassed. Lashing out. The power he had over her, absolute.

There was a soft chap at the door.

"Just a second!" she said. She couldn't check her reflection to see if the colour had flushed from her cheeks, so she just had to wipe her face and hope.

She opened the door to find Arabella, her pointed face perched with worry.

"I'm sorry for making that about me," Bella said.

Verity stumbled. That hadn't been what she'd been expecting. "No, I'm sorry. Arabella, I... in hindsight, I don't know what I was expecting."

She felt herself shrinking, trying to retreat inside her own body. "I shouldn't have shouted at you, I was just…" She trailed off. It wasn't that she couldn't find the words, she just couldn't think of a way to word them that didn't make her feel worse.

"I get it," Bella said. "That's why I did what I did, honestly I couldn't stop myself."

"Parents?"

Bella quirked a smile that was entirely put on. "Parents." Her eyes welled up as she tried to keep the smile. "They didn't like me very much."

"I think my mother loves me," Verity said. "Deep down. Or some version of me that she sees when she looks at me."

Bella laughed. "Well, welcome to the club." She tottered from foot to foot, trying to find the words for it. "It's something most of us get in this coven. They took us in when our bio families chucked us out. Me and Holly…" She huffed, trying to pull words out she didn't acknowledge much. "We grew up together. I think we were like, trauma-bonded by our parents hating who we turned out to be. What we turned out to be. I haven't spoken to my mother in a very long time." She chewed her lip. "It's a shit feeling. They would talk about how their son was dead, as if I wasn't still there, literally being born in front of them. I didn't understand why they couldn't just be happy for me."

"I'm sorry."

"No, it's fine. For all I know, they accepted me after I left. But I don't particularly care to find out. And I've made my peace with not knowing. They pushed me out, and I made a new life. A better life." She took Verity's hands, squeezed them. They felt warm in hers. "Everyone deserves to feel that. I truly believe it. To forge yourself, your real self. And find the people who accept the real you. There's no feeling like it. I hope you can feel that with us."

"It's something I've noticed in the last few days about you witches. The kindness you've shown me, it's not been unnoticed. It seems you're all raising each other up, all the time. Supporting each other."

"I think that's just queer people, to be honest. Though... you should see us when we're fighting each other," Arabella said. "Anyway. I just wanted to say sorry, and I've done that, so I'll leave you to decompress."

"Kids with controlling parents need to stick together, right?" Verity said.

Bella nodded.

They hugged — awkwardly, with the homunculus pressed between them. It gurgled as the liquid inside it settled.

Bella closed the door so Verity had the bathroom to herself once more.

***

Arabella let the door close, standing now alone in the guest bedroom, with the astrolabe and the candle and the bedsheets that cleaned themselves with magic.

This room had been a safe space for thousands of people that she'd met by this point. Their fingerprints were etched on the room. She trailed her own finger along one of the astrolabe's arms. Perhaps Uranus' orbit had been thrown slightly off by it, she couldn't tell.

When she had been the one in this bed, she'd felt so alone. Like the weight of everything she was going through had been more than any human had faced ever.

And she hadn't been wrong, it had been pretty bad. But not insurmountable. She owed that to everyone here.

But this, what she was fighting now, was death. And no-one defeated death. It was rule one of witchcraft. Even Nicnevin's charms had only held it back.

She sat down on the bed, as if it held some restorative power in and of itself, as if the smell of fresh linen would somehow give her the answer.

Her eyes fell on the drawer on the bedside cabinet under the astrolabe, the one that didn't shut properly. It was always left cracked open. Every time she noticed it, she would try to fix it. And it never worked.

Fruitlessly, she wiggled it open, ran her fingers along the inside of the drawer, searching for something wedging it open.

She brushed... something. Something hard, and spiky.

And pulled it out.

It was a pendant. Amethyst crystal. One of those little tchotchkes you would see everywhere, probably made under horrible conditions and sold for a couple of quid to children.

But she recognised this one. The ridges of it in her hand specific to her. Connie had given her this on the first night she'd stayed here, as a throwaway. And she'd held onto it for years. Rubbing it like a lucky penny in the pocket.

It had worked. Her luck had changed. More from the efforts of Connie and Iona, and later Roman.

But her luck had changed.

She lifted the pendant over her head, forced it past her bushy hair, and felt it come to rest on her clavicle next to her usual necklace.

It felt strangely comforting for such a daft little thing.

Her reverie broke suddenly as she realised Verity would probably be coming out of the bathroom any second. Possibly she was waiting on the other side of the door for Bella to leave.

She stepped out, closing the bedroom door behind her, leaving the drawer as cracked as it had ever been.

She passed the room, and saw Munro sitting on her stool, painting. Her hair was tied up to keep it out of her face, and she'd covered her clothes with a smock. The waxy smell of paint drifted through the air.

Bella could've watched her, in that moment, forever. Completely focused on what she was doing. That beautiful woman, lost to the world, lost in rapture and creativity. Bella wanted everything to stop. She wanted everything in the world to stop. It burned her, inside-out, and yet she couldn't look away.

Munro would only be able to do this for so long.

She swallowed, drew her hand over her eyes to break eye contact long enough to drag herself away.

chapter 27

It was hard for Munro to focus on anything.

She realised she had stopped, for the second time, palette poised in mid-air, staring at the canvas as her mind raced. She tried to bring her attention back to the canvas. A pointless doodle, really. The inside of a restaurant she'd gone to with Bella, from memory. She'd been painting it after closing, standing outside on the street, watching as inside the wait staff put the chairs on the table.

She had started it when she'd been more inspired. Something about how the electric fake-candles had reflected the light on the glass and on the window pane had seemed pretty to her. Now it seemed pointless.

Nevertheless, she trudged on.

She smirked to herself. "That should be my catchphrase."

Maybe they'd put it on her gravestone.

It was out there somewhere. Right now. An actual object, waiting to be cut with her name. If they did gravestones, the Coven. It seemed a bit traditional for them.

She should've asked. While she still had the time.

If she cared. Did she care?

She mixed some orange, some crimson, some white, until it turned to peach. She took her knife, and started to paint the highlight on a used wine glass in the foreground, and the window between the viewer and the scene.

It wasn't quite right. She closed her eyes, tried to picture it in her memory, the moment that had once so captured her.

It is cold on the cobbles. I am wearing a big jacket over my furs that makes me feel like a penguin. It smells like cigarette smoke, someone is smoking by the door.

She forced herself to open her eyes. Not again. If she just ignored it she could—

still feel the cold. Snow is out there, and my heart is racing, beating in my chest like it wants to escape because he's all on his own, he's too young and—

She staggered forward, fighting the urge to retch. Still it was rising up in her, she took deep breaths, tried to sit down, but the rickety stool felt like it would tip over the moment she did.

She sat on the floor, put her head between her knees as best she could, and tried to breathe. It was okay... She was going to be okay... She tried to feel the warmth of the room, ground herself. She was in the Archive, in the warm, in the...

The room is too warm.

I sit up in the bed. I am so hot I feel like if I look down I'll see the steam coming off of myself.

"Everything okay?" Nicnevin says.

I turn, to see Nicnevin — younger, as she was when we first met.

She is lying in bed next to me, we're both flushed with exertion and endorphins. She's not put anything on again yet. She's lying stretched out like a content cat.

"Fine," I say, though I'm still out of breath.

"Come here." She beckons, and I come. I lie across her chest, and she fiddles with my hair. The warmth of another body right now feels like burning. I need water, but I don't want to move. I am tangled in the saccharine sweet smell of her sweat. I am high on her.

And then I am in the bed alone—?

There is a cough from the corner.

There she is. Sitting in the old armchair that used to sit in my room. Nicnevin, as she is now.

"I'm... confused," I say.

"I'm supposed to just let these play out, lest I fray your world line, but..." She's blushing. How unusual for her. "It seemed inappropriate in this case."

"Is this going to break my memory of what actually happened?" I ask, before I consider why that's the thing I seem to care about right now.

"I hope not," Nicnevin says. The room feels like one of my paintings now, indistinct, half-finished, a poor imitation of the real thing.

"Living them all out, in a random order," Munro said. "I realised, there weren't many nights like this."

"Oh?"

"I think I just realised how much of my life has been actively miserable."

"I think you focus on the negatives," Nicnevin said. "I have a lot of memories of nights like this."

Munro laughed, leaning back, pressing her back against the headboard. "Maybe."

"I really loved you, you know," Nicnevin said. "I don't think I ever apologised for..." She rummaged her brain for how to word it. "How things went."

"I loved you too," Munro said. She rubbed her face, then stopped. "Wait. Did you think—"

"No, I know you loved me. I just thought, maybe I had ruined the good times with my behaviour at the end."

"You didn't," Munro said. They'd been together for so long, she was so wound into who Munro was, it would be hard for her to think that. "You saved me. And then you kept saving me." She sucked her teeth. "By the time I started saying 'let me go' it must have been second nature to you to hold on."

"That's very charitable," Nicnevin said. "I've spent a lot of time thinking about it. Talking to people about it. The longer goes by, the more I realise how far I'd strayed." She stood, the chair behind her dissolving into colours as she did. "Anyway. I'm sorry."

"Thanks," Munro said, knowing that was what she wanted. Not 'I should be apologising to you', not 'I worry you will feel this way after I'm gone', not 'I want you and Bella to be closer', or any of the other things that would be how she actually felt.

"I should probably find another memory to slip in here for you to relive before I accidentally kill you," Nicnevin said. She lifted her fingers as if she was playing some invisible stringed instrument, or a theremin, and golden strings began to weave through the room.

"It's nice, to have a second to talk to you alone."

Nicnevin smirked. She tried to hide it, but Munro knew exactly how she'd taken it.

"I don't—" Munro started, before holding herself back. No. Not the time.

Nicnevin dropped her hands, halting her ministrations. "You don't what," she said, annoyed now.

Well. If this wasn't the time, there probably wouldn't be a time.

"I don't understand why you and Arabella feel this competition between each other. You two are so alike, why can't you—"

"I'm going to stop you there," Nicnevin said. "I am happy for you, Munro. Truly I am. But that woman has not earned my grace, and I give her more than she deserves already, because you are important to me."

Munro tensed. "Well, I'm glad your grace is so valuable you need to hoard it."

Nicnevin was holding her tongue.

"Go on," Munro said. "Say what you want to say."

"She went into..." Nicnevin started, and then stopped herself. "No.

I'm a big girl, as people are so fond of reminding me." She lowered to her knees, crouched so she was eye-level with Munro. "Our feelings aren't something you're going to be able to resolve. I'm sorry."

Munro furrowed her brow. What the hell did Bella do?

"Don't look at me like that," Nicnevin said. "You don't have much time left. I suggest, as your psychopomp, and as someone that cares about you, that if you want to focus your remaining time on fixing things, aim for things that can be fixed." She placed a hand on Munro's cheek.

Munro's smile betrayed her. "To hell with you."

"Oh, darling, I'm already in hell. Who do you think the throne is for?" Nicnevin said. She turned, and eyed the threads, which had now started to fall into the impressionistic background of the rest of the room. "I'll try and find you a nice one this time."

Munro was already feeling the lethargy take her. "Thanks, Nevin."

"You're very welcome," Nicnevin said, as darkness swallowed them both.

I am on a beach in Newcastle with the Coven. We're here for some kind of meetup. It's rare for them to go south of the border. Roman is remarking about how the seagulls sound Geordie here, and he and Holly feed them chips, talking about how well-behaved they seem compared to Glasgow seagulls.

"It might be because you're feeding them, you numpties." Iona is covering her head in her hands. "Just try not to embarrass us tonight in front of the English."

The grass is warm, and the sun is shining, but there's a breeze coming in off the sea. Bella is sitting in my lap, idly making daisy chains. The four of them continue to bicker, and I smile.

I haven't felt this content in a long time.

She stayed in the dream as long as she could, but all too quickly it was over, and she was back in her studio.

chapter 28

It was Verity who eventually disturbed Munro, tiptoeing in while she thought she wasn't looking.

Munro jumped, enough to knock over the stool so she was left on her feet. "Oh! Hello."

"Sorry, I didn't mean to interrupt."

"No, not at all," Munro said, retrieving her stool from where it had fallen. "I'm sorry your meeting with your grandfather went so badly."

"I don't know how else it could've went," Verity said. She had cried all the tears she was going to cry about it, she'd decided when she left the bathroom. "I'm gonna kill him. I don't know how yet, but I will."

"Wouldn't that kill you as well?" Munro said.

"I'm dying anyway." Verity gestured to the little potato creature on her chest. She leaned in so she could see the painting.

It was... chaotic. Blacks and blues and flecks of green, all painted in acrylic, forming an impressionist seascape of stormy ocean. A score of light blue showed lightning striking the surface of the water, illuminating the roiling waves around it. "Wow."

"It's not perfect," Munro said.

"Art never is." Verity hoped this sounded sufficiently clever. Honestly, critiquing art had always been the realm of her grandfather — a scholarly, pretentious pursuit that had seemed to her to be an excuse to use up the thousand-franc words you had in the cupboard.

But she couldn't argue for the feeling that art put in her stomach. It felt like if she reached out to this painting, she would feel the rain stinging her arm, feel the wind stripping the oils from her skin.

"It's not exactly as I remember it…" Munro said. "Not yet."

"This is real?"

"It's what I remember. It was my fiftieth birthday and a storm came in, and we were separated. My eldest was swept out on a current, and I went out to look for him. I was out all night."

Verity swallowed, still looking at the painting. "Did you find him?" She regretted asking the moment the words were out of her mouth.

Munro said nothing. She painted in the bottom half of a tree on a wind-beaten little island in the background, the top half presumably ripped from the trunk and carried away by the tides.

Verity, as if looking for something comforting to say, looked around the room. The paintings weren't all morose — some of them positively beamed with happiness and vibrant colour. But they all had this style, with the same acrylic paint. It looked like most of it had been done with the dull side of a blade. It rendered them all with a quality that was incredibly sharp in its lines, but made the shape feel overall indistinct and hazy. It was a beautiful technique, thought Verity.

"Are they all memories?"

Munro looked up, as if annoyed Verity was interrupting her train of thought. "No. Some of them I just feel like painting."

Verity approached a stack of canvases leaning on the wall, thumbed through them like records, looking at every one.

"What about this one?" she asked, smugly. It was unmistakeably Arabella, reclining on a chair with her arms raised, topless. A large blue jewel rested on a necklace between her breasts.

Munro raised an eyebrow. "That one was a joke. It's a reference to a film she made me watch."

"I haven't seen a film in…" Verity thought. She blinked. She couldn't actually remember *when* she had last seen a film. She tried to conjure it as she put the picture of Arabella back in with the rest. The smell of the theatre, the old upholstery, the sweat of so many people in the space. The buttery snacks she'd eaten as the opening credits rolled. It could've been any time.

Hell, she might have been making it up.

"It's a horrible thing to live so long," she said.

Munro looked up at Verity, as if she finally had her attention. "Yeah. It is, isn't it." She swallowed. "It feels like you outlived the world. Like it's rotting in your hands."

Verity swallowed. "I don't know if I'd go that far."

Munro looked down, nodded. She'd tried to be vulnerable, and Verity had rebuffed her.

"But it has been horrible to watch the world change around me, so vibrant and full of life. While I... stagnate."

Munro nodded. "Yeah, I can see that. I don't know, I never... I never needed much say over my life. I was a pup, then I was someone's lover, then a mother and a grandmother, then a lover again. Then I died. The first time. Then I was... someone else's. And now I'm here. With all of you. There's been a lot of change. But I was always, in relation to someone else."

Verity tried to look encouraging. "I don't remember before I died." Sometimes she tried to remember it, but it was like remembering before you were born. "When you get turned, your body dies. The brain shuts down, the grey matter dies. And then you wake up, and you're changed. But all memory of the old life is gone. It helps the transition."

"Did Breckenridge name you Verity?"

Verity made a non-committal noise. "Him or my mother. I assume. You take the family name of your brood, but there's no rules on given names. For all I know it was my name in life, but... I could be anyone. They could've picked it out of the phone book. If there had been a phone book."

"If you were to die today, would you have any regrets?" Munro asked. It was very straightforward, in a way that almost bowled Verity over.

"Yes," Verity said. "I've lived off the suffering of humans for hundreds of years. And I need to do something to make up for that." She paused.

Maybe Munro had been asking, so she could speak on this matter herself. She was normally so tight-lipped.

"How about you?"

Munro went back to her painting. "No. No, I don't think so." A smile cracked her craggy face. "I've lived multiple, long, wonderful lifetimes. I think that's the thing that makes it so sad that it's going to be over. For a long time, I was so angry and sad at the world. And now, I'm happy. It seems a shame for it to end."

Verity's heart swelled for this giant woman. It almost gave her hope. She put a hand on Munro's shoulder. "What's been your favourite thing?"

Munro rested the handle of her paintbrush on her lip. "I think... being here, at the end. Seeing through Bella's eyes has taught me so much. About humans, about their little rituals and how they can make happiness out of nothing. Like I finally understand why humans bother with gender!"

"Selkies don't have gender?"

"Selkies have pronouns, but only when we speak your language. That's a human thing. We never had division of labour so gender just isn't something we do in our culture. A selkie's a selkie. You raise young, you seduce humans. That's the deal."

"Hm. Utilitarian."

"It always seemed so silly to me that humans and fey made such a big deal out of their presentation, about the way other people spoke to them, and about them. It seemed so decorative, so unimportant." She smiled. "And then I started to understand gender euphoria, and how being seen, and understood... how that can bring a joy by itself."

"It is nice to be seen," Verity said. "That's... I think that's the thing that makes me feel so helpless when I talk to Breckenridge. That he doesn't even see me. If he can't see me, my words mean nothing to him. He can just wave them away. I'm as invisible as his own reflection."

"He just sees you as himself?"

Verity laughed. "Oh, no, sorry. That doesn't make sense unless you— He doesn't see anything in the mirror. I'm literally invisible."

"Oh..." Munro said. She put her index fingers under her mouth to pretend they were fangs. "I see." It looked very silly.

"Although, I suppose that's another way of looking at it." Verity thought of Bella. About what she'd said about how her parents had viewed her as someone else, their own version of her. "I guess he does just view me as an extension of himself."

Munro was silent.

Verity waited for her to form the thought. Munro had shown herself to be the kind of person who needed space to let her ideas breathe and germinate. Who wouldn't speak until she was absolutely sure what she—

"Wait, so how do you brush your teeth?" Munro said. "If you can't see your face in the mirror?"

Verity burst out laughing.

"I'm serious!"

"We..." Verity was trying not to laugh. "We don't have mouth bacteria and we don't need to breathe. We don't need to brush our teeth. Plus, our insides are a toxic environment to most critters."

"Huh..." Munro was still stoic. "Wait, so you have no idea what you look like?"

"I have... a vague idea," Verity said. "I've heard descriptions."

"Hang on," Munro grabbed a pencil and her sketchbook. "As your new friend I need to rectify this now."

***

Verity was starting to get antsy in the same position as Munro finished up the pencil sketch. She had no idea how long she'd been sitting there in the chair. She wished she'd thought to relax her arms, her hands sitting perched in her lap like some fussy matron.

After what felt like an infinite length of time, Munro said, "I'm done!" and Verity found she was... nervous. Positively trembling. She wasn't sure why.

Her mouth was dry as she said, "How do I look?"

"See for yourself," Munro said.

For some reason, Verity had been expecting an oil painting layout. She needn't have worried about her hands, Munro had only drawn the face. From multiple angles, so Verity could see the side-profile as well.

She stared into the pencil eyes, and they stared back into her. She had a widow's peak, she realised. She hadn't known that. Her nose was massive — she had suspected that, but never been sure. Her hand rose, instinctively, to cover her nose. Her stomach tensed, and she found she was welling up. "This is me?"

"That's you," Munro said. "I don't know if I quite got the mouth right on some of them. That one is the most accurate, I think." She pointed to the picture of her in profile.

It almost didn't look like a human face to her. Like some alien approximation. It was only after staring at it did the pattern form. She was still covering her lower face.

Munro looked confused. "Do you not like it?"

"I—" Verity couldn't form words. "I don't..." She wiped her eyes with her free hand. "I don't understand what my body is doing right now." She laughed at the tears on her fingertips, but they were still coming.

Munro chewed on the silence that followed, as though trying to process what Verity was saying. "I... you're very beautiful, maybe I didn't capture that properly."

"No! No, that's not it, I promise," Verity said. She was sure the picture in front of her was very attractive. But it was like she couldn't make out a person in the image. The other people she'd seen in Munro's drawings popped off the paper, instant representations of the people she'd seen in real life.

But this looked like a collection of random lines. She had to concentrate just to see the face, and when she did all the features looked like they were the wrong size and shape, assembled from newspaper clippings of other people's faces.

And yet, she couldn't look away.

"I'm sorry, maybe I shouldn't have—"

"No," Verity said, and she tore herself away from the maze of her own face. "No. You have no idea how much you've just done for me." She wiped her tears on her sleeve — *God, she'd spent so much time crying today* — and held the drawing close to her chest. "May I keep this?"

"Of course," Munro said.

Verity set the picture down on the table, so she could give Munro as big a hug as she could around the homunculus.

"Thank you," she said. Munro nodded.

That night, she lay in the guest bed, and spent hours staring at that picture. Looking at the contours of her face from every angle Munro had captured, putting her fingers on her own face like she was following them by a map. Tracing the lines of her cheekbones to the tip of her nose, down her Cupid's bow, across her lips onto her jawline.

She smiled, and then fear shot through her, as she felt a twang she hadn't felt in days.

She'd gotten used to her mind being clear so quickly, she'd forgotten what it had felt like. The constant pangs of hunger, the need to nibble, to burst human skin like a peach and drink...

She pulled down her nightgown, to find that the homunculus was rotting on her chest like an old potato.

It was dead.

She dry-heaved. The stitches tying it to her began to dig into her ribcage, sending shooting pain into her that rang through her bones, down her arms, her legs. Like her body had just noticed it wasn't supposed to be wrapped round this thing. She grabbed at it, uselessly, each movement ratcheting up the pain.

She screamed.

chapter 29

Iona got to her first. It made sense, her room was the closest, but God she'd wished it could've been anyone else. To find her lying in the bed with the wet, mossy gunk of the homunculus splattering everywhere. It was bubbling now, trapped air inside it venting as the gases within it congealed and popped. Green slime bubbled all over the crisp white bedsheets and her nightgown.

And yet, all she could find herself asking was "What's going on? Was it him? Did he do this?"

She asked the same questions over and over again as Iona scooped her from the bed and brought her to Roman's room. By one point, they were all in there, though she hadn't seen them come in. Her vision spun, light-headed, until she felt like she'd left her body. Numb and detached. The bloodlust was tickling the back of her cerebellum and the fear and shame and guilt and chemicals, with the stress. She wasn't convinced this wasn't some horrible nightmare.

"It's okay, it's okay!" Bella cradled the back of her neck, suddenly filling her field of view with her big, bushy hair. Verity smiled, remembering the picture Munro had drawn with the pendant, how Verity had known the second she'd looked at it who it was, and then Bella moved away. They were all shouting to each other, shouting at each other, and lying on the table, Verity was staring at Roman's ceiling lamp, an ostentatious chandelier made of plastic...

She stirred.

Her eyelids were heavy. She opened her eyes, thinking for a second it had all been a dream.

But she was still on Roman's operating table. She looked around. It was like she'd blinked, and hours had passed.

Roman was lying on the chair wearing a plastic suit that was completely splattered with green and brown viscera. A thought flashed through Verity's head as she could feel his heartbeat across the room, see the pulse throbbing through his carotid like electricity through a wire. She retreated from the thought as soon as she realised she was having it, and made to sit up.

Her arms were tied to the table.

Now that she was looking down, she could see the line of salt on the floor.

"Shit..." she said.

Roman stirred, waking. "Oh, you're up. Are you... with us?"

"What did I do?"

"We had to put you to sleep," he said. "Sorry." She could see the sincerity in his eyes, but she could smell the fear under it. Thick, pungent. Settling in his armpits, his neck, between his legs. There was no hiding that.

He checked his watch. "Wow, you've only been out for a few hours. It normally takes a day for people to wake up from that."

She swallowed. "Did I... hurt anyone?"

Roman smirked. "Come on. We told you when you got here. No-one gets hurt in the Archive. You're safe here. Everyone is."

Verity breathed, relaxing. "Where are the others?"

"Asleep. We stabilised you and then we weren't sure what to do so we just... left you like that. It seemed like you'd make it till you woke up, at which point we could ask you what you wanted to do."

Verity nodded. "Thank you."

"Can I get you anything?" Roman asked.

She looked at him, directly in his eyes, trying to avoid that bright-golden pulse in his neck. "No. Thank you."

"Do you think you'll last until the morning?"

She nodded, tersely.

"Okay." He looked down to realise he'd fallen asleep in the muck of the homunculus. "Rest in peace, little man," he said. "I'm gonna go clean myself up now I'm not falling asleep on my feet."

Verity let him go, and watched him leave. She could see his pulse through the wall.

She knew, in that rotten husk in her chest, that this was going to be even harder than it had been last time.

***

Holly entered next. Without the homunculus to dull Verity's senses, she lit up with that same firework show she had when they'd first met. Verity closed her eyes, and Holly left a sparkling mark on the inside of her eyelids.

Damn this fucking body.

"Hey," Holly said, hovering in the doorway.

Verity forced herself to look. To look, and not to think. "Hi, sorry."

"I brought you this." She was carrying a mug full of... something. It smelled like boiled leather.

"What is it?" Verity's nose rankled against her will. Her sense of smell was sharp as a razor again, and every new smell cut her.

"Vegan blood."

"W—" Verity said. "What's vegan blood?"

"I don't know, it sounded funny when I said it in the kitchen but now I just feel weird. I'm sorry, this isn't funny."

Verity smiled, despite herself. "No, I suppose it isn't, is it."

Holly made to come closer, but the smell got stronger. Deeply floral herbs, overpowering in themselves, but masking something bitter and coarse. Verity put her hand up to stop her, and Holly stopped short of the salt circle around the operating table.

"Do I have to drink it?" she asked.

"It's this or starve," Holly admitted. "We've got nothing else in our bag of tricks."

"Honestly, I'd rather starve. Can't you smell it?"

"Can't say I'd want to *drink* it, but no." She gave it a huff. "Ooh, there is a bit of... something. What is that?"

"Whatever it is, it'll kill me before starvation will."

Holly put it down on the bedside table, and stood, rolling on the balls of her feet in front of the salt circle.

Verity stared at it, before rolling back in disgust. "I can't believe he did this to me... I finally had *something*."

"Did what?"

"He took the homunculus from me!"

"Who, Breckenridge?"

Verity cocked her head.

"Breckenridge didn't do that. The homunculus just failed."

"No, that can't... It can't be. He wasn't..." Verity said. "I'd just talked to him, and then..."

"Sorry babes. We had to take it off you, we would've found it if he'd sabotaged it somehow," Holly said. There was a silence as Holly watched Verity react. "Isn't that a good thing?"

"I don't know..." Verity said. She felt a pit forming in her stomach, the worry that she'd been wearing a hair shirt for years, ripping it off only to discover it had been keeping her from freezing to death.

She looked at Holly, eye to eye. Her vision had adjusted now. The room was pitch black, and the flames wreathing Holly licked at her but didn't burn.

"You should drink it. I can't promise it'll help much, but it'll help."

Verity's nose still curled against the smell now permeating the room. "What is it?"

"Flour... yeast..." she coughed. "Sweat."

"There's human sweat in it?"

"Oh yeah. Focus on that bit!" She picked it up, and looked at it with the disgust it deserved. "Iona says vampires need blood for the red blood cells, to carry oxygen through your bodies. You need the iron, and you need... the life energy. Sweat was the closest thing we could think of to try and fabricate that."

"How the hell did you even get human sweat?"

"We put one of my old t-shirts in the cauldron." Holly was pretending to be clinical and chill about it, but Verity could even see through the flames the red rising to her cheeks.

Verity laughed. She couldn't help it, this was ridiculous. "That's not going to work!"

"I mean, not indefinitely! We're doing our best here!"

Verity was still laughing, clutching the sides of the table for support.

"Hey listen, if I could just give you my blood I would!"

Verity's laughter stopped, immediately. "Don't..." She swallowed as her mouth began to salivate. "Don't joke about that."

"Okay, sorry!" Holly said. She put her hands up.

Verity couldn't break the gaze. Couldn't force herself to look away now. And even if she could, she could still hear the thumping of her heart sending blood through her body, still smell the perfume drying on her skin, still feel her from across the room, her neck, plump and sweet.

Holly's brow furrowed. "You're... looking at me like dinner."

Verity clutched the edge of the table until her knuckles were white. "Sorry."

"Don't be," Holly said. "I like it."

Another primal feeling stirred, and destabilised the first. Verity smiled. "You are such a fucking chancer."

Holly still had her hands up, but she shrugged. "Guilty." Her eyes sparkled wickedly. "Now are you going to drink my sweat or not?"

Verity tensed like a cat being rubbed the wrong way. "Do I have to?"

Holly grinned. "I'll make it worth your while."

Verity smiled again. "Oh? What's that supposed to mean?"

And then Holly stepped over the salt circle, cradled Verity's face in her hands and kissed her.

Verity's heart raced. That was a new sensation. So much for a husk in her chest.

Holly's lips were soft against hers, and Verity melted. Held against her she felt her arms wrap around Holly's waist as Holly's tongue began to explore her mouth.

Verity's head was beginning to spin, it had been decades since she'd been kissed. It had likely been a hundred years since she'd been kissed like *this*. The little breaks to press kisses against her jaw, her throat. The thumb rubbing circles on the nape of her neck.

Then Holly's tongue touched her canine in just the way that it slid from her gum.

Verity recoiled, covering her mouth. "Shit."

Holly stepped back, face flushed, eyes bleary. "You okay?"

"We have to stop."

"Okay. Sorry," Holly said, still dazed and confused. "What's wrong?"

Verity lifted her hand to reveal that the fangs were now fully unsheathed. When they were out, it became hard to close her mouth — knives jutting out of her upper jaw.

Holly wiggled her eyebrows.

"This is serious! I don't want to kill you!"

Holly sighed. "Nah, you're right. Honestly, I probably shouldn't be letting this happen anyway. You're a guest in our house, you're here for our help, you're vulnerable."

"Trust me, I'm the least vulnerable person in this house. I'm a danger to you all just being here." Verity curled her knees up to her chest. "I'm so fucking stupid."

"Och, okay, calm down." Holly rolled her eyes. "Enough of the 'poor me' act."

Verity furrowed her brow at Holly.

"Listen, this is the hand you've been dealt. I will stand behind you no matter what you choose to do. So long as you choose to do *something*. Don't just sit here and think about how miserable everything is."

Verity nodded.

"Now be a good vegetarian vampire, and drink your piss sweat."

"There's piss in it as well?" Verity retched.

Holly cackled. "No." She made a face like she wasn't sure. "Well..." Before beaming like a mad lady. "No."

"Fuck off!"

"I'll be back for more kisses once you've brushed the sweat out your teeth." Holly turned to leave and gave her a little salute on the way out the door.

Verity fell back onto the bed, bubbling with a cocktail of endorphins that told her on a chemical level she wasn't miserable at least.

***

"I heard the whole thing," Bella said under her breath, washing the sweat pot in the sink. "You're stirring up big fucking trouble, Holly Winter. Why are you such a fuckboy sometimes?"

Holly blinked in Bella's face. "This from the woman who had us kidnap a seal-woman from an Arch-Witch so she could get laid."

Bella threw the metal scourer into the pot and wiped her hands dry on a tea towel. "Well, if you're not going to take me seriously—"

"Stop," Holly said. "I hear you."

"Do you?"

"Yes," Holly said. She paused. "But also that was really nice? And I like her?"

"She's our fucking ward, Holly," Bella hissed. "It's a dodgy power dynamic."

Holly closed the distance and took her best friend by both hands. "Bella. Balleficent."

Bella groaned. "Yes, Holliver."

"Do you really think that woman in there is going to be alive in a week's time?" Holly said, under her breath. "Do you think your weird concoction made of sweat and herbs is going to keep a literal *vampire* going for seven whole days?"

Bella's stomach cramped. "No, I suppose not."

"Then I would think... whatever we choose to do as consenting adults, is between us!" Holly let go of Bella's hands to give an exaggerated shrug.

"I'm not just worried about her though," Bella said. "What if she fuckin' eats yo— don't say it." She raised a finger to stop Holly's joke in the back of her throat. "I'm serious."

"I will be *very* careful," Holly said. "What's the point of being the 'most powerful witch of a generation' if I can't shag a vampire once in a while?"

Bella groaned. "You are going to hold that over me until we're both old cronies."

Holly grabbed an apple from the fruit bowl. "I mean, straight from the mouth of Auntie! It's beyond contesting!"

She took a bite out of it as she rushed off, and Bella was left with only the chiming of the bell that hung over the front door.

***

Time passed slowly in the guest room, with only the occasional visitor, and a pint of the most disgusting liquid she'd ever touched to work through.

Verity passed the time with reading. The books on Roman's shelves were garish and light on actual content, but they kept her busy. Never busy enough though that she couldn't feel the sharpness of hunger whetting. She wondered what their next plan was, when she allowed herself. Their next concoction, now that the homunculus had failed.

She should just ask to leave, she thought, as she turned the page, barely taking in the words. But go where? She couldn't go back to Breckenridge, and if left on the streets she'd eventually put the others in danger.

And yet, something in her still refused to die. Some inviolable seed in her just didn't want to give Breckenridge the satisfaction of dying a starving animal. Wanted to see him look up at her, with a stake in his heart, realising he'd underestimated her.

But from here, on what amounted to a hospital bed, it felt like a maladaptive daydream.

There was a crack from out the window and Verity started from her reverie. It was a tall, thin stained glass number that had likely been very beautiful once, but now resembled the colour of a medicine bottle. Even *her* eyes couldn't make out things through it. But with her sharpened smell, she could make out the seal-skins. Munro, skulking around.

The window was... technically within the circle, Verity thought. The line of salt hit the edge of the room and ran along the skirting of the floor. If she was careful...

She picked at the window latch with her fingertips, and cracked it.

Munro was positioned between the bush and the wall, leaning into the shadow.

The carefully folded sketch in Verity's pocket burned white-hot as she was reminded of it.

"Hello," Verity said.

"Jesus!" Munro shouted, jumping out of her skin. She was holding

an unlit cigarette in her hand.

"No, just me," Verity said, trying to position her head so they could see eye-to-eye through the crack without her putting her head through the salt circle.

"Bella's not with you, is she?"

"No... why?" Verity arched an eyebrow.

"I don't want her catching me." She gestured with the cigarette hand. "Filthy habit."

They stood in silence.

"I..." Munro considered what to say.

Munro weighed her words by the ounce, Verity thought. It was a wonder the witches with their human lifespans didn't lose patience. Maybe they did.

Verity was struggling to see. The seconds stretched out. She repositioned.

Huge, wet tears were rolling down Munro's cheeks, her face screwed up like it was causing her physical pain. Her face was flushed red like an angry boil.

"I'm sorry about what's happening to you," Verity said.

Munro covered her face so she could continue to cry without being seen. "I don't know why I'm so sad. I was happy with my life. I'm two hundred years old."

"It's okay to be sad when something that's good is ending," Verity said.

"It's not that, it's... I finally got everything the way I wanted it, and now it's being wrapped up like a board game at the end of the night. I'm not a board game. I'm a person."

Verity smiled weakly. "You've done a phenomenal job, Munro. You should be proud of what you've done."

The silence broke as Munro let out a sob. A sob like the ground splitting, the kind of seismic shake that toppled buildings. And she crumbled. Fell to her knees, fell back against the window, howling in the dark. "I don't want to die, Verity. I don't want to die. I'm not ready."

She just said it over and over again, and there was nothing Verity could say. Because there was no way to fix it.

She rested her hand on the glass, felt the salt beneath her feet hiss and crackle like an allergic reaction as her skin began to burn. But she held it there, until Munro could feel the heat on the other side of the glass.

Munro finished crying herself out, and turned around as if she was looking at the wreckage. Her eyes were so puffy Verity could barely make them out recessed into her head. "Shit, stop that," she said, as she realised where the warmth from the glass had come from. "Doesn't that hurt?"

"Only for a minute." Verity pulled her hand back and watched as, against her will, the skin knit back together.

"Thank you for listening," Munro said.

"I didn't do anything."

"No, you... you did." Munro finally lit her cigarette. "I struggle to talk about that stuff. Actually," she corrected herself, "I'm just not good at crying in general. I never have been. But that helped. You not being with the others, and..." She gestured between them as she exhaled smoke. "We're the same, kinda."

Verity shrank. "Yeah."

"It helped."

"Well, I'm glad," Verity said. "...So you're not ready?"

"No," Munro said. "But I'm as ready as I'll ever be." She looked at Verity through the crack in the window. "I wanna help you."

Verity looked confused.

"I'm dying anyway," Munro said. She took a deep draw of the cigarette, and instead of the orange, the flame lit up blue. She held it up to the window. "A problem shared?"

"What... what did you do?"

"I'll give you some of my life force."

"What? I can't," Verity said. "I saw you before! You're barely holding on as it is."

"I've only gotten this far, because that lot reached out and pulled me up," Munro said. "Give an old lady someone else to help."

"You were just crying about how you didn't want to die, Munro," Verity said.

"Exactly," Munro said. The tears were coming again. "We're the same. So I know you're feeling the same thing. Let me help you."

Verity looked at it, the cigarette. The blue flame was spitting like a firework. The blood-hunger gnawed in her belly, it recoiled against the cigarette. That wasn't what it wanted.

So she reached a hand out. She'd spent long enough resisting the vampire urges, to know it was a good instinct to follow.

Munro passed the cigarette up through the window. Verity almost smiled at how juvenile the action seemed. She held the cigarette to her mouth, and breathed in its smoke.

For a moment, she could see it. The waking world washing away, revealing the lifeline between them. It was like the Dark Scaffold, but blue. Underwater, a glistening cobalt rope tied them together.

Her lungs filled with the blue smoke, the bubbles around her as she felt a wave rise up—

— she is falling. She is falling from a great height, a rock face, and a thin man is standing at the top.

— a woman with thin hands is staring into a pond. There is nothing looking back at her. She reaches a hand in, like she can find the reflection and pull it out —

And then, others, completely foreign—

— a woman in a seal skin standing on the far side of a stoney beach. Mother! Her mother, beckoning her to swim to her —

— dark clouds part as a lightning bolt cuts the sky in half, splitting a

tree in twain. The tree falls on her leg, crushing it, and pain sears through her, she thinks she is going to die, she thinks she will never feel pain like this again—

— the waters are so choppy they threaten to pull her under, she has never seen a storm like this. The rain is cold, so cold and sharp it threatens to pelt the skin off her wet face and she screams for him, but she knows as she does it's in vain. He's so small, if he is out here he will already be pulled under. She will never feel pain like this again —

— Nicnevin, reclining on the beach, looking at her over a pair of sunglasses like she's a piece of meat, and for the first time in her life there is a feeling in her chest that she is looking at something more powerful than her, and she likes it —

And then, the wind knocked out of her, she was back in the room.

The hunger was tamed again. For now.

Munro had paled. "Whoo." She staggered, held her hand against the wall while she caught her breath. "That takes it out of you."

"Sorry."

"Don't apologise. It feels good to do something good," Munro said. "Let me tell them to let you out. Once they're awake."

Oh.

Verity hadn't thought about how the witches might have taken this.

chapter 30

It was horrible hearing them shouting from the other room, trapped behind the salt circle. Arabella was screaming with rage at the top of her lungs in a way that she clearly was not practiced at. Verity thought back to her lobbing a fireball at Breckenridge. Maybe she'd have to take a fireball too.

If there was a way she could've given Munro that sliver of life force back, she would've. She could feel her vampire bloodlust chewing on it, the dog in her sated by gnawing on a bone. The freedom she'd gained was temporary, but it was considerable. She could think.

She leaned back against the wall. She could feel the vibrations of the argument through the plaster. It seemed so unfair. After all this, she was still living by draining other things. The homunculus' dead heart, Munro's unbeating one. There was no way to ethically keep herself going. A sunk cost she had resolved to keep paying until she put a stake in Breckenridge.

Eventually, excruciatingly, the door opened. Holly entered, head down like she'd been sent to the headteacher.

"I'm sorry," Verity said, echoing the words she'd been rehearsing for the past five minutes. "I betrayed your trust."

"It's not her you have to apologise to." Bella emerged from behind her, scowling, followed by the ever-stony Iona.

Something rankled in Verity. She was right, it wasn't Holly she should be apologising to, but it wasn't Bella either. It wasn't like she'd taken it taken it against Munro's will.

"I'm sorry," she said again, as Munro entered behind her. It was beginning to feel like a firing line up against the salt circle, and Munro was coiled like a snake. Something was bothering her, and Verity expected she knew what.

"I can't give it back," Verity said. "I don't think it's even possible."

"No, we know," Arabella snapped. "So you're free to go." She put a brogued foot forward and broke the salt circle with it. "Get out."

"Well hang on!" Munro suddenly piped up. "Don't I get a say in this?"

"No," Iona said coolly. "She's in no immediate danger, and there's nothing more we can do for her."

Munro just stared at Iona like a lion eyeing a yapping bird. Iona, to her credit, didn't flinch.

Holly boiled over. "Aw fuck off, Iona. Fucking technicalities. I thought it was you who was always saying twisting words is the lowest form of witchcraft."

"Holly if you're going to argue you can go with her," Iona said, gaze still fixed on Munro.

Holly legitimately looked like that had knocked the wind out of her. But Verity knew Holly well enough by now to know how she reacted to confrontation.

Holly flushed. She fizzled. "Oh. That's how it is, is it?" She looked to Arabella. "Is that how it is?"

Arabella looked cold. But Verity could hear her heartbeat, pounding like she was running a marathon. "Don't look at me like that, Holly. I'm fucking angry at you."

Holly lifted her hand and her coat flew, by magic, through the door into her hand. "I'm your best friend, you stupid cow!"

"You're not acting like it."

Holly screamed. "Fuck sake!"

"She put Munro in danger," Iona said. "And her grandfather could come down on our heads any moment."

"That's fucking *Tuesday* for us!" Holly shouted back. Verity was shrinking into the corner. She could see the fire pluming off Holly in the Astral Realm. This woman had spent her whole life screaming at the world.

Holly looked between the two of them. "One of you fucking listen to reason!"

They didn't say anything.

"Fine. Fuck it." She stuck her free hand out to Verity. "Let's go."

"I don't—" Verity said. "Holly, this is your family. I don't want to drive you apart—"

"Of course she doesn't," Bella said, dripping with sarcasm. "She doesn't want to do what she's spent the last two weeks doing."

Holly sucked air through her teeth. "Get. Fucked." She stuck her hand out again. Verity took it gingerly. It was warm, and it gripped her a little too tight.

Holly stormed out, down the corridor, dragging Verity in her wake. "Self-righteous, sanctimonious, fuckin'," she snapped her fingers and the Archive's front door slammed open, as if it was rushing before she ploughed right through it and took it off its hinges.

Verity felt like a recalcitrant toddler being dragged by an angry parent.

Holly spun to glare at the building. She raised her witch's finger and pointed through the front door, aiming some kind of curse, before her better half prevailed and she thought better of it. She dropped her finger, screaming again.

"Everything okay, Holly?" A friendly looking older gentleman with a goatee poked his head out a neighbouring shop's door.

"Fuck off, Julian!"

Julian grimaced. "One of those arguments, huh. Sorry." He closed the door behind him.

Holly stood there, fizzing like a pressurised canister. She shouted out again and shot a jet of fire into the air.

Verity tapped her on Holly's shoulder. "Could you let go of my hand?" She could feel her knuckles popping.

"What?" Holly said, as though she'd forgotten she was there. "Oh. Sorry." She dropped it, and buried her hand in her cardigan pocket.

"You should go back inside," Verity said, now that she sensed an opening. "They're your family."

"Are they? They just fucking chucked me out. They always fucking chuck you out eventually."

Verity put a hand on Holly's shoulder.

"Come on," Holly said, shaking it off.

"Where are we going?" Verity said.

"Away."

***

Bella tensed as Holly became a blurry dot in her vision, pointing at her through the open door, before storming off. The righteous fire in her stomach flickered like a wind had gone past. "I am... I can't... Fucking!" She screamed into the air as well. "That self-righteous, sanctimonious fucking—!"

Roman, still asleep on the sofa bed, threw an empty bottle of Lucozade Sport at her and rolled over, grumbling.

Bella looked at him, actively trying to maintain the rage.

Then she looked at Munro. "What did you do that for?" she said, welling up. She reached out, and pulled her around her like a blanket. "I don't understand!"

Munro swatted her off. "Stop it!" They stared at each other. "You would understand if you were listening to me! I keep trying to make this process easier for you and you keep making it about yourself! I wanted to help her!"

"You have so little lifespan left, why are you squandering it?!"

"Because it's *my* life! If I want to spend it helping people, that's *my* fucking business, Bella, and you have no right to stop me!" Even as she said it, she was beginning to turn transparent. She stumbled back, taken by a dizzy turn.

"Munro!" Bella shouted.

Munro put a hand up to stop her as she clutched with her other hand to steady herself on the banister by the front door. "Stop. Bella. I know you want to trap my last days in a jar like some old hoarder until they go bad. I know you have this vision of what my perfect death will look like—"

"I don't, I don't w—"

"Stop it!" Munro shouted. "Stop it! Stop talking over me!"

Bella stopped. Frozen. A deer before impending death.

Munro focused, and she began to come back into opacity. She sat down on the step. "I can't deal with you mourning me before I'm even gone, Bella. And I can't deal with you trying to take my choices from me. I just want you to be with me." She tilted her head down, suddenly heavy, her eyes closed as she had to focus. She rested her head on her knees. "Just be with me, Bella. Let me do what I want to do."

Her eyes snapped open as she felt a warm hand on her back.

She looked back to see gold thread travelling along her back. "What are you doing?" she said, suddenly charged with energy.

"The same thing you did, you dummy," Bella said.

"Bella, you've got your whole life ahead of you. You have no idea what this will do to you down the line!"

"It's called informed consent, babes." Bella smiled, but even she could feel the unsettling gnaw that she wasn't handling this right. It was like she was outside her body, watching herself over frothing waves of mania. Had she just sent Holly off to be eaten by a fucking vampire? Was she smothering Munro?

Munro slapped her hand away. "Yeah, consent goes two ways."

Bella dropped the thread, and it faded. "Sorry." She didn't know what else to say. Munro pulled her into a hug. "There's just a lot going on right now," she said into her shoulder. Even if it was the truth, it felt piddly in Munro's arms. And she was doing it again. Making it about her. She could feel the thread she'd already managed to tie, holding Munro as Munro held her. Goddess, that was a half-inch off what Nicnevin had done. She looked up at Munro. "I love you. I'm sorry."

"I love you too." She held her hand up and looked as the golden thread revealed itself. She tugged on it, and Bella felt herself sway as if she'd stood up too quickly. "You crazy woman."

"I'm sorry, I should've—"

"What is it with this family and throwing our lives away for people?"

Bella smiled, despite herself. She could feel it disturb the drying tear tracks on her cheeks. The mania was beginning to fade now, and she could feel things properly again. "Come on, it's basically a trans tradition at this point to pass the same twenty quid back and forth. You're actually a bigot if you *don't* take it."

"Oh well in that case..." Munro rolled her eyes.

But Munro was right, she was no Nicnevin. Her magic wasn't strong enough. If she'd tied that spell round Munro any tighter Munro would've died just the same, and she would've been dragged under with her, an anchor tied around her legs.

From the mania, she could see the logic of just letting that happen. What would be the point going on anyway? But she couldn't do that, not to Munro, and not to the other people in her life.

Her head spun, and she sat down next to Munro. "Woo. Gimme a second." She could feel it, astrally. The gale force that tugged at Munro, tried to blow her away. It was tugging at her now too, like Munro was a kite she was holding on the beach.

The open door to the Archive was letting a draft through, and it was threatening to break the line of salt on the door. Bella snapped her fingers, and the door—

Didn't move.

Her brow furrowed, confused.

She snapped again. Nothing.

"Uh..."

She raised a hand, concentrated on it. She swiped her hand left to right like Karate Kid, and the door finally slid closed by itself.

She stared at her hand. "What the hell?"

"Your magic's all tied up with me now," Munro said. "You're doing two things at once." She rubbed the bridge of her nose. "By the tides, Bella, what have you done?"

"It's fine," Bella said. "I can handle it."

Munro shrugged. "Well, you're not wrong there I suppose. You can handle anything."

They smiled at each other.

"Plus, you know, when magic is taken away it always comes back stronger, right?" Munro added.

Bella darkened. "Don't remind me of Holly right now. I'm still angry at her. She knows everything you're going through, and she prioritised a stranger—"

"Holly was right, Bella." Munro interrupted her. "I'm right. The two of us were in agreement."

"Yeah, but I'm still mad at her. Storming out of here."

"You kicked her out!"

Bella faltered. "I guess I did."

Shit.

***

The dew on the grass was wet, and Verity couldn't have told Holly why she'd wanted to come here. Couldn't have told herself. She was literally in Breckenridge's back garden right now.

But the University building standing over them felt comforting to her in ways she couldn't explain.

She reached a hand out to Holly's, and took it in hers. Holly had been silent since they'd started walking, brewing her rage in the cauldron of her belly. Verity could feel it coming off her in waves, that spicy magic that had so captivated her when they'd first met.

This woman was made of steel, she thought. Tempered steel. That was where the magic came from. If the world dropped a building on her, she'd force it to move. Verity suspected Holly couldn't stop herself from doing it. She wondered if she was even aware of it.

"I'm sorry," Verity said.

Holly arched an eyebrow. "For what?"

"Once again we stand here and I'm dragging you into my bullshit, and now your family are pissed at you."

"Ah, they'll come round," Holly said. "They fucking better anyway."

"Why are you even still helping me? Iona was right. They couldn't do anything else for me, and the bloodlust is satiated, for now anyway."

"Because it's the right thing to do," Holly said.

"Is it?"

Holly stared at her. "I guess it's also because I care about you."

"I care about you too," Verity said.

Holly smiled. "Do you?" She reached a hand out, and drew her fingers through Verity's hair. Verity tingled at the touch.

"I do," Verity said. "I thought it was some... animal craving. But that's gone now. And it's only made me care more."

"Something about you..." Holly said, taking in Verity's face. "You remind me of... church."

Verity cocked her head in confusion. She had never been in a church, of course, but what a strange comparison.

"Church as a wee girl," Holly trailed off. "The daylight through the stained glass windows. The terror. The enormity of it. Noah building a boat as the planet floods. Moses parting the sea. The sky opening up as God dwarfs you, and you feel like you're going to disappear into Him."

"I didn't realise you were a Christian."

"I don't think you ever quite get it out of you," Holly said. She snorted. "Have you seen the amount of pagans that are just cottage-core Catholics?"

"What's Cottage Core?" Verity asked.

Holly shook her head. "Was just a joke."

"Making jokes? As the sky opens up and the infinity of God dwarfs you?"

Holly grinned. "Always."

"I love that," Verity said. She was staring at Holly's lips, she couldn't stop herself. She realised how close they were to each other. Holly was staring at her, with those little brown eyes.

Verity's mouth was slightly open, her fangs grazing against her lower lip. Holly smelled of strawberries, her breath sweet and hot. She ran a hand through Holly's hair, her slim fingers, every touch was electric on her skin. And before she knew it, she was leaning in. They drank each other in, Verity's breathing quickening as Holly's lips played across hers, so soft on her chin, and along her jaw. Holly lifted her head back, gently submitting. With a firm but gentle grip, Verity moved Holly's hair out of her way, tilting her head back to expose her neck, and leaning in...

She stopped herself.

"I'm sorry," she said, covering her mouth where her fangs had extended to the point where she couldn't close her mouth anymore. "I got carried away."

"No, it's..." Holly took her hands in hers. "It's okay. I want to."

"Holly, it could kill you." Her voice was toothy, like her mouth was full.

Holly made a mock sign of the cross across her forehead and shoulders. "God rest her soul, she died doing what she loved. Hot women."

Verity laughed, despite herself, still covering her mouth out of modesty. Holly cupped her hands, and gently lowered them.

She tilted Holly's head back, exposing her bare neck to the moonlight. Her grip was light, her fingers delicate. Holly breathed heavily, her heart pounding in her chest. Verity could feel it through their fingers entwined, Holly's pulse. Instinctive. Innate. Hot, quick, rabid. Despite everything, fear.

She could feel her pupils constricting to a pinpoint, her fangs extended, a drip of saliva running down her lip.

And then, like a viper, she plunged.

Holly gasped, the anaesthetic of the vampire venom tickling her spine and the back of her brain as the two of them connected, body and mind. Holly huffed, planting soft kisses on Verity's clavicle as she drank, hungry and panting. She felt light-headed, woozy and pleasant, Verity's hands instinctively finding her wrists, grabbing them tight in a pincer grip.

Holly continued to kiss around Verity's perfect neck, and then was confused when she was finding wet.

Sticky. Black. Tasting of copper.

It was her own blood, dripping down Verity's neck, she realised. She laughed, punch-drunk, and leaned into her lover, feeling the weight of her on her cheek, and relaxed into the lightness of being eaten, knowing she was in good hands.

***

When Holly came to, she sat up slowly, looking around. "Hello?"

Verity was lying next to her. They were still in the grass, Verity's face covered with the red, like she'd buried it in a giant, ripe strawberry.

"Hey." Verity smiled. Her teeth looked pearly-white compared to the visceral red. Her fangs were gone.

"What happened?" Holly could feel the connection start to go back to normal.

Verity smiled, her stomach tittering. She'd never done that before. She'd never fed on anyone, and been able to stop herself killing them. When the mind-link had happened, she'd never been able to feel anything from them but fear.

She didn't know what she and Holly had, but it was something she'd never gotten anywhere else.

chapter 31

Bella chapped the door to Iona's study with her elbow. "Iona? I've brought you a tea."

There was no response, so Bella chapped again. When there was still no response, she said, "I'm coming in, hang on!" She juggled the two mugs into one hand and opened the door.

Iona was drawing on the floor in chalk. She looked pale, like she'd been up for days, and her hair was a crow's nest.

"Iona, are these... witch-proofing sigils?"

Iona jumped, as if she hadn't noticed the door was open.

Bella put the tea down on her study's desk and sat down opposite her. "Iona, we're losing it."

"We can deal with it after, if Holly gets turned she'll be—"

"Iona." Bella took her hands in her own. "If Holly was at risk of being turned, we wouldn't have let her go. Right?"

Iona thought about it, but Bella could see that her brain was just doing Catherine wheels. "Here." She got up and got one of the mugs. "Have some tea."

"No, I need to fi—" Iona looked at it, and then at the chalk in her hand. "Fucking witch-proofing. I haven't had to do this in a century."

"I don't think you need to do it now."

She looked up at Bella. "No. No, I suppose not." She put the chalk down. "What the hell am I doing?"

"Do you have some... history with vampires?"

"If you live long enough, everyone has history with vampires," Iona said.

"Mm," Bella said, stretching to get her own mug. "You are a skilled artisan of dodging the question."

"Cheeky," Iona said. "She…" Her eyes began to well up, and she chewed her lips to try and loosen then.

"…Who?" But, by then, she'd twigged. But how hadn't she known?

"There was…" It was normally so hidden, Iona's grief. Buried under the tectonic weight of work, of duty, of life. Right now, she could see it, straining against its belts. "There was…" She struggled again.

"Connie," Bella said. Iona's wife. Her other mother.

"She, she used to stand…" Iona's voice was warbling like a stalling car. She wiped the tears from her eyes but it did nothing to stop them. "She used to stand out in that plaza. And she had these daft fluffy green slippers, waving her fag about." She laughed, a wet burble bubbling up.

Bella squeezed her hand, she was crying as well now. Goddess, she'd forgotten about all of this.

"No-one would come within ten feet of her. They thought she was mad," Iona said. "She *was* mad." She smiled, and it seemed to break some valve inside her. "She was mine." The dam broke, and she collapsed into Bella's arms, ten years too late. "And they killed her! They put their fangs in her and they killed her, Bella! She was mine and they killed her!"

Bella gripped Iona like she was about to fall, squeezed her tight as they both cried.

"I'm sorry. I'm sorry. I'm sorry, I'm sorry, I'm sorry…" Iona said.

"It's okay, Iona." Bella rubbed circles into Iona's back.

There was a lot of powerful magic in the world, but no magic so powerful as something unspeakable hanging over your head.

"I never told you how it happened. You were so young, none of you had anywhere else to go, your families had abandoned you. It was so sudden, I…" Iona said. "I couldn't let it affect you."

"Connie was murdered by vampires?"

"No," Iona said. "They left her alive. She... asked me to finish the job."

She opened her mouth, then closed it. She didn't know what to say.

Iona disengaged from her, wiped her face for the final time, and took a deep breath as she took the room in.

There was that cold look again, that one that had scared Bella so much the night Verity had turned up on their door. The one that passed through her like radiation. It didn't see her.

And she understood now. When Iona looked at Verity, all she could see was driving a stake through her own wife's heart.

Iona covered her face with her hands. "Stupid, stupid! I taught you all everything I know. Everything except vampires. Because it was too painful. And now I reap the consequences."

Well she couldn't well be getting angry at Iona for grieving wrong after her own behaviour the past few weeks. She looked at the chalk circles on the floor. "I know, we're all in a lot of danger right now, and action is important. But do you think maybe we're running in the wrong direction?"

Iona cupped the tea for warmth. "I don't know. I don't know what to do. I feel like my brain is full of holes."

"Same," Bella said. She grabbed Iona for a hug, and the two of them held each other. "I'm so lucky to have you, Iona."

"I'm lucky to have all of you. You keep me right."

"Even Roman?"

"Especially Roman," Iona admitted. "I have a horrible feeling Holly wouldn't have run away if he'd been awake to diffuse that. God, I'm a daft old coot!"

"Don't tell him that, it'll go right to his head," Bella said.

Iona smiled, as though she was just now realising she was surrounded by chalk scribblings. "What the hell am I doing..."

"We need to go get Holly back," Bella said.

"If she doesn't want to be found, she's going to be pretty hard to scry."

"I know," Bella said. She thought of Munro padding about in the next room, painting. She wondered if she could hear this. She asked, as quietly as she could, "Iona... before, I asked you about... losing Connie."

Iona looked at her. "Yeah."

"You never..." she trailed off. "What do you do? To deal with it?"

Iona popped a finger on her head. "I keep her in here. And sometimes, when I need to, I bring her out like the good silverware and I ask her questions."

"Does it help?"

"Sometimes," Iona said. "It's not like having her back. And it hurts. But sometimes it hurts in a nice way." She finished her tea. "Let me wipe all these chalk marks up, and then I'll find Holly." She stood, and perched to hold Bella's cheek before giving her a peck on the forehead. "You should try getting the silverware out."

***

By design, every witch will have a slightly different process. A different way to tap into the divine, grown and bound by their spiritual beliefs, their upbringing, and their culture. A lot of them focused on ancestry, of asking their forebears for guidance.

For Arabella, there were no ancestors she could ask. Certainly none she would care for the answers of.

No, for Arabella the only important ancestry was the Coven. The family she'd grown around her like a garden, tended to, trimmed when needed. The advice she cared about was of the people she'd entangled with, her social net. Roman. Iona. Holly.

And well, there was one other.

Even as the incense began to burn — orange blossom, Connie's favourite — she could feel the blonde curls against her cheek like the memory of her wrapped her in a hug.

"Hi Connie." She opened her eyes, and looked at the image of the cheery, round woman in front of her. Iona's late wife.

Alright, hen? How's tricks?

She'd had wicked eyes, like she'd shoplifted a thunderbolt and was carrying it around with her, expecting to get caught. Though she'd pinned her hair back in multiple places, she was always pushing it back out of her face. Was it any wonder Arabella's third mother had left such an impression?

"Not great."

Connie sucked air through her teeth. *It never is when you're asking for help.*

Arabella laughed. It was difficult to describe this process. Confabulating half a conversation based on memory. She suspected everyone who grieved did it. She suspected she'd be talking to Munro this way for the rest of her life, and it broke her heart again.

You been eating? You're looking awfy skinny. Can't have you wasting away.

"Yep."

Connie raised her eyebrow that way she always did when she didn't believe you.

Go make a sandwich. And a big thing of water. Choppy choppy.

Arabella sighed, and did it, leaving the darkened room into the blinding yellow light of the kitchen. Cheese and ham and butter on wholemeal bread. She even cut the crusts off the way Connie used to do, as if they'd been little kids and not traumatised seventeen year-olds who'd run away from home.

She returned, and ate the sandwich in front of the altar as her eyes readjusted to the darkness again. "You happy?" she said.

Don't talk with your mouth full. You're a witch, no' a donkey!

Arabella covered her mouth with her hand as she chewed.

She finished the sandwich and drained the pint glass of water in one go, and it was frustrating how it did immediately help.

Right. Gies the goss. She perched on the edge of the couch with her legs curled up against themselves, lighting up a menthol.

"My girlfriend is dying."

Connie's expression crumpled. She'd always been like that. She had this cheery disposition, but somehow other people's bad news would have her looking like the beach on a rainy day.

Sorry, hen. What's happened?

Arabella explained it in her head. She kidded herself she was fast-forwarding, but honestly if she said it out loud she might break for good.

Connie chewed on it. She was a chewer.

"How did you and Iona deal with it?" Arabella asked. "When you were going through everything?"

No response. Arabella became aware she was talking to an empty chair.

That was the problem with this kind of conversation. You could only really talk to them about things you'd already talked to them about when they were with you. It was a pleasant form of torture, reminding you of all the conversations you'd never had. And none of them had ever talked about Connie's death.

She burst into tears, and cupped her face. They ran through her fingers like raindrops.

Connie tutted in the other chair like a mother hen. *Och, come here. It's alright...*

Arabella climbed onto the couch and nestled herself in Connie's legs where the cat used to lie, and cried until she was empty, wailing. She could feel Connie stroking her hair, almost like it was real. The incense had burned down now.

She squeezed the cushion she'd been lying on, and sat up. Wiped her face.

I bet Oanie could give you a hand.

"She told me to ask you," Bella admitted. "Honestly, she would just tell me I was daft to get involved with a selkie in the first place, especially one in Munro's position."

Ooh, you didnae mention she was a selkie! Did you try on her seal skin? Connie mimed throwing a scarf or a feather boa over her shoulder.

Arabella cackled, feeling the hoarseness in her throat from all the tears. She rubbed her face, and swatted at the cushion where Connie's legs would've been.

Promise you'll help each other. She's got to be more help than fuckin', Connie mimed around her, *this. Me.*

"I will."

And she's fucking whip-smart. It's why I married her. Well. That and the—

Arabella wrestled the cushion to cover Connie's mouth, like she was a little kid, worried she'd catch cooties. Connie laughed like a villain.

Eventually, Arabella went to go wash the dishes, and they carried on their conversation until the last of the plates was on the rack, and then she went to go cuddle Roman in his sleep on the couch.

chapter 32

"Thank you again for helping me with this," Verity said, as she waited for Holly to finish vaulting the fence.

"Stop thanking me," Holly said, balancing her feet between the spikes, before lifting her hands so she could jump clumsily onto the other side. "You make it sound like I'm doing this as some charity case." She stood, brushing the gravel from the fall into her jeans.

Verity smiled. "Well, I appreciate it."

"Good!" Holly said. She looked around. "Where now?"

"This way, I think." Verity led the way, pulling up the hood of the thick black cloak Holly had summoned for her. It camouflaged her in the dark, and she peeked around the outside of the building. Here, at the top of the hill overlooking the park, she could feel Breckenridge's beady eyes everywhere. Every twitch of a curtain from a nearby window, every night bird overhead. "He never kept his projects in the house."

"Woah—" Holly stumbled, almost bowled back by an unseen wind. She fought to regain her balance.

"You okay?"

"Yeah, I— I just got a weird feeling," Holly said. "The ley lines we felt last time we were here. They're stronger in here. Like they're all bundled on top of each other."

"This is Breckenridge's study. He keeps all the stuff we're not allowed to see in here."

Holly clutched the fence. "Yeah, gimme a sec, would you?" She breathed heavily, fighting nausea.

"Are you sure you're okay?" Verity stepped up, and as their fingers brushed—

Verity felt nauseous too, waves of it that rolled through her and threatened to carry her away. The world went dark, a curtain thrown over the moon. As her eyes adjusted, she realised she couldn't see Holly, she was seeing some woman, dark-haired and falcon-eyed, and she gasped as she recognised the woman from Munro's drawings—

She snatched her hand back.

"What the hell was that?" Holly said, but before Verity could reply she added, "Okay, time to sit down." Like the decision had been made for her. If she stayed upright, she'd end up falling over. She was eyeing the bushes as a safe place to throw up in.

Verity looked at her hand. "I think we're linked."

"That's nice," Holly said. "God, the cosmic tidal forces are..."

"Maybe we can withstand them better together," Verity said. She reached her hand out.

Holly grabbed it—

The waves hit her, Holly's magic buffeted by the ley lines. She could see them now, through Holly's eyes. The strands of gold and silver light that travelled through the world wherever people went. Slipping up through Park Circus like an old muscle that didn't get used any more. They'd been ripped up and wrapped around this building like an artery, twisted and tangled in string—

"The Dark Scaffold..." she said out loud, but her voice came out of Holly's mouth. "It was made in the image of this... network."

"The dark what?"

"It's the thing that keeps us alive."

"Vampires live because of Dark Ley Lines?"

"If these are ley lines... yeah."

"The world looks so... bright," Holly said, through Verity's mouth.

She reached Verity's hand up, like the moon was a silver coin in a puddle and she was trying to retrieve it. "It's beautiful."

"Wait till the sun comes out and fries you like a potato fritter," Verity said. She looked around, turning Holly's shoulders, wavering as moving her neck made the nausea worse. "Maybe if we get inside, it'll get better."

"It's not like it can get any worse," Holly said. She gripped their hands tighter, and with Verity's free hand, she lifted a rock and threw it through a window. "You know, I always assumed this building was a church."

"Grandfather likes it that way. He thought it was funny." Holly lifted Verity's hand, and a wind blew the shattered teeth of the broken window in. Verity felt a tingle in her — Holly's — hand where Holly had cast the spell with hers. Something so familiar... A memory long since gone.

She stole another look at herself through Holly's eyes, she couldn't help herself. Seeing herself in the flesh for the first time. So that was what she looked like. It horrified her, and entranced her. She couldn't look away. Her image, kept from her.

They dropped hands, and the vision was ripped away. They clambered through the window, and into the darkened building.

***

Verity had always expected the inside of Breckenridge's workshop to be stone. Ancient, Masonic. But the corridors were wood. Hardwood. 1950's maybe? It looked uncared for — but then he didn't let anyone else in here, and she doubted he cleaned it himself.

It was unusual for a vampire to be able to enter a private building without an invitation. Despite herself, a grin crept across her fangs, feeling like a little kid sneaking somewhere she shouldn't. Of course, that restriction only applied to buildings owned by *humans*.

Holly caught her breath and leaned against the back of the wall beneath the window. "You were right, I think." She took deep breaths through the mouth. "It's quieter in here."

"The eye of the storm." Verity looked up and down, training her predator eyes for traps going off, disturbed guards, even Breckenridge himself.

But there was nothing.

"Did he really leave this place unguarded?" Her brow furrowed. Something wasn't adding up.

Holly stood up, her Doc Martens crunching the shattered glass on the floor. "Do you know which way we're going?"

"I don't even know what we're looking for," Verity admitted.

"Well come on then," Holly said. "I doubt we've got long before he pokes that veiny head of his in to see the broken window."

They pushed onwards. The corridors snaked downwards, and they poked their heads in rooms to find old classrooms, chairs up on the tables and overgrown with cobwebs, as though the students had gone home for the summer and never returned.

"This place used to be a school?" Holly asked.

"I don't think so..." Verity said. "I feel like it would've come up at some point."

"How many secrets does this guy have?" Holly said.

Verity poked her head into the classroom, walked between the desks. Searched her mind for recognition, or at least a reason. But there was nothing.

She dragged her fingers over the surface of the desks as she passed. At the back of the class was a bookcase that spanned the room, stacked with books guarded by a thick layer of dust. It was then she turned, and saw the mural.

Someone had painted the Dark Scaffold on the wall. An ornate family tree spanning the centuries. All of their names preserved in gold,

It had been painted by hand, excruciatingly. And she recognised the handwriting.

"Woah," Holly said, falling in behind her. "What is it?"

"It's me. An accounting of every vampire in the world," Verity said. She ran her fingers along the seam of gold that traced parent to child.

Holly squatted at the right hand side of the wall by Verity's name, rendered in gilded curlicues. "It's giving... royal family."

"That's the way they talk about it," Verity said.

"Man, Breckenridge was busy," Holly said. Her eyes followed up to Breckenridge, and then down to the many others. A lot of his direct descendants held his surname, Oakleaf. Many others did not.

Verity didn't recognise most of the names. "I've never met the rest of the family. We're not supposed to talk about them."

No. She had been here before.

"That's *very* royal family," Holly whistled through her teeth. "Hiding the unwanted kids?"

Verity shook her head. "We arrange in broods. The lineage is paramount. But vampires hold grudges that last centuries, and immortals fighting each other is a waste of time."

"Makes sense," Holly said. "I suppose when this" —she gestured to the wall— "is what keeps you alive. Would feel a bit like shitting in your water supply."

"Holly..."

If Holly registered her grumbling, she didn't act on it. "What are these?" she asked. There were huge scores where the wall had been burned away. "I thought it was the wallpaper peeling off but..." She rubbed her fingers on it. "It looks like it was burned off."

"They're the ones who didn't make it," Verity said. She traced her finger on the base of the scorch. "Your parents hold you to this world. A dead vampire will ripple down the generations."

"But that means killing Breckenridge would kill you."

"My mother first, and then me," Verity said.

Holly shifted on her feet. "I can't kill him then. I can't."

"Don't." Verity rubbed the ash between her fingers. She had been in this room before. Breckenridge stood before the mural, drilling it into her. Even now, she could barely remember. "That's my job."

***

"Oh... oh man, that's bleak," Holly said. They had made their way out of the room back into the corridor, and Holly had been distracted by a plinth. On it sat a large purple crystal, the size of a basketball. It looked like the inside of an amethyst, spiked and milky.

"What is it?"

"It's a witch's soul," Holly said. She lifted it up, respectfully. "Taken from the body. I've read about it, but I've never seen it for real."

"Can we fix it?"

Holly shook her head. "It's dead. The soul can't live without a body. The soul isn't a... thing. It's a flame. It only exists as the burning of something else. It's why astral projection is so hard, you're moving th—" She stopped herself. "Doesn't matter, sorry."

Verity put her hand on it. It felt cold to the touch, and didn't respond. She could feel the magic inside it, but it was opaque. Gone.

"This was a witch," Holly said. "A witch with a life, and someone ripped their soul out."

"But why?" Verity said. "Why would Breckenridge do that?"

"I don't know..." Holly said, lifting the soul to her eye level, as if she could glean the answer from looking at it. "I don't think he meant to. It's useless to him. God, that poor person..."

"Can we... help them? I don't know."

Holly looked at her. "Yeah. I need a window."

As Verity opened a latch, Holly said, "Roman told me... when you die, your body breaks down, and your soul with it. It returns to the earth.

Her soul starved to death and now it's just a fossilised lump. We can at least..." She squeezed it, filling it with her fire until it melted into a ball of plasma. She lifted it to the window, and blew. It turned to dust, and scattered. "There. Now it's back in the ecosystem."

It drifted like embers, into the night, until it was gone.

Verity looked at the embers, tilting her head. It looked... familiar. And the window sill. And this corridor.

"I've been here before. I've seen that happen."

"You've been in here?"

Verity clenched her fists. "Let's keep digging."

The workshop seemed to go on forever, down several floors. She wondered how deep into the hill it went, if they were under the park somewhere. It was hard to imagine Breckenridge building this place by hand, but only a vampire would have had the time.

The deeper they went, the more the feeling crept up on Verity that she had been here before. "I don't like this," she said.

Holly stopped. "Do you want to leave?"

Verity paused. Something about her did want to leave. But she could tell whatever this place was, Breckenridge didn't want her remembering. Which meant she needed to know what it was.

"Let's keep going."

"Okay," Holly said. She led the way, slow steps into the dark, the corridor getting smaller and smaller around them until they were almost walking with a stoop.

Verity stopped, outside a door. This far down, there were no windows — she had no idea how Holly was seeing in the dark with her human eyes.

But it had been dark when she had been here before.

"Reintegration," she said quietly.

"What?" Holly, stumbling in the darkness, realised Verity had stopped. She walked back, pawing at the wall. "Oh, for goodness' sake."

She conjured a fireball in her hand. It floated, amiably, casting a wicked glow over the corridor. Verity squinted as her eyes adjusted, hissing, but she could make out the words on the plaque on the door now.

REINTEGRATION

She had been right.

"I've been here," Verity said. She could feel the memories in her brain strain in their cages, trying to evade capture.

"Let's go in," Holly said, putting her hand on the door, but Verity gripped it—

Holly was shaking. Whole-body shaking. Her fight or flight response didn't know how to fly, so she charged blindly ahead. Whatever was in this room—

She pulled her hand away, but it was enough for Holly to stop.

"I saw…" Holly said. "Something bad happened to you in that room, didn't it."

"I don't… I don't know." There was something there. Something she had blacked out? But then… Breckenridge. Her mother. There was no taboo with them about rummaging around in each others' heads. The only thing that stopped her from doing it was that they were so much stronger than she was.

How had it never occurred to her they might have hidden things from her?

Maybe that was part of the trick.

"I don't remember…" she said. All she knew was that she didn't want to open that door.

"Let's go," Holly said. "Let's just get out of here." She put her hand on Verity's forearm, squeezing through the fabric, and Verity pulled back.

"No. I'm going in," she said. The door loomed over them, and she needed to know what was behind it. "Please, just, come with me."

"Of course," Holly said.

Verity put her hand on the door.

The knob turned easily, but the door was heavy. They pushed, and Holly's fireball illuminated a dark cupboard with a humble bed, a bedside table, a chair, and very little else. IV drips hung from truss on the ceiling.

"What the hell was this place?"

Verity clapped her hands to her mouth. She could remember. The feel of these sheets, the itchy plastic satin. That truss, hanging over her as she stared at it for days. And Breckenridge—

She couldn't, she staggered, she was—

Breckenridge had said it was totally normal to find it repulsive.

She couldn't catch her—

The room spun.

It had spun at the time.

That ceiling—

The woman's eyes—

"Verity!" Holly said, as Verity fell to her knees so she wouldn't topple completely. She heaved, her lungs filling and filling but getting nothing—

"Help— help— help—" Verity said.

Was this the hunger?

She was dying.

Oh God she was going to die in this room—

"It's okay," Holly said quietly. Verity stared at her, eyes bulging as she panted and panted but nothing happened. She was going to choke on her own lungs—

Holly extinguished the flame and threw them both into darkness, and for the moment before Verity's vampire eyes adjusted, it hid the scene.

Verity wheezed, and heaved, her lungs full of water, as Holly, seemingly unworried, just held a hand on her back. Letting her know she was there.

After a few minutes, it seemed to subside.

"I don't... I don't like it in here."

"Yeah. I know. I'm sorry, I didn't want to move you."

The woman. She had forgotten the woman.

Her first victim.

Breckenridge had had her on an IV for days, talking up how harmless vampirism was.

The fear in that woman's eyes.

Verity had known, in her heart, that the woman had been someone from her life. Why else would Breckenridge have gagged her, stopped her speech? Something about the curls of her hair. She remembered her.

Whoever she was, she didn't remember now.

She hadn't remembered any of this.

***

They kept walking.

The path grew deeper. Darker. Ever smaller. Into the bowels of Breckenridge's workshop.

They passed a gents toilet, the telltale smell of piss and bleach that never quite disappears. Holly stared at the ceramic urinal along the wall.

"Come on," Verity nudged, moving ahead.

"Sorry." Holly kept looking at it with a puzzled look. "It's just not often you get to see them, you know? They just piss on the wall."

Verity looked at her.

"Sorry," Holly repeated, looking down at her feet.

At the end of the corridor was a thick set of oaken double doors. Verity rattled the tall door handles, and the door shivered, but didn't budge. "I think it's locked from the inside," she said, peeking down the slit in the door. "There's a chain hanging over the gap."

"Pfft," Holly said. "You're talking to the greatest witch of a generation, Ver." She lifted her hands like she was trying to divine the lock from the air.

Verity stepped back to give her space to work.

Holly sniffed the air, circling like she was trying to breathe in the door's aura.

"Is it not working?"

"Shh!" Holly hissed. Then she intoned,

"A secret under lock and key,
Desperate grasping to be free,
Just between us, help you help me,
Gies a hand, open sesame?"

The door rattled, but did not open.

"It didn't work," Verity said, dumbly.

"I can see it didn't work!" Holly grimaced. "Fuck it." She kicked the door, and a bright red glow appeared around the centre, the chains on the other side melting into slag metal and dropping to the floor. She pushed the door open triumphantly. "Well, when the subtle ways don't work..." she said.

"Maybe it didn't like your rhyming."

"Yeah, honestly even my good ones are a bit shite. Improvising is hard," Holly admitted. She summoned a little fireball in her hand and threw it up into the air to light the space.

A gymnasium. Empty. The unvarnished floor had that school gym smell that burned the hairs in Verity's nose. And for a second she thought the paint lines on the ground were just from some sport, but then she saw the intricacies, the shapes... "What is this place?"

Holly tentatively stepped into the middle of the room so she could read the entire thing. "It's a sigil. It's... what the hell is a vampire doing writing sigils on the floor?" She moved around the centre the room, tracing its lines, reading them with her fingers like Braille. "This part is a map." She pointed. There was a section in the corner showing a handful of concentric shapes in ink, all intersected by a thick painted line. Once Holly said it, she could just about make it out as the city if she squinted, and she'd been told. Once she knew the painted line was an abstraction of the Clyde, she could see it.

"This is..." Holly said. "Necromancy. Has to be. And look." Carefully, she scraped at the painted line with her pinkie fingernail and freed the flakes with her thumb to show Verity. Verity didn't need to be told the smell of human blood, even aged as much as this caked-on stuff was.

Holly wiped the blood on her jeans.

"What is it doing?"

"No idea, but whatever it is, it's huge. I mean look at the size of it," Holly said. "I didn't think anyone other than a witch would be able to draw a circle this wide."

"Breckenridge can be resourceful," Verity said.

Holly continued to trace the circle. "The energy around Park Circus, those damaged ley lines. I think this is the circle that did it. It's drawing the power..." She traced the path across the circle and back again with her finger. "And sending it to... the Necropolis? Why?"

"Why indeed," came a feathery voice that stopped Verity in her tracks.

"Mother," Verity said.

"What in heaven are you doing down here, dear..." Alice said, her blonde hair all but lighting the room by itself. "I'm so disappointed in you. First you run away, now this." She crossed the room so fast Verity couldn't even flinch, and held Verity like a baby bird with a broken wing.

"You know about this place?" Verity asked.

"Of course. You would too, if your grandfather had felt you could be trusted." Alice looked at Holly, and her pupils sharpened into pinpricks. "And now you're bringing animals into the house. How could you?" She licked her chops like a cat.

"What's Breckenridge's plan with this circle, lady?" Holly ignored the jibe. "You may as well tell me, cos it'll only take me a couple of minutes to work out."

"Bold of you to assume you'll live that long," Alice said. Verity was locked still, a deer in the headlights in Alice's grasp. And then, Alice pounced.

She flew through the air as though on wires, fangs extended, face contorted with an inhuman glee. Verity screamed, lunged, made to fly after her—

But Holly raised a hand and clenched a fist, and Alice stopped in mid-air.

Verity went pale. Illuminated only from above, her vampire eyes could see the flames. Holly's anger, pluming off her like a furnace. The wrath of a dangerous witch.

Alice hovered in midair, the strings now seized by a puppet master.

Holly's face darkened. "Missus, I don't think you know who you're dealing with." She threw her hand and sent Alice hurtling through the still-open doors.

"*Get out,*" she hissed, no frilly rhymes or setting of intention. Just raw emotion. The doors slammed shut, and then fused together into one slab of wood as though to find a way to fulfil her request.

"Holly...?" Verity approached.

"We don't have long," Holly said, but in the other plane she was still on fire.

"Holly, wait," Verity said. She held her face. "What's the matter?" But even as she said it, the connection between them opened—

Verity felt Holly's tears running down onto her own hands, the coldness of those hands on her, cooling the flame billowing out of her cheeks.

Through the stupor, she felt it through their touch. Holly's feelings for her. The same irrational want, the yearning. The first hopeful embers of love, of being unsure whether they would be snuffed out or burn down the entire forest before suffocating. But somehow that risk just made her want it more.

"I feel it too," *Verity said, and this time it came out of her own mouth. They were one, and at the same time, they were each.*

But she already knew that that wasn't why Holly was crying.

"Oh no."

The circle.

Images of it flooded Verity's mind before she could stop them, before she could break the connection.

Holly wiped the tears from her cheeks. "I know what it's for now."

chapter 33

The blunt end of Munro's knife scored the canvas like she was trying to carve chunks out of it, paint drawn across the back of the blade. She wasn't even sure what she was painting, just that she wanted to get whatever anger was in her out.

How could Bella be so arrogant? So foolish? Why was she, at the end of everything, watching the people she cared about throw their lives around like they weighed nothing?

She'd kissed Bella and asked her to go check on Iona, and now she was painting. When she was alone, it was easier to deal with. Easier to think, to process her feelings. And now, she was furious.

She could feel the vision coming on this time. She almost enjoyed it — the self-flagellation. Which of her memories would be taken out of the box, dusted off and shown to her? Which of her sins would be weighed?

She gasped, pitched forward, dropping the knife—

They didn't find him until the morning.

No.

Please.

When the morning had come, the sun broke through the storm, and a search party could be sent out.

Not this one.

I am staggering across the sand, sleep-deprived, because they have found him, and have sent for me.

I don't want—

By the time I came upon him, someone had cleaned his body. Laid him flat as though he were merely sleeping. Wrapped a blanket around him to hide his broken limbs, closed the wound on his head with a stitch. As though he would heal. As though he would open his eyes again.

Oh God

It makes him look like an object. A ghost. The body empty, brittle and hollow, the shell of an egg from which the life has long since left. I take him, and I hold him in my arms, and I wail, and wail, and wail.

I hold him like I had when he'd been born. I still see that rictus, the collapsing face in my nightmares, years later. His last image. Soiled.

Oh my little boy

Oh, my little boy...

Oh, my little boy

My

my

my

my

my

my

"Don't look, my sweet," Nicnevin says. I gasp, as if pulled from the deep. She is turning my head from the memory, pushing me into the darkness. "Remember something else."

"I don't want to," I say.

"The good times."

"He's d e a d ..."

"He is." She blows, and launches me forward—

Snow is laughing with his brother. Haar was always such a runt, and Snow was old enough and big enough that he could catch him without even trying, but Haar would insist on teasing him. Buzz around him like a fly until he was forced to pay attention.

"Stop it, I'm trying to read," he says. I still have not forgotten his voice.

Haar is poking him, and jumps on his back, but he won't respond. He won't respond.

His chest cavity has caved in and he won't respond, he's gone, he's been gone for hours where is he I should've made them come home earlier I

—

"Munro, stay with me," Nicnevin says. "Your world line will unravel if you don't focus. You're blending things together." Again I am in her hands, again she is weaving the strands of fate around me. "I'm losing you, don't you let go."

"Is this it?" I say. "Is it just this forever and ever until I die?"

—

Of course this is how it ends. It's how it's always been. He's gone. Every morning I wake up and he's gone. The mornings stack into years, and into decades, and each one is heavier than the last

—

"Munro, don't you dare," Nicnevin says. "I can't let you fall here. Hang on, let me—" she is weaving the world together, I can feel it, every leaf on every tree and every drop of rain. She always was too clever for her own good. "Munro! I can't—!"

I am falling.

The stitch flips. I am in the dark, and I am watching the flickering, spectral strand of seaweed, like a fishing line tumbling upwards. I watch it. I smile. I want to take bets on when it will finally give up the ghost.

I am on a bench, watching Snow pick up a snail. He inspects it.

I am in the Archive, and Iona has gotten me my first set of paints in as long as I can remember.

I am walking down the street, we have come into the village for supplies. Haar is walking ahead with Lily, and she has decided she has walked enough, so she just hangs so he will lift her forward a few steps at a time.

I am in the Elf-hame Wars, and a troll brings a club down on me, but he's too clumsy, and I tumble away.

I am on the beach, and a beautiful woman is picking flowers. Arabella. This is the day we met.

"Morning, sleepyhead."

"This... this isn't what happened." *The picture is fracturing.*

"Nicnevin can't find you. I need you to hold on. You're losing yourself."

"I can't."

"I have never seen you fail anything in your life."

That's because I never speak about it. The image that burned into my mind every day, that made me so quiet. "Help." *I say it although I know there's nothing she can do, that I'm circling the drain.*

Suddenly, the memory shines through.

Bella is laughing, though she's blushing like a fire engine. "Do you talk to all the girls that way?"

I... remember this.

"Only the beautiful ones," *I smile. I am a selkie. Wooing humans is second-nature to us.*

I enjoy watching her not know what to say. She takes a tulip from her basket, and puts it in my furs. "You suit a green one. It matches your eyes." *She pats the fur down on my collar, and her hand lingers on my collarbone a little too long. My heart is racing, which I don't, at the time, expect.*

I grip the tulip, crush it tight in my hand.

And I realise it is not breaking.

It is Bella's hand

Something real. "Stay with me. Stay with me, Munro."

"Bella, I'm scared."

It hurts so much. My every nerve ending is on fire. I am so tired, and tired of being tired, and tired of being in such pain.

It would be so easy to just let it swallow me...

Time has stopped.

I teeter on the precipice.

Come on, you old bear. Like you told Haar. One more breath. And then another. And then another. No-one can steal your last breath if you refuse to give it up.

Time starts.

There is a moment between seconds, where I no longer exist.

I gasp, and open my eyes.

I hadn't known, until right this moment, whether I was going to fight until the end. But now I did. Now, with only hours left.

I wasn't going to give into these flashbacks. My life, my whole life, had been worth living.

The Reaper was going to have to take me kicking and screaming.

***

Bella twinged as Munro gripped her hand so tight that she could feel her knuckles about to pop.

And then her eyes opened.

"Hi," Bella said, softly.

"I'm here. I'm here. I'm..." Munro said. Her eyes were flitting, panicked.

"You're here."

She looked down, and relaxed her grip.

"That was horrible..." Munro said.

"I know. It's okay, you're safe," Bella said.

"I'm not though, am I?"

Bella chewed her lower lip.

"Thank you," Munro said. "For coming to get me." She grabbed her for a hug, and held on.

"Thank you for not giving up."

Munro's entire body was cold and clammy, drenched in a layer of sweat. She sat up, rubbed her face. "I didn't... did you see all of that?"

"I did."

"I didn't... I didn't mean for..."

"I'm so sorry," Bella said. "I had no idea. It wasn't your fault."

She buried her head in her hands. "I didn't realise it was still hanging over me. I can't handle this. I can't keep doing it."

Bella sat, leaning against her shoulder, like pressing weight against a wound. There was nothing else she could say.

"Let me go... wash. I want a shower." She sounded like she was still in shock.

"Okay," Bella said. She sat on the bed, and let Munro leave.

Nicnevin was in the image of the full-length mirror on the other side of the room. Bella didn't flinch when she saw her, once Munro was out the room.

"You're stronger than you look, Arabella Morrow."

"I told you," Bella said. "If it's for her, I can do anything."

"Don't go stealing my job, psychopomps are territorial."

"It's not a job for me, Nicnevin."

Nicnevin paused. "Well done," she said, begrudgingly. "I would've thought that magic beyond a mortal."

Bella tried not to show how tired she felt, as the adrenaline left her. "Thank you."

"It will only get worse though, I fear."

"I'll cross that bridge when I get to it."

"And then?"

"I'll cross that bridge too."

Nicnevin smirked. "You do have some redeeming qualities."

Bella glared.

Nicnevin turned, and the image in the mirror rippled like a lake, and Bella was just looking at herself.

She wanted to throw something at the mirror.

She wanted someone to talk to.

She needed Holly.

***

Munro felt the water run down her, scalding hot. It wasn't heating her up. She couldn't bring herself to move.

She wanted the visions to stop.

She wanted to rush them, to skip to the end, for every moment she lived to flash so fast she couldn't register the pain.

But she knew that once that happened, once she ran out of guilt and pain and trauma to burn, that would be the thing that killed her.

She turned the water off, and sat on the floor of the shower cubicle.

"Can't I wait?" she asked herself. "In this moment? Just a little while?"

chapter 34

Alice banged on the door, threatening to tear it from its hinges.

"What are you doing?" Verity shouted, as Holly rummaged in her pockets.

"New magic," Holly said, she pulled out her very old, very beat-up smartphone and took pictures of the whole thing. Then, she sat on the floor, legs crossed, and began to breathe. "Come on guys. Come and get me."

***

At that exact moment, Bella was using her pendant, circling the map of Glasgow in a scry.

"I don't know why you're bothering," Roman said, riffling through scrolls for more potent magic. "If she doesn't want to be found, she'll block it."

"I trust her." Bella focused on the pendant.

"You've been at it for twenty minutes, she's not going to come through. We need—"

Bella whispered, blocking Roman out. "I know you're looking for me, Holly, I know it. I've got you, don't worry."

The pendant stopped.

Bella's heart sank. Like the spell had stopped.

But right before she could do anything else, a tiny spot on the map burst into flame.

"Goddess!" Bella shouted, patting it out with her hands. She lifted it to inspect the damage.

"What did you do?"

"I don't think that was me..." Bella said. She held the map to the light, where the burn mark shone through a street corner in the middle of Park Circus.

***

"She's getting through!" Verity shouted. "That door won't hold her for long!"

"It's only got to hold until they get here!"

"That's what I'm saying, I don't think it will!"

"It will," Holly said. She said it with the same certainty she'd told the door to lock Alice out. Every word spoken by a witch created the very truth it carried.

"We have to get out of here!" Verity said. "We'll find another exit! We can fight through her and get away!"

"Do you trust me?" Holly said. She still hadn't opened her eyes.

Verity stopped. "I... Of course I trust you."

"They'll be here," Holly said. "As sure as my—"

With a crack, the door was ripped from its frame, thrown bodily across the room to come to a stop on the ground a few feet before them.

Verity had expected to see a crazed monster, but Alice was just standing there. Her mascara was running down her face.

"Why are you doing this to yourself, Verity?" she asked. "Why are you doing this to us? We're your family!"

"Mother, I..." Verity said.

"What did we do to deserve this?" She fell to her knees. "My own daughter, destroying the Scaffold..."

"Destroying the... What the hell are you talking about?"

"Yoo hoo!" came a disembodied voice. *"Em'dy ask for a lift?"* It was Roman.

The scene around them began to dissolve, warm and fuzzy, like last time. The universe unpicking their stitch and weaving them back into the Archive instead.

"Wait!" she shouted. "Mother, what do you mean?" But it was lost in the tumult, and then the gym was gone.

***

"Welcome back," Iona said, as the scene resolved into candlelight. The Archive's warm embrace. The sudden waft of incense almost knocked Verity off her feet, and she struggled to stand.

She and Holly were standing in the centre of a summoning circle, and the three witches sat around them. Munro stood watch. They clocked eyes with each other, and Munro nodded.

"Don't cut it so close next time!" Holly said.

Bella grabbed her in a hug. "I'm sorry."

"Hey, I was only kidding, I—" Holly started, before leaning into the hug when Bella didn't let go.

Bella looked at Verity over Holly's shoulder with... was that shame? Verity ducked her head. Gave her the space. Verity didn't have the right to do much more.

"We have news by the way," Holly said, when they parted. "Breckenridge doesn't just want Verity back, those ley lines you felt? It goes way beyond Park Circus."

She pulled out her phone and showed them the pictures.

"That's..." Iona said. "No... it can't be..."

"That almost looks like witch magic. It's far too complicated for a vampire." Roman scrunched up his face. "No offence," he added to Verity.

"Whatever he's planning, I expect he's been working on it for a very long time," Verity said.

"He's binding... dead bodies," Iona said. "Ugh, for goodness' sake Holly, can't you make it a bit bigger?" She was stooping to try and see what was on the dim, cracked phone screen.

"Have you got that laptop?" Holly asked.

Bella snorted. "It takes an hour just to warm up."

"I'll draw it," Holly said. "Gies a bit of paper, Roman." They pitter-pattered around the room.

"Actually, while you do that," Bella said, putting a hand on Verity's sleeve. She spoke quietly, "Can we have a word?"

chapter 35

Verity's silent begging for help as she was led from the room had been met with a shrug from Holly and an encouraging smile from Munro, neither of which did anything to make it less awkward as Bella closed the door to the guest room.

"I want to apologise," Bella said.

"Wh—" Of all the things Verity had expected her to say, it wasn't that. "I took your girlfriend's life energy."

"You did," Bella said. "Or, Munro gave you it. And I have problems with that. But it's not on you. And I shouldn't have made it about myself."

"I see…" Verity said. "Well, I'm sorry anyway."

Bella exhaled. "Let's just start from the beginning. I'm Arabella." She held her hand out. Verity shook it.

"Lovely to meet you, again," Verity said.

"I wanted to say, I think we're very similar," Bella said. "I should've seen it from your point of view."

Verity screwed up her face. "We're nothing alike. You're all so…" She looked through the door, pondering a better word. But she didn't have one. "Alive."

"I know what it's like to have a family that doesn't have your interests at heart, I mean," Bella said.

"Not like this, though," Verity said. "They think I'm a failure, and I don't even know if I want to succeed."

Arabella laughed.

"What?"

But it only made her laugh harder. She doubled over as it triggered another peal of cackling.

"Sorry, sorry," she said, taking another second to recover. "Man, I needed that."

Clearly it still showed on Verity's face how confused she was.

Bella scoffed. "Verity, I am trans-fucking-gender," she said. "My *whole life* has been being told I'm failing because they've got me sitting the wrong exams."

Verity shrank, thinking back to the family tree. The giant sigil on the floor of the gymnasium. "That's nice, Bella. But... this really isn't the same thing."

"No, listen." Bella took Verity's hands in her own. "If your family are telling you you've only got one choice, it's usually because they're trying to make that choice for you. You'll be happier if you make your own decision, and let them decide what to do with it."

"Even if it kills me?"

"I was..." Bella stumbled over her words. "I would've said yes. Especially then. But with everything that's happened with Munro..."

"She's trying her best for you," Verity said. "I know she appreciates you, how hard it's been for you."

"It shouldn't be about me," Bella said. "And I keep making it about me."

"It's because you care," Verity said. "If you didn't care, what would be the point? It hurts because it's real."

Bella welled up. "It must be really real, then."

"You're doing well," Verity said. "And you can take it from me. I've seen a lot of death."

Bella flinched at the word.

"Sorry," Verity said.

"No," Bella said. She squeezed Verity's hands. "Munro told me about how you're going to try and overthrow your grandfather. How she wanted to help. And I want to help too."

"You've both done so much for me," Verity said. "You all took me in; I can't... I can't ask any more."

"It's an oath on the door, Verity," Bella said. "Anyone who asks for help, will get it. It sounds selfless, but it's the only way we survive. People like you, people like them." She motioned with her head through the door. "And people like me. It's a promise we make. To look out for each other, because no-one else will."

"I have your back, and you have mine?"

Bella nodded, closed her eyes like she was reciting a mantra. "We create the world that will bear our weight, or are crushed by it. We make space to stand, with people we can trust, because there is no alternative in a world so full of people who refuse to understand us."

It was a weighty promise to make, and Verity felt it settle deep in her heart. It felt good.

"You're right. I'm not going back to him," Verity said. "I'll be there for you, as long as I'm still here... I don't know how long that'll be, but..."

"It'll be a long while, if we can do anything about it," Bella said. "Let's do this."

***

They arrived back in the kitchen to find Holly had turned it into a War Room. Candles hovered over the table, casting their light and dripping their wax on their map of the city. Sitting over it was a huge sheet of what looked like baking paper, scribbled on, anachronistically, by Sharpies.

"What am I looking at?" Verity asked.

"A spell," Iona said. She was marking out a line like rope wrapped around the Necropolis. "It's an incredible amount of power, and it's... skilful." She said it like she had Judas in her tongue. "I know you said he'd had a long time to think this up, but... no-one but a witch should be able to do this."

"He knows a lot about everything," Verity found herself saying, before she could even stop herself. It sounded a little too much like admiration for her liking, but she did it instinctively. Excuses as trained behaviour.

"The problem is," Holly said, pointing right at the terminus of the line Iona had drawn, at the entrance of the Necropolis, "he's gathered all this energy and it just stops there. He's not channelled it anywhere."

"The Bridge of Sighs..." Roman said. "Why is it always an ominous bridge?"

Verity leaned in and looked at it. "The Bridge of Sighs is one of the pillars of the Dark Scaffold."

"Pillars?" Holly said. "You said the Dark Scaffold was like ley lines. Ley lines don't have pillars, they're worn in. People's footsteps, their life paths, you know."

"That makes sense," Iona said. "I've been telling you, vampires are against nature. The structure they rely on needs to be built." She averted her gaze from Verity. "Sorry."

"But why would he take all that power and dump it on a pillar? He could bring the whole thing down on top of u— himself," she said.

"You tell us," Holly said. "What do these pillars do?"

"They're load-bearing. They're all over the world, anywhere there's vampires, anywhere there's death. He said they were like keystones," she said. "They're held up by all the weight pressing against them, and they hold everything else up."

"That sounds like how you described vampires working in general," Holly said. "Tying each other down until you—"

"Yeah, I remember." She rubbed her stomach. "Listen, I don't like it any more than anyone else."

"Hey," Holly said, putting a hand on her forearm. There was that tingle again. They locked eyes, and Holly smiled. "No-one is judging you here. If we were, you'd not be here."

Verity swallowed. "Sorry. I'm just antsy."

"I get that, I do," Holly said. "But they are *probably* on their way here right now, so what you thinking?" She gestured to the map again. "I know he's ripping the ley lines apart for something, I know he's messing with the city's life force. But why?"

"I think..." Verity closed her eyes. Thought of the Bridge of Sighs, with its thousands of invisible black ropes tied around it. Millions. One for every person who'd ever died in city limits. "That energy you were talking about, the twisted ley lines. That's life." She opened her eyes as she realised. "He's bringing life to the Necropolis."

Munro glowered. "We've just spent weeks talking about how it's not possible to bring back the dead."

"Not true life, they wouldn't be alive. They'd be like that heart." She looked to Roman. "Animated."

"Zombie vampires?" Roman quirked an eyebrow. "That's not—"

"No, not vampires. Millions of new bodies, tied to the Dark Scaffold. Under his control. They'd be walking bags of labour. Reliquaries to keep him fed. An entire underclass to live off. Like the homunculus."

"But why? This structure doesn't sound like it could take that kind of weight. And if he's already immortal, what does he get out of it?"

Verity swallowed. "If he can live on them, he'd not need to drink blood anymore." Of course. Of course he'd had the answer to Verity's problems right from the start. She thought of the homunculus, how it had gurgled, and turned to mulch as it rejected her. What would that look like, scaled up? What would be the experience of these reanimated creatures?

He'd said...

How is this monstrosity better? he'd said.

Her individual act had been a monstrosity. When he did it on industrial scale, it was just common sense.

"I don't think... Surely not," Roman said. "They would reject him, like the homunculus did."

"Would they?" Verity said. She tightened her fist until she could feel her bones strain to pop. "They'd probably reject each other before they could get to him."

"But why does he need you for this?" Roman asked. "He'll be—"

He fell silent.

There was a soft knock on the front door.

***

Verity stepped back, seeing the shadow on the frosted glass of the door. Holly stepped between them, holding her arms out.

"It's okay," Holly said. "We're safe. He can't come in."

The shadow ducked low, and the letter box popped open.

"Come on dear, let's not be silly about this," came that voice, slippery and firm at the same time. "Are you going to open the door?"

"No soliciting!" Bella shouted. She turned and added under his breath to Iona, "The defences are up, yeah?"

She nodded, summoning her broomstick and pointing the handle at the door like a spear.

"Oh, for goodness' sake," Breckenridge said. The letter box flipped shut.

They stared at the door, waiting for something to happen, waiting to see if their prayers would hold.

"This place is impregnable," Holly said. "No-one's ever gotten inside it."

"Why do I not feel reassured by your tone of voice?" Verity asked.

Holly swallowed. "I wasn't saying it to reassure you, I was saying it to reassure myself."

The door handle began to glow a bright orange, wriggle in its recess.

Iona stamped the broomstick down on the ground, where it stood straight of its own accord. "He's not getting through," she insisted, raising her arms. Light sigils began to paint themselves over the doors, chains forging to hold it shut. "You are *not* getting through!"

In response, the door buckled, ripped outwards, as he threw it across the plaza outside. They stood, face-to-face, Iona's golden chains latticing between them.

"You can't even come in if you're not invited!" Verity said. "That's rule one!"

"Rules, child, are for other people."

He put one foot through the lattice. His trousers burst into flame, his dress shoe melting, until his leg was slag. His face tensed as though he was pulling out a splinter, and he continued to push.

Iona screamed. "I can't hold it!"

Arabella waved her arms, and her pixie helpers appeared, scattering around the lattice, pulling it tight. Others hit him, shattering into dust as he continued to stagger through the barrier.

Iona fell to one knee, gripping the broom as it threatened to topple. Roman stepped up to her. "Come on hen, up you get!" He helped her up and threw his power behind helping Iona. "Munro!" he shouted.

Munro leapt forward over them, pouncing. She punched his face back as it pressed through the barrier, bending and melting. A left hook, then a right hook, before leaning back to kick him out—

The molten claw of a hand caught her foot. "Oh, you're all but gone, aren't you?" He grinned, bright white teeth in a burnt and cracked husk of a face, his eyeball shining bright orange like a piece of coal.

Realisation seemed to cross Munro's face. Shock. Hope? A smile.

She kicked her leg, breaking his grip. "You're right. I've got nothing left. You, on the other hand…" She gripped his face, tight, and suddenly in the hold of her hands he looked tiny, frail. The glow of the world lines lit up around them, and her eyes glazed over. He hissed, smoke pouring off the two of them as she drained *his* life force.

"Munro, don't!" Verity shouted. She moved between them, and broke the connection. Munro's hand was burnt black and charred. "It'll kill you, it's poison!"

Breckenridge laughed. Munro was zoned out, in another world. "Poison," he said. "Is that really what you think, my dear? After all this? Our life's blood? Our birthright?"

"Our birthright," Verity scoffed. "Grandfather, we have no birthright. Only a debt that will never come good." She grabbed a sharp chunk of wood from the door that had fallen on the ground, felt the wood burn against her skin. She placed it against his chest, looked deep into his eyes, and saw... nothing.

While they'd been talking, Iona, with a wave of her arms, had wrapped him in golden chains.

He smiled.

"Go on then," he said, calmly. "Do it."

She hesitated.

He blinked. "Do it."

A smile began to creep across his face.

Iona started to inch closer, holding the chains with her mind. "Verity, give me the stake. I'll do it."

"No," Verity said. She hadn't known if she'd actually have the strength, until that moment. Until she saw him smile about it.

She plunged it into his chest.

He screamed. Bucked. Writhed against the chains.

"I did it," she said. "I can't..."

Iona, still focusing on holding him down, grabbed her by the sleeve. Verity looked at her. Her hand was shaking, and she couldn't take her eyes from the chains, but she worked her way down from the sleeve and grabbed her hand, squeezed it tight. "Well done, petal."

He curled against the agony, silent.

"Wait, but you said..." Holly said.

And then... he smiled.

"Adorable."

He straightened, took a deep breath... and the stake turned to dust, the wound in his chest closing.

Iona gasped, throwing up a shield which shattered as he loosed some kind of blast. It threw them bodily across the room, hitting the wall and falling to the ground.

Verity stumbled to her feet.

"Munro!" Arabella shouted, rushing to her. She was still in her trance, unmoving, her body flickering like videotape.

Verity reared up, fangs bared—

"Wait!" Holly hissed, grabbing her hand. Verity turned, looked at her, face still contorted in rage. "I have an idea..."

***

Arabella slid to the ground by Munro's side. Her eyes were white, half-closed. "Munro?" she asked, hesitant, as the body was still flickering in and out.

She reached out a hand, worried she'd pass straight through. She'd never been so relieved to feel a shoulder. She pulled her close, pressing her head to her heart. "It's going to be okay," she said, manifesting. "It's going to be okay."

Munro stopped flickering. Still unconscious, but stable.

"I've got you. I'll be right back," she said.

She lay Munro down gently, and stood up. She was boiling over. She turned, and saw the Coven, barely on their feet. Breckenridge had shaken off the chains, in the centre of the room.

Good. She'd have the pleasure of kicking him out herself.

"He's reforming!" Iona shouted. She waved her arms, and a plume of incense followed her motion, rising from the censers and surrounding him. She lifted another stake from the table like it was a butcher's cleaver.

Roman was wrestling the cork off a bottle of holy water with his molars. "I got it, I got it!" he shouted, mouth full.

"For fuck's sake, Roman, just throw the whole thing!" Iona was swilling the incense; it grabbed at Breckenridge with its tendrils and tongues. She waded into it as it tried to hold him down, raising the stake—

He swung his head round, face still in burning pieces, and turned his gaze on her, sending her flying again.

"How the fuck is he doing all this?" Roman shouted. He hurled the bottle of holy water and it shattered on Breckenridge's chest. It burned, sizzled, and then evaporated.

Breckenridge smarted, as if it had been a flute of champagne on his best shirt. Then he turned on Roman.

Bella screamed, summoning her pixies and telling them to descend. *Descend like a cloud of locusts. Pick his skin clean. Even if it makes you sick. The Rule of Three. What pain he inflicts will return to him three times over. And she wasn't going to wait for the universe to do it for her.*

He swatted at them, hissing as they pecked and nibbled at him, before closing his eyes, and then Bella was hitting the wall—

Some kind of sound wave, had knocked her off her feet. Knocked them all over, scattered the pixies to dust. The room was spinning, she staggered to stand up—

Holly was scrabbling back. "How? How are you living off the ley lines?"

"What do you know about me, little witchling?" Breckenridge smirked. He was fully reformed now, not so much as a ruffled collar. He lifted Holly off the ground. "Where did you put her?"

"I'm telling you nothing, you pompous—" Holly said, but Breckenridge rolled his eyes and threw her to one side. He looked around.

"Oh…" he leaned over the table, at the plans. "You've managed to put a fair bit together in a short amount of time. I'm almost impressed…" He leaned further, and pounced.

Holding Verity by the scruff of her neck like a kitten, he tutted. "Really? You think I can't see through an invisibility spell?"

Verity scrabbled at her back, trying to reach his hand.

"Put her down!" Bella shouted. She focused herself, trying to ready another spell.

Breckenridge groaned. "I grow weary of this game." He snapped his fingers—

chapter 36

— Bella's ears were ringing.

For a second she couldn't see anything, only shapes. Shapes and light. She tried to move her head, but the world spun and her neck was heavy.

Eventually, she pushed herself up, and the world began to resolve. Flames. Flames and soot and plaster all around her. "Where are we?" she asked.

Roman was on his knees, bawling.

"What happened?" she said. "How long was I out?"

Iona had her hand on his shoulder. "Come on. I need your help with the others."

Bella stood, touching the sides and back of her head. No blood. That was good. She looked up, and saw the night sky above her. The moon watched them indifferently.

Her gaze came down, and she saw the plaza beyond Iona and Roman, beyond the wreckage. The same plaza they'd walked through every day on the way home.

She looked around. Among the rubble, the odd charcoal table leg, piece of banister, warped by heat and fire but recognisable all the same.

"What happened?"

"It's gone!" Roman wailed. "It was our home! It was the only place I'd ever—"

"It's only brick and mortar, Roman," Iona said, desperately.

"Please, I need your help." She looked up and saw Bella standing there, and breathed a sigh of relief. "Bella, he's gone, the others, they're—"

Bella spun back, a spike of adrenaline shooting through her. *Munro*. She tore off into the skeleton of the building.

It was Munro she found first. Crumpled against a wall, her eyes closed. Her body was fading like an old photograph.

She approached, reaching out, tried to catch her before she faded.

There was a loud, sustained groan from Bella's side, and she threw up a forcefield, standing between the noise and her love—

It was Verity. Her body was mangled by the half-ton of brick that had fallen on her. Even now though, she was knitting herself back together. She reached out with a stump of a hand and pushed the weight off herself as her fingers snapped back into their sockets.

Bella dropped the forcefield. "Are you okay? Do you need help?" She was reluctant to leave Munro's side.

"I'm good," Verity said. "Thanks to Munro. She shielded me. Shielded Holly. Jumped in the way."

"I think I missed that..." Bella said.

"You didn't miss much," Verity said. She tested her weight on her previously trapped leg, and limped over to Bella. "He ripped through us like we were nothing. It was witch magic. I don't know... I'd never seen..."

Bella kneeled down to Munro. "Not yet, babe. Not yet."

She could tell, she could feel the embers of Munro's life fading before her. This was the end.

She would give anything. She couldn't see through her tears.

"One more day..." she said. *"Just give me one more day with her."*

It would cost her everything, but she would pay it in a heartbeat.

She lifted Munro's cheek from the ground, saw her own fingers through the translucent skin, the bone. She pressed a kiss into her lips, and transferred the rest of her magic, the power that animated her.

She felt it go, felt herself panic as it left her, the deep reservoir of creativity and love she'd always had, so foundational she couldn't see it. It emptied out from under her. She tightened a fist, riding out the feeling, and smiled as she felt the heat return to Munro's cheek in her hand.

***

I am Munro Selkiefolk, and I have lived many lives.

In my first, I was a matriarch, the protector of my family. In the second, I was the consort of the most powerful witch in Elf-hame.

At first, I tried to integrate the two lives.

I was not successful.

We are all standing in the shallows, water up to our knees. Everyone is watching me. I have never felt so alone, them all standing facing me like a wall.

"Haar..."

"No," Haar says. The years have grizzled him, but his eyes still look like Snow's. I can still see them behind his leathery face, glittering like geodes.

"Please, let me just explain—"

"You've had years to explain, mother," Haar said. "And you would choose now?"

"I can't turn back time." His anger is usually a flash in the pan, this is new. He isn't thinking clearly.

"Maybe she can turn it back for you," Haar says. He nods into the ocean, into the mist. Keeping a respectful distance, they can all make out Nicnevin's silhouette in the cloud.

None of them can make eye contact with me. Cowards.

"Why is it so wrong?" I ask. "Don't I deserve some amount of happiness, after all this?"

He makes a move, like he's going to hit me. I flinch. Damn my reflexes, I flinch.

He withdraws. "Don't fucking talk to me about happiness," he said. "We buried my happiness with Snow."

This time, I make the move. I punch him.

Punch him right across the cheekbone, to make up for all the times I coddled him. How dare he. How dare he, of all people? "You—"

Even now, I can't blame him. He was only a child. We had told him not to go swimming in the currents. I must have wasted months daydreaming, that it had been me who had realised he'd gone, and not his brother. His attentive, quiet older brother, just old enough to feel responsible, and just young enough to think he could handle it by himself.

Haar blames me. He blames me, because it feels better than blaming himself.

I know that. I've always known that. But it doesn't make it hurt less.

Lily has begun to cry. She is straining against her mother's grasp, trying to get to her dad. He is ignoring the blood starting to bead at his cheekbone.

He takes Lily, strokes her hair with his free hand. "Hey, it's okay, wee pudding," he says, as she inspects his face. She turns to look at me, and she looks... terrified.

Something in me goes cold and hard in that moment, as I see Lily's tiny face contorted in fear and misery. There's no path forward with them now.

"I'll go," I say.

And I hang my head, turn, and walk into the mist, where Nicnevin is waiting for me.

I watch this happen, the end of my first life, and if I could only do it again, I'd fight. I'd scream and flail and thrash. I just let them cut me out. Hell, I cut myself out.

I strain and buckle against the memory, but it won't move. It's done. The choices were made long ago.

I wish... I'd been brave enough back at the house, to try to reach out to

Lily before she left.
I don't know if it would've worked.
Now, I suppose I never will.

***

Munro's eyes batted open, her big eyelashes like a baby lamb. She swallowed so she would have the moisture to speak. "Bella... you're alive. What happened?" Then she tensed, raring for Breckenridge to come out of a corner.

"He's gone," Verity said.

"Wait... but he can't be. He came for *you*," Munro said. She felt her stomach. "How am I...?"

Bella squirmed under Munro's gaze.

"Bella... what did you do?"

"Nothing," Bella said. "It's gonna be fine."

Munro's face contorted with sadness as she realised. "Why...?" She covered her face. "I didn't want you to do that. The cost..."

"I'm sorry," Bella said. "This was no place for you to die."

"Why does this always end up happening? Why do I have to watch the women I love wither and die to keep me alive?"

"I'm not going to *die*, Munro—"

"You don't know that!" Munro shouted, with a sudden and righteous fury that made Bella jump. She'd never heard her raise her voice like that before. "You don't, you don't know that."

"I'm sorry," Bella said. She would say it, over and over, but she'd do it again in a heartbeat. She tried not to think about how naked she felt without her magic. She couldn't feel the heartbeat in the breeze, or the tug of the moon, or the rolling of the seasons. She couldn't have told anyone she'd felt them before, but now that they were gone, their absence was deafening. And her heart broke, as she realised Munro probably felt like this all the time.

Munro looked at Verity. "I'm glad you're okay."

"Holly," Verity said.

"Where is she?" Bella asked.

"She's with him," Verity said, as the last of her wounds closed and her eyes fixed on them, black as pitch. "It was her final gambit."

***

It was different, connecting from this far away. It wasn't fuzzy, like Verity had expected. She wasn't in Holly's body, she floated above it.

"Are you okay?" she looked down at Holly, seeing her red hair through the raven black glamour that disguised her as Verity.

Holly stirred. *"For now."*

Verity pushed against the vision, trying to get a vantage point. Holly was in a cage, around it chalk circles drawn. Witch circles.

"I was right." Holly smiled. *"Whatever he's doing, he needs your mother and you. You're the final pieces."*

"He doesn't know he's grabbed the wrong person yet?"

"He was in a rush. I don't think he's looked at me twice since he threw me in here."

Verity felt her ghost move through this place like butter on a frying pan. *"He's creating his army alright. I can feel it. But what would it do if you're in that circle instead of me?"*

A sly grin cracked Holly's face. It was strange looking at the glamour — the complete stranger who looked back at her. *"You are gorgeous."*

"Shut up," Verity said. *"I'm trying to figure out what this thing will do to you."*

"Better come get me out then."

"Can't you break out yourself?"

"I was trying until you showed up," Holly said. *"Not without alerting him. And even I'm not thick enough to think I could take him in a one-on-one. Not after..."* she trailed off. *"Is everyone okay?"*

"They're alive. Not so sure about okay," Verity said.

"Tell them I love them."

"Why are you saying that like you don't expect to see them again?"

"I owe them my life," Holly said. *"My identity, my soul…"*

"What is it with everyone in this godforsaken house and throwing themselves on the pyre?" Verity hissed. *"Hang on, I'm going to find out where you are. Don't do anything daft."*

She floated silently out through the wall, and up, up, up. She breached white brick, finding herself—

Outside.

The sun was coming up over the park, its rays rising up the hill like the tide coming in. She felt it warm her skin, and two hundred years of learned behaviour kicked in as she started to panic, started to—

Nothing.

The sun's rays passed right through her astral form, warming her from the inside out. She took a deep breath and closed her eyes to enjoy it.

And then she let herself open her eyes to watch her first sunrise in two centuries.

After a few minutes, she heard Holly's voice, from a hundred feet under the ground. *"Well, where am I then?"*

"You're under the church tower. Looks like we found our lightning rod."

chapter 37

Roman was still in bits when Verity came out of the trance, blinking and groggy. The first thing she saw was him picking amongst the rubble between sobs, collecting shiny nothings like a grieving magpie.

They had moved her into the shade while she was out, and propped a parasol up just in case.

"Hey," she said. She wanted to move to embrace him, but she'd be chargrilled before she could. She could already feel the sun's fire turning its eye on her from here.

The impossibly tall, wiry older guy next door had come round with a brush and shovel that must have been symbolic more than anything — they were comically ill-equipped to do anything about the chaos around them. He was speaking to Iona in hushed tones, but Verity's vampire ears could hear everything.

"God, Iona, I don't even know what to say," he was looking around at everything, the enormity of it.

"It's like I told Roman, it's just bricks," Iona said. "We can worry about it later. We'll build it again."

"Will you?" the man said. "How?"

Iona was chewing her lower lip. "I don't know. Honestly Julian, I don't know. It was Connie that did it the first time."

The man gave Iona a hug. It was strange seeing Iona hug. Like watching a wolf walk on two legs.

"I'll be here to help," Julian said. "If you need somewhere to crash, if you need a pair of hands—"

"I appreciate it, old friend," Iona smiled. She rested a hand on his shoulder. She was a tall woman but she seemed to need to stand on her tiptoes to do it. Verity sensed there was magic at work. "But I think the first priority is to cut that vampire's head off."

Julian smiled a toothy grin. "Well, that I *can't* help you with. But I'll be here."

She nodded, before turning. "Witches!" she shouted. "Who's for a bit of revenge?"

"We're coming!" Arabella said. She and Munro emerged from the rubble. She was holding the canvas of a painting under her arm.

"Everyone over— oh. Yes." She saw Verity and realised she couldn't come out. She traipsed over. "Everyone over here!" Julian pottered off, leaving them to it.

Roman arrived, wiping his tears on his sleeve.

"This man has come into our home," she said. "He's taken our home from us, and now he's taken Holly. We have two advantages. One: He thinks either we're dead, or we'll be too busy licking our wounds to retaliate." She let it sit. "Two: He took Holly, but he needs Verity."

"I don't know if that's an advantage," Verity said. "I think if he does whatever he's doing, and Holly's still in my place, it'll kill her."

"Then time is even more of the essence," Iona said. "What did you find out? Were you able to speak with her?"

"She's under the church tower in Park Circus," Verity said. "You know, that one where it's just the tower standing by itself?"

Iona exhaled. "Okay. Then in that case—"

"There's... something else I should disclose," Bella said. "I've got no magic."

Iona furrowed her brow. "What?"

"I'm currently... binding Munro to the plane."

Iona paled. "I knew it. I knew it."

"Don't get mad—"

"I told you, you *ridiculous girl*—"

"Hey," Munro said, stepping between the two of them. "You need all the help you can get right now. And as... loath as I am to admit it, I am a big help."

"We have until sunset to prepare. He's not going anywhere until then." Verity chilled. It might possibly be the last sunrise Breckenridge would ever have to fear.

"I have... an idea. A way to even the odds," Bella said. "It occurred to me while I was getting this." She raised the canvas under her arm.

"What do you need?" Iona said.

"A few hours," Bella said.

Munro looked at her, puzzled. "I'm going with her."

"Okay. In that case, let's meet at the Bridge of Sighs come sunset," Iona said. "Roman, help me, I can't seem to summon Holly back but maybe if we..." She trailed off, taking Roman by the hand and leading him away.

Verity looked from them walking away, to Bella and Munro, from her little shaded spot.

"We gotta go," Bella said to Verity. "Good luck." She took Munro by the hand, and led them away.

She stood in her tiny island of darkness, with no idea what to do, feeling the shame and the fear rising in her—

"Verity!" shouted Iona, looking back over her shoulder.

"Yes?" She was shaken from her reverie.

"Don't just stand out there with your mouth open, you're catching flies." She tensed and a section of flooring lifted off the ground, until it was suspended over Verity's head, giving her a shaded path into the more enclosed section of the broken building.

She walked across the darkened path gingerly, breaching the distance between her and Iona.

"I wanted to apologise for what I said about you," Iona said.

"No, you don't need to apologise," Verity said.

"I do," Iona said. She put a hand on Verity's shoulder, and squeezed. "Welcome to the Coven of Merchant City."

"But I'm not even a witch."

"Welcome home, petal." And a crack in that icy exterior of hers showed. A smile.

Iona Howell had a heart after all, Verity thought. And she'd shared it with her?

"I don't... But you're like a family. I've never had a family before, not a real one."

"Like I said." Iona smiled. "Welcome home."

***

Arabella was taking the streets with considerable pace, considering she was lugging that big painting under her arm.

"Where are we going?" Munro said.

"You know where we're going."

"And why are you carrying that around like that?" Munro tried to take it, but Bella was a woman on a mission, and wouldn't stop to let her.

Night In Ullapool, it was called. It depicted a night in Ullapool. She was never particularly imaginative with the names. She'd lain on the bank of Loch Broom and watched the stars. That had been before Bella's grandparents had probably been born.

"Bella. Stop."

Bella stopped. Finally. She was shaking.

Munro crossed in front of her, and gave her a hug.

"I love you," Bella said.

"I love you too." Munro finally prised the painting from Bella's hands, and looked at it. "I don't even like this one."

"You don't?"

"I mean, it's fine. It's just... another painting. I did it in an afternoon."

"I'm going to get more if we have time. There's so much damage in there, so many of them are broken. I just figured they would start to deteriorate if they were left out in the dust and the rain, and I wanted to start with a big one. I can go back, I can—"

"We have a vampire patriarch going to kill us in eight hours, and you're busy saving my scribblings that I do for fun?"

"I can do both, I can multitask, okay!" Bella said.

"These are worthless, babes."

"Not to me! And if you really are..." She took the painting back. "If you're not gonna be around..." She still couldn't say the word. "They're all that'll be left of you."

Munro looked at the painting like it wasn't worth what Bella was valuing it. "I didn't think of that, I guess."

They kissed. It wasn't a pretty kiss, wet as it was with their tears.

They pulled apart. Bella pressed her forehead to Munro in their embrace. "I still don't understand why you did it."

"Did what?" Munro said.

"Gave up that life energy," Bella said. "I respect your choice, but... I don't understand why. It's such a risk, and, and now you only have a day."

"Bella. Look around us. Nothing is stable. Everything is a risk. All of this could collapse around our heads at any moment."

"Exactly! So why roll the dice?"

"Because if everything could fall over at any time, I can't waste all my time hunting for stability! I need a stronger compass than that. I have to do what I think is right. Or what's the point?"

"Us. What we have. It's more important. It's more important than anything. You're safe here, with us."

Munro took her hands. "I'm sorry. I need you to understand this though. Because when I'm gone—"

"Don't," Bella said. She was shivering. "Don't say that."

"When I'm *gone*," Munro insisted. "You're going to have to rebuild everything."

"No." Bella shook her head. "No. I can't. I couldn't."

"Everything ends, Bella," Munro said. "Happy endings, sad endings, they're all just endings. If you let your compass guide you, you'll be able to guide yourself to the next safe harbour."

"Don't talk like that, Munro. You're not going anywhere, not yet, we still have time."

"We don't," Munro said. "We have one day." She used the back of her hand to wipe her tears away, before taking her furs off and wrapping them around Bella. "And it's gonna be a good day! We're gonna kill this guy!" She held her tight. "The universe is a horrible place, especially for people like us. Everything ends, and it's arbitrary, and it's cruel. But I've always rebuilt. And you can too."

"Stop talking like this."

"I think the—" Munro stopped, overcome. "I think the saddest thing is that I don't know what you're gonna do next. I'm so sad I don't get to see your next joy."

Bella's knees gave out, and she dropped. "There isn't any. We're all we have. Roman, Holly, Iona, and you." She sputtered, like a guttering car engine.

"I want you to promise me," Munro said, sitting so she could grip Bella in a hug, "I want you to promise me, that when this collapses, when I'm gone, you won't let it take you with it."

"I can't, I—"

"Promise me, Bella."

"I love you."

"I love you," Munro said. "Now promise me."

Bella wailed into her sleeve. Munro's touch felt cold, distant. Like it was already gone. Like everything she'd built for herself was already crumbled, and she was a scared little girl again, sitting at a bus stop with a hastily-packed suitcase, knowing she was never going to see her parents again.

She looked in that pit, for the diamond Connie always said formed under pressure. The piece of her that said to grow, despite everything. But she'd only powered that feeling with pride, or spite, or anger.

She would simply have to find another way.

"I promise."

***

Bella had put the painting on the kitchen table back in the flat, and spent too long staring at it, as if it would fall if left unobserved for even a moment.

Munro was staring out the window, watching the cars drive past. "Are you sure this is a good idea?"

"No idea, but it's the only card I've got left to play, so I'm gonna play it."

She took Bella's hand. "Then let's play." And they left.

The Bridge to Nowhere was empty. She felt nothing, standing at the crossroads, even while people were walking past, while cars zipped to and fro along the motorway. It put a pit in her stomach. Before, she'd been able to feel the occult thrum, even in the middle of the night, when the roads were quiet and the Clyde was busy blowing all the dust and exhaust out to sea. Suddenly, she wondered if he'd even show up for her now.

But she needn't have worried.

"Well, well, well! Looks like Ms. Thing's lost her magic!" Preston leaned against a bollard like a discarded rake. "How *embarrassing*. God, that looks like it must be sore, having it sucked out of you like that."

Bella spoke with gritted teeth. "It was better than the alternative."

"Don't I know it, sister. My whole business is 'better than the alternative'." He stepped towards them, and she felt Munro hovering over them. He was in the driver's seat now, and he knew it. "So what can I do for you?"

"The dead of this city are about to climb out their cots," Arabella said. "I want your help to stop them."

He whistled through his teeth like a mechanic pricing a repair to some old clunker. "That's big magic."

"It is," Bella said. "But this is bending every ley line, every law of nature. Your little patch won't be unaffected. I'm assuming you'll take that into account with the price."

He grinned, sparkling white teeth. He raised a hand, and a scroll and quill appeared. "Let's draft a contract."

chapter 38

Park Circus is built in circles. It's in the name — the 'circus', the disc. Three concentric circles of streets, a pristine circuit of sandstone and brick, glittering on the hilltop.

And right at the entry point, is a huge white tower with no purpose other than to be there — an ornament on the most ostentatious wealth in the already ostentatious West End.

It was originally part of a church, built in the 1850s. Park Parish Church stood untouched for a hundred years, ownership passing from the diocese to the Church College.

Over the decades, the parishioners began to file out, finding other things to do with their Sundays, until it was eventually demolished in the 1960s to create a block of flats.

With one exception.

The church tower, viewed as an 'essential part of the skyline', was kept. The entire church was painstakingly demolished by hand, all so the tower could be preserved. Now painted white, it still stands today, a bleached lily in a field of sandstone.

Without context, without purpose. A head on a spike.

One wonders just why it was so vital.

***

Verity watched Iona draw chalk on the Bridge of Sighs. Roman had been dispatched to divert people away with magic. It was a wide space, no pavement, just tarmac, and it was proving a large, slow canvas.

She busied herself watching the movement of the sun over the hill, trying to work out when it would be safe to come out from the shade.

Iona looked up from what she was doing as she got close to Verity, off to one side, huddled under the shade of the tree. "Oh. Sorry, could you—"

Verity shuffled around the edge as Iona drew under her feet. At one point, she moved, just a little too quickly, and Iona flinched.

"Sorry," Verity said.

"No. No. It's not you," Iona said.

"It is," Verity said. "But that's fine. Or... not fine. But—"

"I wish there could've been another way." Iona was looking at the chalk in her hands. "It doesn't make me feel good to admit it. I'd have been happy to let you rot in that house, just so I didn't have to think about it." She took a deep breath. "It's unbecoming. It's not how I was raised."

"If it helps..." Verity said. "I spent my whole life afraid of them. So I don't think it's shameful."

Iona looked at her, like she couldn't even begin to formulate a response.

"Sorry," Verity said.

Iona looked over the hill. "Do you think it's dark enough yet?"

Verity looked at the space between them. "One way to find out." This moment, the twilight, was always the most risky — but in that moment, the separation was excruciating. She didn't want to be on her own anymore.

She reached out her hand to Iona, feeling for the telltale prickling of the skin that preceded her arm bursting into flame.

But it never came.

She took a deep breath, and stumbled out, crossing the distance between them, almost tumbling into her.

If everything went to plan, that would be the last time she'd have to fear the sun. Her eyes stung as her resolve tensed. She gripped the stake she'd been keeping in her belt.

"It's okay," Iona said. She touched her arm, so softly, like a whisper.

"It's not," Verity said. "They say time heals all wounds, but not this one." She was trying not to cry. "It's infected. Every day I hate myself just a little more."

Iona chewed her teeth, uncomfortable. "It's not your fault. None of this was your fault."

"No, but it's my responsibility." Verity said, and she was able to steady herself. "And sometimes that's the same thing."

Iona sighed. "I am sad I couldn't know you longer, Verity."

"Me too," Verity smiled. "I've only known *myself* since meeting you." It seemed so chronically unfair that she could live forever, passive and complicit, or she could die, instantly and in agony. There was no in-between, no compromise.

"Here, help me," Iona said, picking up and passing her the basket of chalks and her broomstick. She seemed to sense the silence and wanted to fill it with something that didn't require speech.

"Is there anything else I can do?" Verity asked, relegated to carrying something that had previously been sitting on the floor. "What is this for?" She looked at Iona's sigils. Looping, concentric art that wrapped the bridge like ivy.

"It's a barrier. He's warped the ley line, he's trying to steal its power. But he can't access it directly, because he's a vampire. He has no connection to it. So he's pouring it into your Scaffold."

Verity looked at the art again, tried to imagine the witches' art like a blanket over the bridge, the keystone.

"If I can insulate it," Iona said, "It might stop his trick from working."

"That sounds like a temporary measure."

"It is," Iona said. "But if he's planning this ritual, if he's going to widen that channel... If he opens his veins to let it in and there's nothing coming through..."

"I might have a shot at killing him," Verity said.

"Well. I was going to say *we'll* have a shot. But yes."

The more Verity looked at the tapestry Iona was drawing, the more sense it made. The pattern she hadn't finished, Verity could see where the lines would be parallel, where they would be convergent. "I think you're right. It will make him vulnerable."

She remembered Breckenridge, painting the family tree. How he had lavished care and attention on it, how one day, a branch of the names he had spent sacred time painting had burst into flames. How she had been told to forget that name. How the way he had said it made them sound like sinners. That tree was everything. Pruned and tended like a garden. At the time, she had been too afraid of being the next person who disappeared, to think about how fragile it must be, if it needed such a tender hand.

"What are you doing?" Iona asked.

She looked down. She'd taken the chalk, without thinking, and begun to finish the lines. Parallel lines never to meet, brought into convergence. Seventeen runes in a circle with the largest oriented east so it would catch the sunlight first. Concentric information, truth nested in truth nested in truth.

As above, so below.

On Earth, as it is in heaven.

"... I don't know." She looked at the hand like it had betrayed her, the chalk dust coating her fingers. "I just..." She pointed at the circle she'd drawn, the symbols. "Finished the pattern."

Iona was looking at her with a suspicious eyebrow.

"How did I...?" Verity said, looking at the sigils she'd drawn. She had never seen them before in her life. "I don't understand."

"I'm beginning to." Iona took the chalk from her, and continued the pattern. "Burying a thought. Burying magic. It always, *always* makes it louder. You really are just like Holly."

"What are you talking about?"

"There are a million vampires in the world, he has all this lineage. But you and your mother, are the ones he keeps close. The ones he's pulled into this ritual. Why? Why does he need you specifically?"

"I always thought…" Verity's mouth was coppery. "It was because I was the weakest. Because I had the least will. And my mother, she loves him. Against all reason."

"I don't think that's it…" Iona said. She buried her head in her hands. "It doesn't make any sense. He has a needle in the ley line, all of this life energy, tapping its power, and he can't access it…" She rubbed her eyes and groaned. "I can't see the whole design."

Then, she straightened her back, took a deep breath, and went back to work.

"Wait, but—" Verity said.

"It's not the way I would do it, but it works," Iona said, looking at the part Verity had drawn. "Make yourself useful, help me cover that pillar." She gestured up.

And it was then, she got it. The way Iona worked. There was more going on over their heads, always more, a tumbling maelstrom of chaos. But before them, was the work they could do. The craft.

There was always work that could be done.

"Yes, ma'am," Verity said, and she took her chalk in hand.

***

"How's it goin', hen?" Holly asked, still in Verity-guise, languishing in the bottom of the cage. "It's starting to feel a bit… claustrophobic in here."

"Not long now," Verity said. Mentally, she put her hand on Holly's

shoulder, felt the warmth despite the distance between them. *"Iona has a plan."*

Holly laughed. It sounded like a bark. "Iona always has a plan."

She said the next bit quietly so Iona couldn't hear, standing a hundred feet away, at the base of the Bridge of Sighs. *"Do they always feel like they're clutching at straws?"*

She felt her skin tickle with Holly's mirth. "Only the best ones."

She looked up at the orange band along the horizon, coating the entire city in the warmth of sunset. The heat was starting to come back out of the ground.

"You know, in the Mediterranean I bet vampires probably get fried even in the shade."

"I thought frying things was one of our *specialties, dearest,"* Verity said, voice dripping with sarcasm.

"Op. Something's happening here. Stay safe, I'll see you later," Holly whispered.

Verity didn't reply, just in case he could hear it somehow. She ran up the Bridge of Sighs, to help Iona with her chalk circles.

"What can I do?"

Iona put her hand up, scanning her work like exam questions before handing them in. "No. I think we're done." She took a deep, juddering breath. "I'll be honest, petal. I don't think we're going to get out of this one."

"Holly's in there," Verity said. "Have faith. I think it might be your turn to trust me."

Iona smiled. "Hell mend us." Then she looked over her shoulder. "Where on earth have you been?" she shouted.

Verity spun. It was Roman, wielding a thin blue plastic carrier bag and a bottle of wine under his arm.

"Am I fuck dying on an empty stomach." He put the bag down as he reached them, the smell of grease and fat and starch wafting into the night. "Or sober, at that." He thrust the bottle into Verity's hands so he could rummage. He was doing a good job of hiding it, but his makeup was running. Thick, wet tracks of foundation and tears down his face like war paint.

He dove into the bag, handing Iona a steaming paper package as he excavated it and a few bunched-up plastic cups. "Gies, gies," he said, almost rabid, gesturing to the bottle in Verity's hands. It flew back as though he'd sucked it back on a yo-yo string. The cap screwed off by itself, vanishing off into the dark like a frisbee, as he started filling the cups. Wine spilled around the outside as they rattled, the liquid weighing more than the container.

Verity thought better of asking if they should be drinking before doing this. Roman was right. If not now, when.

He unwrapped another paper bag and started tucking into a sausage supper, washing it down with wine. He groaned. "Man, I just realised I haven't eaten all day."

"It's funny how you just forget to, isn't it..." Iona said, quietly. She nibbled at the roll and fritter in the paper in her hands. The carbs seemed to give her an energy spike because she started to well up.

Roman patted the ground next to him. "Sit down, missus."

She did. Plonked herself down, her dress splayed around her. She ate, with huge, hungry bites, like she was trying to fill some hole inside her.

"You were right..." she said, mouth brimming with potato and tears running down her face. "It was a good idea to get food."

Roman laughed. He eyed her handiwork on the bridge. "Ooh, okay," he said, cocking an eyebrow. "That could work."

"It was the only thing I could think of," Iona said.

"Someone would still need to kill him though," Roman said.

"Don't—" Iona said. "I can't think about it while I'm eating." She had been deflating like a soufflé since the first bite had crossed her lips.

"Mm, too right," Roman said. He fished in the bag again. "Do you want—?" he looked up to Verity, who was still standing.

Verity shook her head. "I can't."

"Mm, fair enough," Roman said. Then his gaze fell on the wine bottle. "I mean... it's also a red liquid." He held it up.

Verity laughed. She paused, considered it.

"Sure. Why not."

"Eyyyy," Roman grinned. He hunted for another cup. "Ach, fuck it, use mine." He passed it up.

She drank. It was bitter, thick. It coated her lips and her teeth, but she could taste the grapes. Feel herself lying in the vineyard, watching the world go by.

"It's good." She passed it back.

"I mean, it's the best you can get for a fiver." He grinned.

"Hours from death and you didn't splash out?" Iona asked.

"I feel like if you spend a tenner on a bottle of wine, you've already lost, to be honest."

"Oh, I don't know about that," Iona said. She smiled, secretly. Like she was remembering something nice.

"What's this, the Last Supper?" They turned to see Munro, traipsing towards them. "Bella said you would be here."

"Where is she?" Roman asked.

"Finishing up. She'll be here," Munro promised. She took a deep breath, and tried to force herself to lower her shoulders. With her back straightened she towered over them all. "I'm not going down like that again."

"We got this," Roman said. "Here, have some—"

She took the bottle from him before he could finish the sentence and necked it. It ran down her face, dripping down her clavicle and into her selkie furs. She stopped when she needed air, wiping her face with the back of her hand and closing her eyes to soak in the light of the moon behind her, just peeking through the pink and purple.

She handed the bottle back to Roman. "Thanks," she said, getting into the zone.

Roman couldn't hide the fact that he was pissed off about how little was left in the bottle now. "No worries…"

"How long have we got?" Munro said.

"Not long." Verity could already feel the grass around them tickling. Like underneath the soil, thousands of follicles were waiting to sprout. And as the last kiss of the sun whispered away behind the horizon, Verity felt the whole earth quiver. Like someone had just walked over every grave. "It's starting."

***

"What's going on?" Verity asked. "Are you okay?"

"Uhhh…" Holly was standing now, as the ground around her began to sweat ectoplasm through the floor. "Yeah, not feeling this."

Verity could feel it. The Scaffold, groaning. Creaking as its limits were tested. The entire structure opened in her mind's eye. Her stomach turned like the ground she was standing on was being thrown.

She could see her mother. Under the old school. No cage for her, but a similar room. She looked… sad. Like she didn't want to be there either, but she'd made her mind up.

"Mother!" she shouted.

Mother put a finger to her lips like Verity was interrupting. "Your grandfather is speaking."

She could see him as well. Emerging from a crypt in the Necropolis, rising into the night sky. He could fly?

She could see it in real life too, off in the distance. The dual perspective was making her nauseous. Or maybe that was just him.

He spoke to the whole Necropolis. *"We are one.*

Your flesh, is my flesh.

Your work, is my work.
Your life, is my life.
I take this, for you.
Take this, in memory of me."
"More witch magic?" Holly shouted. "Where is he getting this from?"
Breckenridge... twitched. "What is she doing in here with us?"
"I let her in." Verity clenched her fists.

"Wait." And for the first time Verity could remember, confusion crossed Breckenridge's face. *"You're supposed to be in the—"* She flinched, as she felt his gaze descend on her.

"Yoo hoo!" Holly grinned. She was hanging on the cage like a jungle gym now to stop her feet from touching the slime filling the room. She waved a hand in front of her face, and the glamour vanished. *"Remember me?"*

"That's not... Get out of there!"
"Gladly," Holly said.
And then there was fire.
Fire and smoke and glee.
"You hurt my friends," she said, deep in Breckenridge's head. *"And I was too busy trying to be a wee wide-o with a switcheroo to stop you."*

Verity's heart swelled as she felt it. The incandescent joy of Holly Winter, in her power, bringing an entire building down.

The blue vein on Breckenridge's temple quirked, as she tumbled across the Glasgow sky like a comet, a tail of fire streaking behind her.

She touched down on the Bridge of Sighs as Breckenridge floated up to them. Her eyes and clothes still caught with flame. "How d'you like that, bawjaws?" She cracked her fingers like a pianist. "Everyone okay?" she asked quietly to Iona.

"You irritating little wasp," Breckenridge said.
"Who you calling a wasp? Wasp," Holly said.
Breckenridge made to speak, but stumbled. For a moment he

almost fell out of the air, but caught himself. "The spell."

"Yeah. Doesn't work so well when you put the *wrong person in the fucking cage, does it?*" Holly stuck her middle fingers up. "You really should keep a better eye on your hostages."

"And yet, you brought her here," Breckenridge said, drolly. "The Bridge of Sighs, the exact gateway point. You're not the sharpest tool in the shed, are you?"

"No." Holly growled. "I'm the sledgehammer." She clapped her hands together, and Breckenridge burst into flames.

"That's my line," Munro growled. She took a running jump, and leapt, easily ten foot in the air, grappling him and trying to pull him down. The flames licked at her furs.

"Holly," Verity said, as she looked around the Bridge.

Hundreds of black tendrils were starting to creep round the edges, like troll fingers. Verity arched her back, swiping at them and hissing, retreating. They needed her to complete the circuit. But why? *Why?*

Iona summoned her broomstick. "Roman! The seal!" The two of them circled each other, and the runes they'd drawn on the bridge lit up. A protective circle opened on the bridge, extending out into the air. Breckenridge was pushed back, pulling Munro with him. The shadowy tendrils screeched as they sizzled and vanished, already creeping back in, searching for a way in like moss on brick.

Breckenridge laughed, cackled despite himself as Munro hung onto him for dear life. "It's too late, you silly girl! You're only delaying the inevitable!"

And he was right. She knew he was right, because she was on the Dark Scaffold too.

The ground under them wriggled as fifty thousand of the city's lost stirred, and reached for the surface. The Necropolis was about to burst its banks.

The city was bringing out their dead.

chapter 39

It started slow. Like waking up from a long rest. Or the aura before a migraine. First, a low whine in the back of her neck. Then, the eye sockets. And then, all at once, the dizziness.

She could see them. "The spell worked!" she tried to shout, but her mouth was slurring her words.

Holly lit a ring of fire around her to stop the tendrils' advance, but even now she was stumbling to the ground. "Verity!"

Verity didn't have the strength to answer, her whole body was limp. Something was draining her, taking her essence, and using it...

She could see, in some third eye, the first hands begin to breach the surface.

The first gravestones began to tip backwards and collapse as their foundations were moved. "They're powered by... me?"

"By all of us," Breckenridge said. *"They'll give us a better life. No silver, no garlic, no ray of sun..."*

"We already have a better life than we deserve," Verity said.

"It's a small price to pay, Verity. They were dead. Their resources were just sitting there."

The anger rising in her was making her more dizzy, more queasy, but that was just pushing her harder. She pushed herself up so her arms took her weight. "Their resources?" she spat. "They're human beings! Can't they even get peace after they die?"

"What a senseless waste that would be," Breckenridge said. He had

successfully shaken Munro off now, and was rising higher and higher into the sky.

She noticed he didn't seem to be suffering the same ill effects she was.

Munro screamed as she dropped, and Verity gasped, watching her tumble towards the ground.

And then, she stopped. In mid-air. Like a massive invisible hand had caught her.

"Sorry I'm late," a voice said into the night. A voice she recognised. *"I brought backup."*

Arabella, floating on another broomstick, swarmed by a million golden pixies.

"Look who got her groove back..." Holly grinned.

"I don't... but where?" Iona asked.

"Nowhere," said Bella and Munro in unison.

"Never mind that, he's getting away!" Verity shouted, gesticulating at the sky. She could still barely sit up, let alone fight.

"What's wrong with you?" Roman said, as he tried lifting Verity to her feet. "The vapours, bitch? Get up!"

"He's done something to me... to all of us," Verity said.

"I understand now. I understand all of it," Holly said, and her voice rumbled with mania. "Verity... you said you have no memory of being a human?"

"None. It's part of the process that turns y—" Through her stupor, she suddenly had the time to process that before she said it. "Breckenridge always said vampires have no memory of their previous lives."

"You. And your mum. The Dark Scaffold has all these vampires on it, but you're the ones who are important to him. And he's got you wrapped around those ley lines like a fuckin' knot. Even though no vampire can access the ley lines directly," Holly said. "But a *witch* could."

Verity could feel the entire weight of the scaffold on her, the power of the ley lines dragging on her like the tide. "We... we were witches?"

"He didn't want just anyone as family. He needed witches." Holly's hands were burning, her steps setting fire to the earth as she moved. "That's how we couldn't stake him. You two give him direct access to all the magical energy in the city. This bastard has been sucking us dry, and now, he wants even more."

"Thousands of homunculi." Roman was blinking like a fish. "Just one was enough to keep you alive."

"I was worried about a treaty," Iona said. She was very cold, and very still, and it gave Verity the creeps. "I was worried about a treaty, and he was turning our sisters? He was lifting them out of their graves?"

"How much backup did you get?" Holly said, to Arabella.

"A lot." Now that they were up close, Verity could see it. She was glowing like the fey, all gilded and gold and glittering. "I don't know how long I've got it for, but it's—" She made a chef's kiss and a shower of sparks burst from her mouth. "Oops."

"I'm not going to think about what you're going to end up paying for that..." Iona said.

"Who cares, look at her!" Roman grinned. "Let's just drop a nuke on him and go!"

"It won't work," Iona said. She looked. The tendrils were creeping in. The seal was beginning to flicker and gutter like an old bulb. The first of the shambling horde had made its way down the hill to them, back up the Bridge of Sighs, the wrong way round. "Every single one of those things is keeping him alive now, like your homunculus. How do we lay to rest so many lost souls...?"

"They're not lost," Verity said. "They're in bondage." She retched, her body juddering. "I can feel them. Their misery..."

"It's going to be okay." Holly moved to help Verity up.

"Where the hell is he going?" Roman looked up, trying to make

Breckenridge out in the darkness and failing.

"To get a better view of his new world," Iona said.

"No," Verity said, feeling his mirth herself in the back of her head. "He's taking a run-up."

***

With the power of a million dead things, Breckenridge struck like a comet.

Even seeing it coming, their seal was never going to last. The Bridge of Sighs buckled, groaned. They were sent scattering, the shadows rowdy and restless — and then came the horde.

There was a moment, after the strike, where Verity's head cleared enough for her to get up.

"Come on, Holly." She shook her.

Holly blinked, groggily. "Shit, shit! Sorry!" She jumped up as Verity checked the others were able to get to their feet.

Breckenridge was inspecting his nail beds. One of his drones started to walk towards them, but he held a hand up — gently, ever so gently. It obeyed without question. "I think you're beginning to understand your situation. I'm not unreasonable."

"That's how it always starts," Verity spat. "How you always start. With the platitudes, and the fake concern, and the tut tut tutting, and the pretend patience. Until you've convinced me that everything I've ever thought was wrong."

"Verity, dear. This is a family issue. Let's not have this ugliness in front of our guests. We can discuss your grievances later."

"No!" Verity said. "You took my life from me. You wiped *everything* from me. You're harvesting our dead, for your own benefit—"

"For *your* benefit too, my love. Or are you not a part of this family?"

"I don't, want it!" Verity said. The nausea was starting to come back, and she fell to her knees. "What is... what is going on with me?"

"Bit of an adjustment period, I think," he said, laughing, to the witches, as though Verity was a little girl who had peed on his rug. "Come along, dear."

"No!" Verity swiped at him. "Stop trying to take me away from everyone else!" She clutched her head as a wave of pain and suffering swept her body away like it was at sea.

Holly adjusted her weight to hold Verity up. "Here, I don't want to give you the wrong idea, Breckenridge," she said. "I think you're a twat, and I am always gonna think you're a twat. So we can stop with the lah-de-dahs of it all. But one thing I don't get. Why isn't this happening to you as well?" She gestured with her chin to Verity, who was all but convulsing. "If this is some grand sacrifice you're all making for the benefit of vampires?"

Breckenridge grinned, held his hands up. "I'm just older. Had longer to get used to it."

"Wow," Munro said. "Verity made you sound like some master manipulator but that was the most shit lie I've ever seen."

"I'm not lying!" He guffawed. "Good lord, you're all paranoid, aren't you?" He looked between them, smiling as if they weren't all closing on him like a pack of wolves. They looked at each other, all seemingly working it out in unison.

"There was a moment where I was fine. And it was right after you put a big dent in the Bridge of Sighs," Verity said.

Bella stepped forward, gold dust falling off her as she walked. "You've built some huge pyramid and put yourself at the top."

"Don't be silly." Again Breckenridge was laughing, as if they were going to just turn around and leave the army of zombies, come round to his way of thinking. "Not at all, it's just—"

"It's those poor dead people on the bottom in mindless servitude, and then the witches you harvested as 'family' in constant pain to keep this running," Bella said. "And then, you."

Breckenridge's face darkened. "Okay, I've had enough of this. If you're going to make threats, you'd best be able to back them up."

"Oh!" Holly said, in mock surprise. Shock! Disbelief! "Threats? *Threats?* We're just trying to understand, Breckenridge! We must simply all be paranoid, absolutely losing our marbles! We're all just being irrational!"

"Okay, I'm tired of these games," Breckenridge said. He waved a hand. "Kill them."

Behind him, a wave of bodies began to charge.

"Yeah, you really shouldn't have let us know about that big weak point in your whole structure," Holly said. She raised her hands, feeling the ground around her, and the entire bridge began to shake.

He stumbled, looking more confused than anything else. The zombies however, stopped where they were. For a moment, it was like they'd remembered they were inanimate. And when that moment of realisation was over, they started to fall—

"That's a fancy trick," Breckenridge said. He nodded, pointing out Verity, now shivering on the floor. "But look what you're doing to your so-called friend."

"He's lying..." Verity said. "It's him that's doing it. It's not you."

Holly hesitated.

Breckenridge smirked. "Funny how the tables turn, the wheel spins, and everything comes around again. Wasn't it *you* who was just telling me what a horrible person I was? You hypocrite, you're hurting my granddaughter."

"Don't put fucking words in my mou—"

"Holly," Bella said. She looked at Verity, who was trying to get to her feet.

"Verity!" She grabbed her, held her up.

"You have to do it," Verity said, seriously.

"I can't hurt you," Holly whispered.

"Holly. He's doing it again." How funny it was, now that Breckenridge had finally let her in his head, that he was so easy. He had one move. Blackmail.

Holly opened her mouth.

"You're thinking she's lying to keep you safe." Breckenridge smiled. "You're right. She is."

Verity smiled.

Holly grinned.

"Mate. Do you think I would trust *you* before her?" She gave Bella a thumbs-up. "Bella, let's do this!"

Energy transferred between the two of them, bursting where they met like a far-off quasar. Everyone else was blown back, as it seemed to swallow the Bridge of Sighs around them like a burning hole in a photograph, growing outwards, outwards...

Breckenridge was screaming, as the black tendrils were severed. Whatever this was, it was doing the business. The most powerful witch of a generation, and whatever Bella had taken from the Bridge to Nowhere...

Breckenridge was screaming, and—

No. That wasn't screaming.

"You're just making it stronger! Anything you do, it just assimilates!" He was laughing.

But Verity could think again. With the zombies at bay and this pressure on the wound, she could think. She could act.

Beside her were Iona and Roman's unconscious bodies. She picked up Iona's stake, and charged.

He was still laughing so hard he didn't see her coming. There was a scuffle, and they fell into the black hole.

chapter 40

When Verity came to, she wasn't on the bridge anymore. At least, she didn't seem to be.

Everything around her was dim, dark, some grey gel filling the cracks of everything. Breckenridge was standing over her, watching her dispassionately. "Well done."

"What is this place?"

"We're inside the Dark Scaffold," Breckenridge said. "I haven't been here since…" He cracked his neck.

"It's a real place? It exists in space?"

He didn't answer.

"Wait, so that's it? It's over?" she said. "Are we trapped here?"

"No," Breckenridge said. "There's always a way out. I just wanted, what I have been asking for from the very beginning my girl. To speak to you, *alone*."

"What's the point?" Verity said. "You're just going to tell me I need to think of the greater good, which seems to just mean 'your best interests'. I'm going to disagree, and then we'll be at each other's throats again."

"We're immortals, Verity. When one is immortal, one must be very careful before holding a grudge." He sighed. "What if… I could offer you what you want?"

She looked up at him. "What?"

"Join me. At the top of the Scaffold. With the drones doing the dirty work, and the other vampires dealing with their little headaches. We could have it all. Real life. Forever life. No death in the sun. No *need for* blood-drinking..." He took her hand, and she batted it away.

"Are you joking?" Verity said. "If you think I would accept that, you don't know me at all."

"You're so short-sighted. Always thinking of the... little people. But don't you see? If you were at the top, you'd be free! You'd be making the rules! And the people that make the rules, don't have to follow them."

She screamed at him. He flinched. "Why don't you just take the mask off?" she said. "Why do you pretend everything you do is inevitable? That your cruelty is just the way the world works."

He scoffed.

"You do! You've done it my whole life! You've weaselled your way into my head from the day you woke me up on that stupid rock! I don't know who I am when you're not whispering in the back of my head!"

"You're a child! And you're to shut up and sit down!" he barked.

She fizzed. Finally, the quiet part, spoken out loud.

"You're always so fucking ungrateful, spitting it back in my face. I gave you life! Your mother and I gave you life! And you're acting like I cursed you. Well, if you need to know how the world works, there it is! I'm in charge! I rule this world, from morning to night. And if you want my spot? If you want my life? You come, and you take it from me! And if you can't, then you *do as you are told*."

She swallowed. She looked at her feet. For a moment, she was almost tempted to acquiesce. She was so tired. And then, she saw under her feet, in the grey and the black and the dirt and the wood and the tubing.

A puddle.

And for the first time in two centuries, it had Verity's face in it.

She watched realisation dawn on her reflection's face. So *that* was what she looked like.

Not a description.

Not a drawing.

Not through someone else's eyes.

She pressed her free hand to her face, the other hand limp with the stake. Pressing it, and watching it change as she did.

This was a completely different woman.

"You didn't give me life," she said. The memories. It was all coming back now. Now, on the other side of the Scaffold, where they were just people. "You took it."

"What?" he said, absently, like she was an annoying fly.

"You took my life."

Breckenridge looked at her.

"You pushed me off that cliff. How many witches have you killed to build that new Scaffold?"

He spread that grin like butter. "Oh, come on. Now you're just being—"

"What?" Verity said. "*Irrational?*"

Breckenridge stepped back, raising a hand. Suddenly realising all his power was on the other side of the portal that had dropped them here. Here, they were just people. Here, they were mortal. "Verity. I know you're angry. But if we can't discuss this like adults…"

"What was my name?" Verity asked.

"What?"

"My *name*, Breckenridge!" Verity shouted. "What was my name before you hollowed me out into your perfect grandchild?"

"I don't… Verity, I don't know what to tell you. These things you're saying I've done, I can't even… I don't even—"

Verity let him spin. She could remember it herself. She didn't need anything from him.

"Next you'll be saying I'm running the world governments! If I'm such a Machiavellian psychopath how exactly d—"

"Emily."

He started.

"My name. In life, I was called Emily."

"I don't like the way you're looking at me."

"I know nothing about her."

He was retreating along the walkways of the Scaffold as she approached.

"You killed her, and let me take her place. How many times have you done that? And now, with your drones…"

"Verity, sit down."

"You sit," she said, and hissed. He hissed back.

"I want you to remember, Verity, that after all this. After all this, I'm still your patriarch. If you get any bright ideas about harming me, it will trickle down to you as well."

"Good," Verity said. Her eyes were misting over with tears. "This wasn't my real life anyway." And she lunged.

It seemed like, with all those souls weighing him down on the other side, he was slower now. Or maybe Verity was just angry enough that it didn't matter. She could've ripped the entire Scaffold apart by hand if she'd needed to.

But she *didn't* need to. Because its architect, was here.

His fingers scrabbled uselessly at the stake in his chest, flapping his gums, eyes wild with fear. "I didn't. I don't. I can't," he said. She had him gripped by the throat, he was going nowhere. "How did…? I don't want to die."

"No-one does," she said. "I didn't."

"I gave you life…" he was crying, silently. "I gave you life, and you do this?"

She leaned in, extra close, smelled his foul breath. "We get one life," she said. "One. And sometimes it is short. Shorter than we would like, or shorter than is fair. But you don't get a do-over. And I am done, *done*, wasting mine listening to you."

It was like his body remembered all at once it was over a thousand years old. His skin turned to papyrus in her hands, before flaking into nothing, his skin, muscle, tissue dissolving, his bones turning brittle, then crumbling, then ashes. The wind scattered him.

She could feel the groaning weight of the Dark Scaffold under her. It felt like it was ready to tip. She smiled, and closed her eyes, dedicating it to that strange witch she half-remembered. Emily.

Something about strawberries... she thought. She loved strawberries. Or maybe she was allergic. Or both?

***

"Hello, sunshine," Holly said.

Verity blinked.

"What am I doing here?"

Holly just looked at her. She blinked back tears.

"Oh, come on, Doctor. Don't mince your words now, I've been dying for ages." She looked around. The zombies. They'd turned to dust, like Breckenridge. But the energy of all those people brought back. So many rules broken. It was like a tidal wave, snapping back. It looked like Bella was fixing it though, with her Mad New Powers. She would need to ask her about those...

About the...

"What's going on?"

"Verity," Holly said. "Verity, stay with me."

"I don't understand, what's going on?" Verity asked. Her head hurt. She thought. No, it didn't.

Nothing hurt. There was nothing to be hurting.

"I love you," Holly said.

"Don't, don't say goodbye yet. I don't... where is everyone?" She tried to understand what she was. She was losing her train of thought.

The others were dancing in the background. Like they had back at the barbecue. A dance to relax restless energies, to put old feelings to rest.

She felt it lifting her.

"Guys! Can we take a fucking second, please?" Holly shouted.

Verity giggled. Always with the arguing, this lot.

Munro came up. "Hi, Verity."

"Oh good, you're okay. I was a little worried with the Dark Scaffold…"

"Nothing to do with me, it seems," Munro said. "You changed my life."

She didn't like it. Everyone talking like they were never going to see her again. She didn't want this. Curse herself, in the end, she really didn't want to die.

Holly lifted her up, and Iona peered in. Verity saw a reflection of herself in Iona's glasses. She was a little pink and orange fireball in Holly's hand. Like the crystal they'd seen in Breckenridge's workshop, but pulsing and glowing with light.

"Goodnight, Verity. Pleasant dreams, and safe passage," Iona said.

"Man guys, you're gonna make me cry, I hate this," Verity said. Holly laughed through sniffles, wiping her nose with her free sleeve. "Can I just say, since I get the chance? You guys saved my life."

"Shut up," Holly said, blubbering.

"It's true! I wasted, *hundreds of years*, with that man's poison in my ear. On that family, and their expectations. I wasn't even who I thought I was…"

"You did amazing, babes," Roman said.

"I did, didn't I?" She beamed.

Bella dropped down next to them, her strawy hair all golden and bright now. She was trying to hold it together. "See you around, sis." She raised a pinkie, and they had a little pinkie-swear. Verity thought. It was quite hard to keep track of anything.

"This is great, guys. I don't know about you." Oh. She could hear it now. It was like she was on laughing gas, and they were all being nice to her but she must have been talking a power of shite.

"What?" Holly said.

"Nothing," she said, bubbling with warmth. "Is it nearly over?"

Holly nodded, crying.

"Then I'm gonna go out like a firework!" Verity shouted. "Bright, and beautiful, and short!" She beeped Holly on the nose on the way past. "Like you."

Holly laughed again, but now she was fully crying. Her face was fighting for the steering wheel and going six different ways.

The others took Holly in a hug as Verity flew off into the night sky, just like Holly had arrived earlier.

Verity Oakleaf was halfway into the upper atmosphere, when she fell asleep for the last time. Her final time of death was 9:01am. The sun had come up forty minutes before.

chapter 41

Over the course of the next few hours, people went missing. They were missed. Pillars of their community, people who had been there so long, everyone just assumed they'd always been there.

The prime minister died in his sleep. So did the pope. Newscasters were baffled.

Breckenridge's greed had taken the whole thing down with him. The Dark Scaffold, as evil as it was, could just about hold up a few thousand vampires. Whatever Verity had done, it had knocked him off the top, and the new, top-heavy structure came right down with it.

"Iona will be happy," Holly said. She tapped her foot on the ground like she was anxious to leave, even though she'd been the one to ask to come.

Bella understood. Holly was looking for Verity. Everywhere she could think of. Looking for places Breckenridge might have hidden away was a good excuse.

The wall Holly was looking at was burned to cinders.

"Why will Iona be happy?"

"This is, um... it's their family tree," Holly said. "It updates itself, I think."

"Huh." She looked at the charred remains. There were a few names tucked into the corner that were still alive, but it almost looked like someone had dropped a bomb on a name in the middle that had exploded radially outwards. "I hope it doesn't come back to bite us."

"I mean, if four witches could just do that by ourselves, don't you think we'd be at war still?"

"I guess," Bella said. She shuddered. "Right. I'm heading home. Are you gonna be okay?"

Holly nodded. They hugged briefly, and Bella started the walk across Kelvingrove Park towards home.

***

Bella was walking past the fountain when she saw him.

Sitting halfway up it, hunched gargoyle-like against its pillars like she had done as a kid, one hand leaning on a sandstone horse for support, Preston smiled at her knowingly, in the way all loan sharks do, and wiggled his fingers at her.

She pulled her coat tighter around herself, and kept walking.

If he followed, she didn't see him.

Munro was waiting at the gates. "Hey." She sounded exhausted. They embraced.

"Ready?" Bella asked, hiding the knot in her stomach.

Munro gave her a thumbs up.

They found a quiet place under a tree, squeezed their hands together, and stared up at the sky until their eyes saw nothing but green and yellow when they closed them. And then, they invited Nicnevin into the dream space.

She was silent, solemn. She didn't even say hello, just got to work. It was like sitting in a doctor's waiting room, watching her walk amongst the world lines, hover over Munro's threadbare life.

Eventually, she looked up, tears welling up. "You killed her," she said, looking Bella right in the eye. "She has less than a day now."

Bella was silent.

Munro buried her face in her hands.

This was her fault?

All the parts of Bella that tried to keep the peace — that tried to hold everything down, that promised her if she just kept everything civil it would all work out — tensed, and snapped.

"How dare you?" she said, quietly. "I did this? How dare you?"

Nicnevin went steely, but didn't say anything. She didn't have to. She'd already said it.

"You weren't there. She was disappearing in front of me, and you were in your faraway mansion," Bella said.

"You... told me... to leave her alone," Nicnevin said. She was trembling. "You cut the cord in the first place, all of this is your doing, and now that the bill comes due, you're blaming this on me?"

"Nevin!" Munro shouted. "Bella!" She interposed herself between the two of them. "Stop it!"

"I am tired, you little twerp," Nicnevin said, towering over even Munro. "I am tired of you speaking to me like I'm your serf. I am tired of you blaming me for everything when I've done everything I could to hel—"

"No," Bella said, raising a finger, the gold light of the crossroads hushing the space. "You are tired of not being the only one who could pull her back."

Nicnevin's jaw dropped.

Munro stepped back. Bella had never seen that look on her face before. Like she'd betrayed her.

"Don't fucking look at me like that, you know it's—" Bella said, before she was knocked from her feet. Nicnevin brought her hand back and slapped her across the face.

"W— wait!" Munro shouted.

Arabella got to her feet, dabbed her lip, and inspected the blood. The light that bounced off it was gold and glittering. She scoffed.

"Oh, I have been waiting for this," she said.

She reached into herself, to the place where she would find her magic, and unleashed that golden light of the crossroads. The flare of a million high-beams in the rain, all the little sufferances and angry prayers that had been made on that road.

She lifted the M8 junction into the air, and dropped it on that hateful, hateful woman.

"Bella!" Munro shouted, as the rubble and the tarmac dust washed her back. "Bella, wait!"

A voice in her head whistled, impressed. *"You sure this is a good idea? It's not in the contract. It's gonna cost you."*

"Shut up," Bella said, and she floated into the air, and just as Nicnevin was getting to her feet, Bella swung her hand round and sent the 12:03 Larkhall to Dalmuir train barrelling into her.

Nicnevin looked up, and saw the lights of the train, and said something that Bella couldn't hear over the roar of the traffic. The train seemed to strike her, and hit nothing but air as she turned to blue smoke and curled around the edges of the carriage, thick and deadly and seductive as a trail of cigarette smoke.

The smoke began to coalesce over their heads, a cloud. A storm. And in that storm, a face took shape. A face full of such anger, and resentment, and rage that you could live a thousand years and never feel it.

But Bella could. She felt it right now.

She felt it more.

She flew towards the cloud, and the gaping mouth screamed, a scream of agony and vengeance. She tumbled into it, head over heels, and brought golden fists down on its centre. If she could bring herself to bear, if she could make Nicnevin pay—

A manicured hand reached out and grabbed her by the windpipe, the golden light spilling out of her blinding her to the rest of the cloud, as Nicnevin pitched them forward and slammed her into the ground.

The cloud, the light, all of it faded, as Nicnevin pinned her down.

She scratched and clawed at her face. Nicnevin, leaning back so Bella couldn't find purchase, pulled at her hair.

Bella screamed.

Nicnevin screamed back.

It continued like this, until Nicnevin pitched her head back enough to see something that made her grip relax.

Bella, sensing her opening, broke Nicnevin's grasp and reared back to launch another spell—

She wasn't even looking at her.

How fucking dare she, she wasn't even looking!

What was she—

She turned, and saw.

Munro was lying curled in a ball, sobbing.

They both looked at each other, and disentangled, as though they had only just realised that it wasn't appropriate for them to be fighting like Looney Tunes cartoons.

"Munro?" Bella said, approaching.

"It's not fair, it's not fair," Munro said. She said it again and again.

"It's not fair, you're right," Bella said. "It s—"

"No!" Munro pushed back at her. "No! It's not fair that I have hours left, and I am still regulating your feelings!"

Bella looked back at Nicnevin, whose hair was now a mess, and who was looking at her feet in embarrassment.

"You two don't care about me at all," Munro said. "You're just fighting over me like a fucking football."

The guilt in Bella's stomach tensed.

"You don't give a shit about me," Munro said. "I am walking to meet my maker before the sunrise, and the first thing you do is go at each other's throats."

"I'm sorry," Nicnevin said.

"I do— I do care," Bella said. She was blinking back her tears, she didn't want to add 'manipulative waterworks' to her list of crimes. "I do care, Munro. I love you."

Shit, what had she done…

"I was ready to go. And you guys talked me into fighting. And now it's here. The end of the line. I didn't think I would have to spend my last precious few hours dealing with your bullshit. So I won't. Fuck both of you." She sat up, wiped her face. "I came into this world alone, I'm more than happy to leave that way."

"No!" the two of them said, and Bella could already feel it even before Munro recoiled. The fawning, the rushing forward. No wonder Munro felt this way.

"You're right," Bella said. "You deserve better."

"You deserve *everything*," Nicnevin said.

"I don't want to *deserve* anything, I just want you two to behave like human beings and not fucking animals!" She stood, and took a deep breath. "I'm going to wake up now. I want to spend some time alone." She rocked where she was standing. "Don't look for me."

She vanished in the blink of an eye.

Bella's vision spun. Shit. What had she done?

She might literally never see Munro again. Munro might meet her end by herself. And it was Bella's fault.

"This is all my fault," Nicnevin said, slumping to her knees. "…Shit."

"No, it's mine," Bella said.

"Are we going to fight about this too?" Nicnevin said. A smirk crossed her face, but she looked too exhausted to actually wear it.

They sat in silence, alone, together.

"I was so jealous," Nicnevin said.

"Shut the fuck up. What the hell did you have to be jealous about?"

Nicnevin screwed her face up. "The love of my life found me wanting, and chose you."

"Nicnevin, you're literally Queen of Witches. You are a ten-foot tall goddess who has magic no-one could ever compete with, who could literally have any woman she wants."

"None of that means anything if it's not what I want," Nicnevin said. "I said it, you *read* it. I don't like that I feel this way. I should be happy, but I'm not."

Bella sighed, rubbed her eyes with her palms. "Me too. And Munro's right. I've not been focusing on the right things. It's just... there's nothing I can do to help her."

"You've *been* helping her. For the record," Nicnevin said. "Not just magically, though honestly I was pretty impressed by that as well, which didn't help how I was feeling." Bella looked at her, and she groaned. "Her dreams. I've been seeing all her dreams. I see how good you are for her."

"I hated that you would get to do that," Bella said. "It felt like such a violation."

"I hated doing it," Nicnevin said. "I truly did mean it when I said, I am happy for you two. I don't want her back."

"Then why all of this!"

"Because I hate you!" Nicnevin said. "Are you happy now?"

They both stopped.

Bella snorted. She couldn't help it. The snort made Nicnevin chuckle, and then before they knew it the two of them were laughing.

"After all this time," Nicnevin said. "I'm just a frivolous little girl."

"Same club, sister."

They had both been sitting there, pretending they were fine, pretending these emotions were abhorrent and unique.

The two of them hugged. It was a little awkward with Nicnevin still taller than Arabella, even on her knees, but it felt warm. Bella exhaled.

"Why *did* you read my diary?" Nicnevin asked, when the laughter had died down, and the silence had settled.

"I..." Bella crumbled. "I thought you must have been spiking the wine."

Nicnevin looked openly confused.

"I thought this was some elaborate ruse, and you were trying to steal my dying girlfriend back."

When she said it out loud, it sounded like something from a conspiracy wall.

And in the light of everything that had happened, she finally reached a truth.

"I would give her up, if it meant she could live," she said. "How about then? Could you save her then?"

Nicnevin shook her head. "I'm sorry. I did everything I could already."

"But... but she's... but she's dying."

"Yeah," Nicnevin nodded.

"We have to save her."

"We *did* save her. But she can't live forever. She can't outlive her great-grandchildren."

Bella stepped away. "I'm sorry that I treated you this way. I'm sorry I let my jealousy cloud my mind."

"Me too," Nicnevin said. "I'm just ashamed it took this long for me to realise it." She stood to her full height. "You should go. You may not get another chance to say goodbye."

"What about you?" Bella said.

"I'm a psychopomp," Nicnevin said. "I get a front row seat either way. But really..." She took a deep breath as she internalised it. "It's you she wants on the stage with her."

Bella swallowed. "Thank you."

"Don't thank me, thank Munro," Nicnevin said. She grinned. "All this time, and she still knows exactly what to say." She looked straight ahead, snapped her fingers, and vanished.

chapter 42

It was still strange seeing Iona and Roman walking around in her pokey wee flat. Like seeing teachers in your house.

"Really Bella, Holly, I had no idea you lived like the Lost Boys. Must you keep things so messy?"

"I don't mind," Roman said. He was playing Holly's old PlayStation that had been gathering dust under the telly for years. It was nice to see him distracted, he was still visibly shaking about not having the Archive.

"Iona," Holly said, with mock incredulity. "A witch should never judge another witch's lifestyle — especially when she's invited you into her home!"

Iona grumbled. "Quite right. Though with me and Roman sharing your living room and adding to the clutter it would d—"

Bella strode past:

"We've got a small room,
And the family's come to stay.
For the next few days,
Put yourself away."

The mess began to dutifully pick itself up off the floor.

Iona pouted. "There's no substitute for hard work."

"Have you seen Munro?" Bella asked. "I have to find her."

Iona furrowed her brow, then nodded to the other room. "She came back half an hour ago. She's having a nap."

Munro was lying on her side, dozing.

Bella curled up to her, and Munro lazily lifted one eye to see who had disturbed her slumber. "Hello you."

"I'm sorry," Bella said. "You were right. You've always been right."

"That's nice," Munro said, still half-asleep. She smacked her lips as she wet her mouth. Then her eyes focused. "Oh yeah. Shit. I forgot about that." She sat up. "I take it from the fact that you're still here, that you and Nicnevin worked it out?"

Bella nodded.

"Good."

Bella made to kiss her, but Munro put her fingers in the way. "Morning breath."

"Mmmm, my favourite," Bella smirked. She moved the fingers to one side and kissed her. Soaked in the feeling of her lips, thick and soft pressed to her own. Ran her fingers through her coarse hair, wild and knotted like hair did when you slept.

They settled into a warm hug that was deep as an ocean. "You okay? Sorry I woke you up."

"I'm fine," Munro said. "Just tired."

But Bella could tell, when she lied like that. She was saving her waking hours.

They lay in each other's arms, Bella fully dressed and still wearing her shoes, Munro in her nightie and under the covers.

Bella looked up at the wall. "Interesting." More of Munro's paintings had hung themselves, in the shape of a pentagram. "Did you hang those?"

Munro shook her head.

Maybe she'd done it with magic...

Well. It couldn't do any harm, a protective sigil on the wall, she thought.

She ran her thumb across the back of Munro's hand, feeling this new power that supplemented her own. She wondered, tried to focus on the golden sparks...

But they bounced off.

She had hours, she knew it. She would need to work out another way to save her, to use this power. Preston had been ironclad in his contract that she couldn't dump his entire power to save Munro like she had done herself.

But she was clever. Surely there would be...

"Let's go for a walk," Munro said. "Yeah?"

Bella was shaken from her reverie. "Sure."

***

Arabella stood with Munro on the Squinty Bridge, summoning stones out of nothing in her hand, and dropping them over the edge to watch the splash.

"You're still thinking about it, aren't you," Munro said.

Arabella watched the stone drop, inevitably, into the water and disappear under the waves. "You could always read me like a book."

"You're quite the page turner," Munro said. She sighed. "Look at me."

"I can't," Arabella said. Try as she might, it was like trying to look into the sun. There was nothing she could do. She'd run out of time to save Munro for good.

"Hey, you never know. I might last another month."

They both knew that wasn't true.

She had had all this time and she'd wasted it. Wasted it. Wasted it.

Munro pressed a hand to Arabella's cheek, and turned so they were looking at each other.

They kissed like they were drowning. Like they were going to sink and all that was holding one up was the other.

Munro pulled back. Took a deep, happy breath. Leaned on the

railing, to look out over the river, and the setting sun. She reached out and held Bella's hand. Arabella squeezed it tight.

"It feels different this time," Munro said. "It feels like the chairs are packed up and they're asking everyone to leave, and you're getting pulled away…"

"Then I promise," Bella lifted their interlocked hands, "to never let go."

Munro smiled. "You numpty."

Munro looked back up at the sky. The two of them were bathed in the purple and pink of it. Munro's eyes were glittering. "My mammy used to say it was the Fairy Queen's robe."

Arabella bubbled, feeling the soft warmth of Munro's hand, running her finger over her calloused knuckles, tracing their outline. She was so lucky. She'd been so lucky. To have this woman in her life.

"You can't see the stars in the city," Munro continued. "But they're still there. It's just too bright down here to see them. Man, you should see the stars back where I'm from. It was too cloudy that weekend we went away."

"I'd like that," Arabella said. She smiled to herself, a memory now rosy in its age.

She noticed her shoelace was untied, and dropped to tie it.

"What should we do tomorrow?" Munro asked, still stargazing, her hand gripping the railing tight.

"I don't know," Bella smiled, daydreaming. "Let's get coffee. Or a walk in the park. It's Tuesday so the place will be empty." She stood back up and reached to take Munro's hand again—

But there was no hand on the railing.

Arabella turned. There was no-one there.

"Munro?" she asked. She could see for a hundred metres in every direction. She was alone.

She dropped to her knees, mind racing, and that was when she saw it.

A tiny pile of grey ashes, right where Munro's feet had been.

Bella's lip trembled like a wean.

A breeze lifted the ash, and scattered it to the Clyde.

Bella watched it go, in shock, the last remnants of Munro.

It pierced her. That absence. Pierced her like a spear, hurled by an unflinching and indifferent universe. It pierced her like a balloon. She folded under its weight. Felt it knock her off her feet as she rolled with the impact.

With all the expectation, all the waiting, all the dread, she had not expected to be surprised when it happened. But now that it was happening, now that it was right in front of her, she had realised how ridiculous that had been.

It punctured her like a spear, and now her love was spilling out of her, nowhere left to go. She stumbled forwards, wracked with the pain, silent and shaking, breath ragged. She fell to her knees, grasped with feeble fingernails against the concrete—

She screamed. She bawled. So loud they could've heard her in Elfhame. And as she screamed, it ripped the Squinty Bridge to ribbons around her.

***

Lily watched the sun go down, through the blanket of mist. House Nicnevin cast no shadow.

She didn't know why she'd come back.

She looked down the hill, and for a second, she thought she saw a person. An indistinct shape coming out of the mist.

She squinted, trying to make it out. "Gran?" she said, and then made to call out, but by the time she'd blinked, the shape was gone.

Weird.

She stepped forward, making for where she'd seen it, when she saw—

A feather, trapped in the grating of the fence.

And she didn't know how she knew, but she knew.

By the time Nicnevin came out and found her, she was already in bits. It had snuck up on her.

Nicnevin held her, like a crying babe.

She had been so used to the scar tissue on her heart for her grandmother, that she hadn't expected it to hurt.

Silly, silly girl.

***

Munro smiled, feeling the last of the sun's rays on her face. "What do you want to do tomorrow?"

Arabella didn't respond.

"Bella?"

She turned, and Bella was gone.

She turned again, to check behind her, and Bella was walking towards her over the bridge.

"Bella."

She didn't respond. Just kept walking.

"Bella?"

She passed her, not adjusting her pace.

She turned, the bridge being completely empty now, and followed Bella, in a daze.

There was no-one in the streets. No cars driving past.

Not a soul, but Bella.

She was led, slowly, to the Archive. Intact. As it had been.

"What the hell..."

She took the steps into the foyer, gingerly, a little light-headed.

"Hey," Bella said, loudly.

"You took your time!" Holly said. She was sitting at the big table, still wearing her leather jacket from years ago. Across from her, Iona did receipts.

"Here, come see this!" Roman shouted.

He scampered up to them, and Munro took another few steps into the room.

She didn't try to get their attention. Just wiped her own tears, as Bella walked behind them, skooching past to get the biscuits out the cupboard.

She popped one in her mouth, and looked up at the doorway, like she expected to see someone.

But of course, she didn't.

So, this was what it felt like.

Bella walked down the corridor into the back of the house. Munro made to follow her, and as she stepped past the threshold, she found herself in her old bedroom, in House Nicnevin. Where she'd died the first time.

Nicnevin was making her bed, wrapping the sheets down tight under the mattress.

Munro watched, quietly.

Nicnevin fluffed the pillows, and then looked up. She'd been crying.

She looked right at Munro. "Goodnight, my love."

Munro smiled, through her tears.

She tried to be brave.

* * * *

acknowledgements

There are many, many people without whom this book would not exist. I can't pass up the opportunity to thank:

My entire writing group, for their perspective, their wit, and their patience. In particular, Ryann Fletcher, my critique bestie. You were the first to read a working draft of this book, and punched me in the gut with the structural problems I'd been avoiding.

Winter James, who provided sensitivity reading for Bella — a task I'm sure is not easy when I make her more unhinged every book. Knowing your tastes, I knew that if you liked this story, I was onto something.

Shona Kinsella, my structural and copy editor, whose insight has always been invaluable, and who never has a bad word to say about any of this nonsense.

Jenni Coutts, who delivered the phenomenal cover art for both this book and the second edition of Witches of Merchant City. (I'll always be fond of my home-made cover looking like a pirated DVD case but what a difference getting a proper artist makes!)

The Wee Witch Book Club, who kindly asked me to ramble at them for a few hours about the last book. I was on cloud nine all the way home knowing it had found its audience.

The people who keep Glasgow libraries running. I spent hundreds of hours drafting and editing in the library in 2024, and it's great to have a place to write where you don't have to buy litres of coffee or worry that you're hogging a seat. (I won't say it's a distraction-free environment, but at least the distraction is on-theme!)

Also, anyone who harangued me about when this book was going to come out. Trust me, no-one was more annoyed than me about how long it was taking.

I wrote Witches from first draft to publication in ten months. The sequel took four years from first words to first sale. I have never been so unsure if a creative project would resonate with anyone.

Because of that, I would like to say thank you, reader, for making it all the way to the end.

If the spirit moves you, a review on Amazon or Goodreads helps me immensely. You can check out my other books and future projects at lukebelcourt.com, including the upcoming final act in the Glasgow Witches trilogy.

Until then, thank you again,
Luke

Made with love in Glasgow, Scotland
22nd June 2025

about the author

Luke Belcourt is a writer of LGBT adventure fantasy novels, born and raised in Glasgow, Scotland.

You can find info on future instalments of the Glasgow Witches at **lukebelcourt.com**, or on Bluesky @lukebelcourt.com – providing he still hasn't managed to escape social media and go live in the woods.

"Your magic's all tied up with me now. You're doing two things at once. By the tides, Bella, what have you done?"

"It's fine. I can handle it."

"Well, you're not wrong there I suppose. You can handle anything. Plus, you know, when magic is taken away it always comes back stronger, right?"

The story will conclude in...

WITCHES

BREAK

GLASGOW

www.ingramcontent.com/pod-product-compliance
Lightning Source LLC
Chambersburg PA
CBHW030604170726

48283CB00002B/463